DEAR GIRLS
ABOVE ME

DEAR GIRLS ABOVE ME

*Inspired by a
True Story*

CHARLIE
McDOWELL

THREE RIVERS PRESS
NEW YORK

Copyright © 2013 by Cloudbreak Productions

Published in the United States by Three Rivers Press, an imprint of the
Crown Publishing Group, a division of Random House, Inc., New York.
www.crownpublishing.com

Three Rivers Press and the Tugboat design are registered trademarks of
Random House, Inc.

Library of Congress Cataloging-in-Publication Data
McDowell, Charlie, 1983–
Dear girls above me : inspired by a true story /
Charlie McDowell. — First edition.
1. Self-realization—Fiction. 2. Neighbors—Fiction.
3. Dating (Social customs)—Fiction. 4. Young women—Fiction.
5. Humorous fiction. I. Title.
PS3613.C3948D43 2013
813'.6—dc23   2012049640

ISBN 978-0-307-98633-7
eISBN 978-0-307-98634-4

Printed in the United States of America

Book design by Maria Elias
Cover design by Jessie Sayward Bright
Cover photographs and styling: Christine Ferrara / Call of the Small
www.call-small.com
Author photograph: Kate Danson

10   9   8   7   6   5   4   3   2   1

First Edition

For Nell and Edna,
the original funny women

AUTHOR'S NOTE

This book was inspired by real people and events in my life, but ultimately it is a work of fiction. In some cases, composite characters based on real people were created, but ultimately most names, characters, places, and incidents are fictional. Any resemblance to actual persons is entirely coincidental.

CHAPTER ONE

"OMG, if someone ever writes a book about me, it should be called *A Beautiful Mind*," said a voice still filled with the glory of having uttered some profound cliché.

"I think that's already a book," I responded out loud, to nobody. "And a movie."

"And I'll write the sequel, *A Beautiful Fashion Sense*. Fashion is totally my seventh sense. My sixth sense is seeing ghosts wearing last fall's line," chirped another voice in keeping with the enthusiasm.

I glared at my ceiling fan, hoping that this wasn't going to turn into a trilogy. These voices, the voices of the girls who lived above me, had become the Greek chorus of my life. As a guy not new to city life, I expected the intrusions and boundary violations that occur when one lives with only a few inches of wood and stucco between himself and his neighbors. Random footsteps, muffled television programs, maybe even the occasional sentence fragment. But I most definitely did not expect to be the unwilling audience of a twenty-four-hour slumber party between the Winston Churchill and Benjamin Franklin of the *90210* generation.

But let's back up a bit. To a more innocent time. Before the girls rearranged every idea I'd once had about life and love, and the biggest challenge in my daily routine was walking my dog.

I stood on the freshly cut lawn of my apartment building and looked around to make sure no one was within earshot. There was the girl across the street chatting on her cell phone, but she seemed much too preoccupied by the argument she was having with her boyfriend to notice me. So, I cleared my throat.

"Go pee-pees outside, Marvin. Pee-pees outside," I said in the most high-pitched voice humanly possible.

These are the words I must say to my dog every morning in order for him to go to the bathroom. Not a day goes by that I don't regret taking him to that dog trainer. I'm not totally sure, but I think she was legally a "little person" (which I Googled), clocking in at approximately four foot ten, and the pitch of her voice was commensurately high. No wonder dogs listened to her. So, now, any command I give to Marvin, I must deliver with this Mariah Carey screech. Otherwise he'll just sit there and stare at me as if he has no idea what we're doing outside. We go through this routine at eight A.M. every single morning. If I wait till eight thirty A.M., I'm screwed; the grass will be damp from the sprinklers and Marvin won't go near it. Even the smallest drop of water frightens him. I guess that's one of the drawbacks in rescuing a Hurricane Katrina–survivor dog.

"Good boy, Marvin! Good boy!" Compliments must also come in this piercing frequency. I don't know how much longer my vocal cords can take this.

"Bro, you shouldn't talk like that where people can hear you. They might think you're a homo." This unsolicited morning advice came courtesy of apartment 4E, the guy who calls himself "the Con-Man" but whose real name is actually Conor. The Jesse James of my apartment building. What kind of person puts "the" in front of his name anyway? I guess the very same guy whose wardrobe appears to be sponsored by Ed Hardy.

"Good morning, the Con-Man. How's your day going?" I said with complete disinterest.

"Awesome. I've already taken a dump and trimmed my pubes this morning," he blurted out.

"Wow, Conor—I mean, the Con-Man, that's a lot of information I don't really wanna know about you," I said with complete sincerity.

"Stop being such a pussy, bro. It's science; it's the human body; it's education. Learn to love it."

Why didn't I rescue a cat? There would have been no reason to converse with him and his freshly trimmed nether area if I were a cat owner. Felines are smart; they go to the bathroom inside, just like humans. They are loyal and don't whore themselves out the way dogs do. If I had been a cat, I'd have scratched the shit out of the Con-Man by now.

"All right, bro, I'm gonna go annihilate ten egg whites for breakfast. Maybe a splash of POM juice if I'm feeling *craaazy,*" he said. A real trailblazer. "Remember, bro, keep your voice *down low, like this!*"

"Yep. Got it. Thanks." I was thankful—thankful that I was looking at the back of him as I said this. I watched as the Con-Man air-drummed his way over to his hydraulic truck and peeled out of the parking garage, almost running over apartment 6A, Mr. Molever, the on-site landlord. Mr. Molever is another person I can't bear to talk to. Not because he's a weasel like the Con-Man, but because I frequently forget to pay my rent on time and he loves to let me know it. I wish I could avoid him forever, but he's made it impossible.

Just last month, he'd implemented a new policy stating that "every check must be hand-delivered to ensure ultimate safety (do not fold check)." Don't get me wrong, he's perfectly nice, but boy can that man talk. And when he does speak, it *only* has to do with the apartment building. Over the last couple of years, I've literally become an expert on shingle-removal tools and copper piping, something I had previously hoped to never think about in my entire life.

But maybe Mr. Molever hadn't seen me yet and I still had the chance to make a smooth getaway. I picked up my dog, who was carrying out my command mid-pee, and I hid behind the nearest tree. Marvin expressed his discomfort by heavily panting. But that's because he's unable to breathe through his nose. When you're browsing at the shelter, they only tell you the positive stuff. They don't mention how a particular breed is not good for hiding behind trees. I put my hand over Marvin's mouth, praying that he would at least try to suck air through that little pug nose of his. It worked for three seconds, and then he began wheezing and shaking around. This caught the attention of Mr. Molever.

"Charlie?" He stared at me with a silly smile on his face, one that only he could muster so early in the morning. "Do you realize you're the only tenant who noticed the trees were trimmed this morning?"

"Yeah, and it's not even Christmas," I said. Hopefully this brilliant turn of phrase would serve to distract Mr. Molever from remembering I was late on my rent payment.

"Oh! You've done it! Now, that, sir, was funny." He laughed hysterically in a way that walked a fine line between being the nicest guy in the world and being a serial killer who wasn't afraid to target women and children.

"Well, time for me to get my coffee on. Have a good day, Mr. Molever," I said politely.

I put Marvin on the ground just in time for him to take a much-needed breath of life and swiftly made my way toward the entrance of the building. I was almost at the front door, free from any more neighborly interactions, when Mr. Molever defied the laws of physics and suddenly appeared in front of me. His demeanor had shifted and he was not laughing anymore. Now it was my turn to pee.

"Slow down there, Mr. Usain Bolt. Now, if my calculations are correctamundo, and let me tell you, they always are, then you are one day and eight hours late on your financing agreement with this building."

I summoned my theatrical genes and showed him how sincerely shocked I was. "Wow, I can't believe I let that slip my mind. I will go write you a check and slide it under your door right away, Mr. Molever," I said.

He leaned in toward me like an enemy entering a no-fly zone and whispered, "Now, please don't tell me you're forgetting policy number seven? 'Every check must be hand-delivered to—'"

"'Ensure ultimate safety.' Yes, I know." I couldn't let him finish that goddamned sentence without my head exploding.

"Well, good. I'll be seeing you in, let's say, thirty-five minutes. I can fill you in on last week's mandatory tenant meeting, since you were too sunburned to make it."

My sunburn sounded like a bullshit excuse when Mr. Molever said it out loud. And in this particular case, it was. Because who besides a deranged maniac would want to sit through a routine meeting of complaining neighbors anyway? All they ever do is look for things to criticize about the building. Like, seriously, who gives a shit? I don't have a problem with the "color of the trim in the courtyard" because I've never even noticed the trim before. And I hope I never do.

BULLSHIT EXCUSES I'VE USED TO GET OUT OF TENANT MEETINGS

- My grandmother died.
- It's my grandmother's birthday (my other grandmother).
- My other grandmother died.
- My grandfather is getting remarried.
- My stepgrandmother died.

I tugged on Marvin's leash, trying to pull him inside. He held his ground, staring up at me with his bulging eyes, as if to say, "Oh hells no, I still gotta take a shiiiiit." For whatever reason, I picture Marvin's human voice to be that of a middle-aged African-American woman from the South. I probably should've mentioned that earlier. And it's not racist, because he's a dog.

I stood there and actually debated whether or not it would be worth Marvin's crapping in my apartment to just go inside already. Saner minds prevailed, but by probably too narrow a margin.

"Poo-poos outside. Come on, poo-poos outside!" Sadly, that's not one of the commands that dog trainer taught him. If I'm going to pay someone a large sum of money to train my dog, at the very least, I expect him to know how to crap on command. Lucky for me he really needed to go. Or maybe Marvin *was* able to poop on command. Either way, I was in the clear.

As I pulled Marvin along, leaving his feces for the flies to argue over, a frantic voice screamed out from the heavens, "You can't do that! I know for a fact! I know! I know! I know!" This was Sally, apartment 3A, an elderly agoraphobic woman, who ought to leave her eyes to science since she lives on the third floor and was able to see Marvin's minute poo. Supposedly she hasn't left her apartment in more than fifteen years. Mr. Molever, as much as I can't stand him, is kind enough to drop off food, supplies, dry cleaning, or anything else she might need. I'm not quite sure why she would even need to get her clothes dry-cleaned, considering she doesn't interact with the outside world, but I can only assume that even hermits like to look nice. Just, by themselves, sometimes. Actually, Sally is kind of my hero. I can only hope to one day grow up to be a man who never leaves his own personal space and has some guy drop stuff off for him outside his door. She's a genius if you ask me.

"Apologies, Sally," I yelled up to her. "It won't happen again." I waited for a few moments but didn't get a response. I assumed that she was too delighted by the fact that I had paid attention to her to care anymore about the excrement dotting the lawn. Besides, let's be honest, what was she going to do, chase after me?

I had already filled my good-deed quota for the day by acknowledging Sally, which I can admit would probably not be categorized as an act of kindness for the average human being. But, for me, if I do anything I don't want to do, then I'm committing a friendly gesture to the world. I miss those gold star stickers Mrs. Felcher used to give me for doing something good when I was in the third grade. Unfortunately, life doesn't work that way when you get older. Society really sets a standard for you early on in life (gold stars) that only gets worse and worse as you grow up (no stars). Not fair. Perhaps if grown men were issued gold star stickers for proper behavior, there would be less crime.

Finally, I made it back into my apartment after another typical series of nightmare encounters with my neighbors. I was already exhausted and needed to take a nap. But it was only nine in the morning, and I had the rest of the day ahead of me.

CHAPTER TWO

I was sitting in my apartment, wondering if today would be the day I'd finally hang artwork on my walls. I had enough framed art to fill every square inch of my place, but for whatever reason I could not get myself to do it. So each piece lay propped up against the wall on the floor, nail and hammer ready, as if I had literally just moved in. I had actually been living in this apartment for just over two years now. To be fair, I had spent most of my time at my ex-girlfriend's place, so it was there that I made my home. I even spent an entire day hanging up all of her artwork on her walls. But all that domestic bliss ended when she shattered my heart into fifty million-billion-cagillion-tregazillion pieces. . . .

. . . We were enjoying a wonderful lunch, where the both of us ordered our usual chopped salad, hold the onions. It was a bright summery day and it was *hot*. I was sweating like a pig. Although I've never seen a pig sweat. I was sweating like a hypothetical sweaty pig. When I look back on it now, I was very uncomfortable with the high temperature, but I was so in love with this girl that nothing else mattered. At that time, not even the little things in life bothered me. Now everything bothers me.

I distinctly remember her telling me how proud she was of all the "potential work stuff I had going on" (FIRST RED FLAG) and that I should "never stop believing in myself" (FLAG ON FIRE). For most people, compliments are a positive thing that make them feel good, but to me they mean somebody either wants something from me or is laying the groundwork to break up with me. I started downing cups of lemonade out of sheer nervousness, knowing deep down that this would quite possibly be our final onion-free salad together.

After the last supper (lunch), outside "our" restaurant, we got into her car and the talk began. By the time we arrived at my apartment building, four minutes later, we weren't together anymore. I can recall a few of her cited reasons for destroying my life, like "I want to be with other guys, especially when I go to Miami in a couple of weeks," and "You care about me too much, it's exhausting," and "I feel like I'm moving forward and you're moving sideways." But to be perfectly honest, my main focus in the two hundred and forty seconds while I was being dumped was how badly I had to pee. She also had a tendency to drive over every single bump in the road, which felt like the perfect metaphor for our relationship, and my bladder felt as if it were playing a game of *Mike Tyson's Punch Out!!*. Regardless of my extremely uncomfortable urination situation, I didn't want to get out of the car. I feverishly tried to think of something I could do that would both force her to forget the huge mistake she was making and get me to take my mind off my bladder. What if I faked one of those seizures where my eyes rolled to the back of my head and I started foaming at the mouth? You'd have to be a real monster to break up with someone while they're seizing. In retrospect, that probably wouldn't have been the most attractive way to get her to want me again. Also, I haven't carried spare foam with me in years. Regardless, absolutely nothing in the entire world could make me open that car door. Because if I did, I knew she would be gone forev—

She kicked me to the curb and drove off (bumping over the pothole at the end of my block, of course). I stood there for a moment, or maybe it was forty-six minutes, not knowing what to do or where to go. I finally stumbled into my building, trying so very hard not to cry and pee in my pants. A messy combination.

As I traveled down the long dark hallway to my apartment, I kept my head down and focused on the mangy green carpeting, trying to put my attention on anything other than what had just happened. Yup, the carpet was still mangy and green. Just then, my two next-door neighbors (2B), Jimmy and Elisa, an annoyingly happy couple, stepped out of their apartment.

"Hey, man," Jimmy said, beaming.

I kept my eyes on the carpet. My hope was that he was talking to an imaginary friend behind me. I knew that if I stopped and chatted with these people, there was a possibility I would collapse into an uncomfortably loud sob.

"Charlie? Are you okay?" Elisa asked. She was onto me.

I bit my lip, choking down my emotions. I raised my head just a little bit, giving them some acknowledgment, and then performed a kind of half bow, somewhere between a nod and a kneel. Both of them stared at me, mouths agape, with the same look of concern. I couldn't handle any more of their insufferable empathy, so I turned away from them and faced the wall. They must have thought I was on an afternoon peyote adventure.

"Did we tell you we just got married?" Jimmy called out brightly.

I wanted to respond, "Yes! You tell me literally every single time I am forced to communicate with you. And it's time to drop the 'just' from that sentence. You've been married for eight long and I'm sure boring months now since you have to tell me about it every single time." But instead I sprinted away, giving them a congratulatory thumbs-up, and ducked into my apartment.

I bolted for the toilet, which was where I simultaneously started peeing and scream-crying. Definition:

scream-cry *(verb)* To hold in one's sadness until it hits the boiling point and one can only wail pathetically. Much more effective if one has to pee simultaneously, because the sound will then be drowned out by the force of one's urine stream.

Soon after I was able to collect myself enough to curl up into the fetal position on my couch. And I've been stuck there ever since, *metaphorically* speaking. (My legs have a tendency to fall asleep when curled.)

Sadly, for the month after we broke up, I wasted much of my precious time wandering down the dark pitiful path of "I'm going to win her back." Rarely does this idea result in victory, but for some reason, in heartache, I resort to that type of thinking. I repeatedly forget that when someone breaks up with you, that means that they *don't* want to wake up beside you anymore, not the opposite. Even if I go around telling people, "I know she's still in love with me, I just have to remind her by way of a plane banner," or "I'm going to get her back by re-creating the *Say Anything* boom box scene, but with an iPad," it doesn't mean that I should actually follow through with these ideas. In trying circumstances, I am someone who calls for desperate measures. Here are some of my most pathetic post-breakup moments:

I dropped off a cherry Slurpee from 7-Eleven on her doorstep with a handwritten note that read, "I just happened to be in the neighborhood and thought you would want one of these. It's cherry flavor . . . just like you."

I pretended to "pocket-dial" her while I was in my car singing along to REM's "Everybody Hurts," thinking that would make her realize the huge mistake she had made.

I asked her what I should do with her custom-ordered birthday present, especially because it was "too big to fit in my living room."

I texted her best friend, Lauren, "She was the one," knowing very well that she would pass the message along to my ex, while they would probably go on to discuss how romantic I was and what a huge mistake she had made. . . . But Lauren texted me back, "No she wasn't."

I texted Lauren once more, this time with a different approach: "Can you keep a secret? I've always had a thing for you. . . ." Again, Lauren would be sure to tell my ex, who would probably freak out in a jealous fit and need to get back together with me just so I wouldn't sleep with her best friend. Funnily enough, I never heard back from Lauren and

when I tried to reach her a third time, I realized she must
have coincidentally changed her number.

Once I realized that the chances of winning my ex back were slim,
I decided to join an elite group of individuals by becoming "a beard
guy." This took months of focus, determination, and maturity. There
comes a period in every beard's life where it decides to be incredibly
itchy. My guess is the beard is going through its teenage years, where
it has no respect for authority (my face), it goes places it shouldn't
(up into my nose), and it occasionally retreats into infancy (ingrown
hairs). But then, one day, out of nowhere, my beard decided to grow
up. I'm sure my constant love and delicate care had something to
do with it. I mean, I did give it a biweekly shampoo and conditioner
treatment, as well as downward strokes with a fine-toothed comb.
But honestly, I think it'd just had enough rebelling for one growth
cycle. You can only fight the good fight for so long. Now my beard
was living the good life and nothing could get in its way, except for
maybe . . . my mother. She couldn't stand my beard. There had even
been a few moments where I was certain she was trying to sneak up
behind me and destroy my beard by way of electronic shaving device. But luckily for me, facial hair made me more alert. Superhero-
like, if you will.

"What are you hiding from?" my mother continually asked me.

"People," I grunted from behind my shield of hair.

"You're drawing more attention to yourself with that roadkill-
looking thing on your face." She was probably right, but I would
never let her know it.

It's terrible how an abrupt and devastating end to a relationship
can turn an ordinarily cheery person into Virginia Woolf. She was

that depressed poet lady with the big nose played by Nicole Kidman who committed suicide by way of drowning. I don't think she killed herself because of her nose, though. My point is, I wasn't always harboring such a negative outlook on life. In fact, back when I was happily in a relationship, I used to actually enjoy my daily interactions with people and considered myself rather good at "small talk." Even from an early age I was quite adept at listening to people while simultaneously making them feel like they were the most interesting person in the room.

This trait most definitely comes from my father. He is the master of this. And he doesn't have to remember your name to do it. In fact, he only knows the names of about ten people in his life, and they're all immediate family members. Everyone else he simply refers to as "darling!" This, of course, only works when you have a cool British accent to rely on, and unfortunately for me, I do not. I learned this the hard way when I was fourteen years old and forgot to do my biology homework for Mr. Sommers. "Oh, darling, I'll hand it in to you tomorrow. All right with you, darling?" I said with such confidence. He responded by immediately sending me to Principal Nolan's office for inappropriate behavior toward a teacher. Since then I have settled for "buddy" or "bud." Although it's not as good as a British "darling," it works well with my American accent. But I digress. . . .

. . . I couldn't believe it had been a year since the breakup. What had I accomplished in that time? Well, let's see. I obtained my open-water sailing license. I still had yet to use it, seeing as I didn't own a boat. But if I was ever forced into an emergency situation where someone needed me to captain a sailboat that was under thirty feet in length, then, with the help of my *Intro to Sailing* textbook, I could probably have pointed the ship in the right direction (depending on the conditions). Other than "sailing," had I done anything this past year? I thought not. Anyone who says a breakup brings "inspiration" and a "strong work ethic" is full of shit. The only thing it brought me was misery and an unemployment check (I was fired due to "excessive groaning" while on the clock).

Thankfully, my friends and family gathered around me in this time of need and made sure I got through the year with only a few sudden-outburst scream cries. It's moments like a breakup where all of a sudden the people you're close to become incredibly opinionated and don't censor themselves as to their true feelings. It had always been my understanding that everyone had a deep affection for my ex. Her presence had consistently been requested by my nearest and dearest, who extended open invitations to all birthday parties, weddings, family gatherings, and quinceañeras. She had practically become a part of the family, at least until the second I announced the news that we had split up. Then all bets were off:

> Whenever I tried picturing her as my daughter-in-law, I got severely depressed.
>
> —*My mom*

> I wish her the best of luck controlling someone else's life.
>
> —*My dad*

> I'm pretty sure she was the person who farted at my ninetieth-birthday dinner.
>
> —*My grandmother*

> I always hated her nail polish choices.
>
> —*My sister Lilly*

I was the one who farted at your grandmother's
ninetieth-birthday dinner.
            —*My friend Alex*

She reminded me of a wounded pigeon, especially when
she drank margaritas.
            —*My mom's friend Leone*

I tried masturbating to her once and could barely keep a
hard-on.
            —*My friend Luke*

Maybe they were all right, but still, a year after the fact, I thought
about her constantly. I will admit that this longing, to some extent,
had to do with the reality that I was dismissed by this person. I'm
sure a part of me was seeking her acceptance as a way to deal with
my fear of rejection. And if this were the case, then my desire to be
with her had nothing to do with true love, but instead it revealed
my need to be loved. At least that's what Dr. Phil discussed in an
episode that was surprisingly similar to my situation. I don't care if
that particular show was about a transvestite diving instructor and a
Mormon father of twelve, Dr. Phil was talking to me, damn it.

As I lay in bed trying not to think about cute little cartoon sheep
(because when I do, I stay awake the whole night obsessively counting them), I opened up my writing notebook (not to be confused
with a diary) to a new page. I read on some trashy website that if
you physically write out the best part of your day before going to
bed each night, then you increase your chances of reaching a deep
peaceful sleep. I didn't necessarily believe this, but as long as no one
found out I was doing it, then it didn't hurt to test the waters. Plus,

I didn't need to spend any money on this exercise, because for my birthday a few years back, my aunt had given me a beautifully constructed writing notebook. The label called it a diary, but I think that was just a misprint.

I thought for a few minutes, recalling all the motions that formed my day. I reached under my bed, found a pen, and then I wrote this:

The best part of my day . . . was when I found out that Starbucks is bringing back the Gingerbread Latte this holiday season.

I smiled on the inside, but I didn't have enough energy to smile on the outside. I turned off the light and got ready for my night of triumphant slumber.

CHAPTER THREE

"*Aahhhhh!*"

A scream woke me up. Then came the following:

"Oh my God, does pubic hair turn gray as you get older?"

Was that God speaking? I wondered. I looked at my cell phone, which read "2:17 A.M." If so, what was he doing up so late? Maybe heaven operates in a different time zone? Also, why was he referring to himself in the third person? Oh right, God can do that. He probably invented the third person.

Another voice chimed in. "I sure hope not! Otherwise, I'm gonna schedule a waxing appointment for every week until the day I die."

Now I was fairly certain this was not God. Instead, these voices came from the two girls who live in the apartment above me (3C), Cathy and Claire. They'd moved in a couple months ago and had quickly become the number one annoyance in my life.

I don't know if it's because of the way my apartment is positioned, in the corner on the second floor, or because my building has paper-thin walls, or just because they are freakishly loud talkers, but I'm able to hear at least a portion of every conversation these girls have with each other. It's as if I were a fly on the wall at a "no boys allowed" sleepover. Only I don't get to see anything cool, like a pillow fight or a boob. I'm just forced to listen. People say that your home is supposed to be your safe haven, where you can tune out all the stresses that life throws at you. My home used to be my castle. But with the recent addition of the girls above me, it has become my dungeon.

This situation might be more manageable if I were living below someone like Albert Einstein or Socrates or even Michael Lee Aday, better known as Meat Loaf. Then I would at least be overhearing discussions on world-altering theories, the meaning of life, and what "that" actually means. Instead, I'm living underneath a couple of Kardashian wannabes who spend their time gossiping, starving themselves, and throwing noisy parties. This might have been more amusing to me when I was in my early twenties, but I'm quickly approaching thirty and have zero interest in hearing, "If we don't go buy tampons in the next hour, I'm going to die of toxic shock syndrome." I went onto Google to look up toxic shock syndrome and I sorely regret clicking "Images."

I never had a noise issue with the woman who used to live above me, Mrs. Skiffington. But then, she was approaching three hundred years old, weighed about as much as an apple, and lived all alone with her massive collection of Beanie Babies. I kept expecting that one day I would hear a tiny thump and then I'd know that she had moved way way way upstairs. But it didn't go like that. My landlord, Mr. Molever, broke the news:

"She's gone."

"What?! Oh, no. How did it happen?" I asked.

"She left a note."

"A note?! Suicide? She couldn't have waited just a few weeks longer to die of natural causes?" I was in shock.

"What? No, she moved to Florida. Took the Beanie Babies with her."

"Oh. So what do you mean, she left a note? Who does that for moving?"

"Old people."

From the incredibly important knowledge that I've gathered, it's my understanding that Cathy and Claire became "BFFs" when they met freshman year at college. At first I believed they were sisters, because they would refer to each other as "big sis" and "li'l sis." It wasn't until what seemed like a hundred loud, obnoxious "sisters" showed up to stay with them one weekend that I realized their "sisterly" bond was formed not in the womb, but in a sorority.

Right away I felt weird about knowing the intimate details of their lives without even having met them. I know that they're both cranky when they have to wake up before ten A.M. I know that it takes five Patrón shots for Cathy to start talking in "fluent Japanese," even though it sounds more like bad French. I know that Claire thinks her shower singing is "*American Idol*–worthy," but in actuality, it's pitchy. I know that they're both planning to put their children on leashes and hope that when that time comes the rope will be "wireless." And I know that I'm stuck with these girls for the next year, because they just signed their lease.

Their main source of income comes from their parents. Both families seem to do quite well financially, although I'm a little worried about Cathy. She constantly talks about how she has the biggest crush on her dad's bookie and that one day she's going to "ride him like a racehorse," which, I believe, would only result in fast-action money laundering and body bags. I would love to give her some neighborly advice, but unfortunately for me, my relationship with the girls is one-sided. In fact, they have no idea I even exist.

For whatever bizarre reason, Cathy and Claire cannot hear me. I've tried everything to win their attention: shouting at the top of my lungs (I lost my voice for three days), blowing an air horn (which just blended into the beat of their Katy Perry songs), tap dancing (I think I just wanted any excuse to buy the cool shoes), and banging on my ceiling with any item I could find (my fishbowl was a huge mistake). In the end, I think I figured out what the problem was. It's the only way this disconnect makes any possible sense. My hypothesis is that my apartment unit is uniquely positioned in some sort of black hole. Things can come in, like annoying conversations from my neighbors, but nothing goes out, like my pleading for them to shut up.

Sometimes I feel bad for the girls because they aren't exactly the sharpest tools in the shed. In fact, they're more like a couple of dull butter knives that were left in the grass outside of the shed. Of course, it's unfair for me to judge, considering the fact that I'm privileged enough to get insight into their uncensored conversations, but at the same time some things aren't meant to be said aloud. . . .

"This might be a stupid question, but do fish, like, drink water?"

"Oh my God, the power just went out! *The power just went out!* Turn on the lights, I can't see!"

"I know we got bin Laden, but my question is, did we ever get the bastards who flew the planes?"

"Have you ever realized that you can't become a grandma
without having kids?"

The first time I actually laid eyes on Cathy and Claire was in our
building's shared laundry room. I was peacefully folding my boxers and looking around for a lost sock when two familiar voices
barged in.

"Honestly, if Kelly talks shit about me one more time, I'm gonna
start flirting with her boyfriend, like hard-core," I believe Cathy said.

If you piss a guy off, he'll use his fist. I guess if you piss a woman
off, she'll use fucked-up mind games to take you down. I coyly
looked up and laid eyes on my two mysterious girls for the first time.
In my head, I had pictured them both tall with doctored blond hair,
gorgeous in that plastic kind of way, basically Paris Hilton types,
but they were nothing of the sort. Both girls were standard height;
one had long brown hair while the other was a strawberry blonde.
Claire (or the one I identified as Claire from what I remembered of
her voice) wore a tight white tank top, cutoff jean short-shorts, and
sandals, whereas Cathy was dressed head to toe in her Lululemon
workout clothes. They were cute—not in a jaw-dropping kind of
way, but they were above average.

I stood there frozen, with a pair of polka-dot boxers halfway folded
in my hands. They continued with their conversation on how to ruin
poor Kelly's relationship, as if there weren't another breathing body
in the room. I will admit I was completely captivated by these girls.
They were so wrapped up in themselves that they weren't even conscious of my presence. I felt like a National Geographic documen-
tarian, stumbling across a never-before-seen interaction between
two majestic specimens sitting comfortably high on the food chain.

I was able to study them, examine their every move, all from the confines of my folding station.

Unfortunately for me, I suffer from a severe allergy to dryer sheets, which one of my idiotic neighbors had left over as a present for me in the dryer. I tried holding in the sneeze for as long as any human possibly could, but my nose felt as if it were on fire. I let out an enormous convulsive explosion of air through my nose, which echoed through every washer and dryer in the room. I had made myself visible. Cathy and Claire quickly put their discussion on hold and stared at me as if I were a life-form from a distant planet. In this case, I sort of was. I grabbed my folded belongings and kept my head down as I made my way to the exit. A sock fell to the ground, but I left it behind. I figured it was a happy accident, since the dryer had already eaten up the other one. I heard one of them whisper on my way out, "That guy needs to get with the times and make the transition from boxers to boxer briefs immediately." That was my traumatizing introduction to the girls above me. And I will have you know that I've since become a proud owner of Hanes Comfort Flex boxer briefs, even though I do miss the air circulation I once had.

"**Look at this** picture. Suri Cruise is wearing the cutest top ever!"

"Sooo cute! She's been out of the mags for a while; thank God that little fashion diva's back."

Really? At two thirty A.M. the girls needed to discuss Tom Cruise's child's T-shirt? Not that I would condone this type of behavior during the day, but I especially didn't that second while I was trying to sleep. And now, for whatever nonsensical reason, I could only picture what Suri Cruise's top might actually look like. Long sleeved with black and white stripes was coming to mind.

Possibly a matching bow in her hair? I should have been taken away in handcuffs immediately for even picturing such a thing. Five minutes ago, I had been fast asleep having an awesome dream where I was a James Bond–like spy, saving my family from an evil talking rainbow trout. This corrupted fish was forcing us to colonize underwater, which I knew would kill us because we didn't have proper breathing equipment. It was utterly terrifying, but I figured out a way to lure him onto the land, where *he* didn't have proper breathing equipment. My family was surprised by my courageous acts, and ultimately, I think they were proud. Which was a rare occurrence, even in my subconscious. And now all I could think about was a toddler's fashion consciousness. What had these girls done to me? But more important, what shoes was Suri matching with her top? Little flats, I presumed—ahh! That was it, tomorrow I was going to put an end to this madness.

At this point, I was too disgusted with myself to go back to sleep. I opened up my computer and logged on to Twitter to see if any of the people I follow had something interesting to say. Elijah Wood was wide awake as well due to the pain from his root canal surgery. Rob Zombie was thanking Berlin for a "kick-ass crowd." And my sister had posted a picture of her and the rest of my family out at dinner. Hey! Why wasn't I invited?!

I had recently joined Twitter and immediately realized that it was my kind of website. A place where antisocial people can be social without being social. But I had yet to tweet my first tweet. I felt so much pressure trying to come up with the perfect thing to discuss with the entire world. Okay, maybe I was exaggerating a bit since I only had three people "following" me. (Two of whom were my friends; the other was a gorgeous blonde named Gezibelle who followed 742 other people but oddly had no followers of her own.

Maybe that was because she tweeted way too much about calling cards.) But still, what if that one mysterious person was just waiting at his computer for my first tweet, getting ready to pick apart every one of the hundred and forty characters I typed? It needed to be great.

Suddenly I heard, "I feel like I'm gonna die. I texted Chad four hours ago and he still hasn't responded."

Perfect, I thought. My first tweet would have to do with the girls above me. At the expense of their pain and suffering, I began typing.

"Hey, girls above me, where's Chad?" No, no, that's not it. Much too on the nose.

"Hello, me ladies who dwell in the chamber aloft. Where art thou, Sir Chad of no Replyingham?" Interesting, but I didn't want to set an Elizabethan tone with my first tweet.

"Yo, bitches above, Chad's probably textin' yo mama instead." I actually scared myself with that one.

As I stared at my IKEA reproduction coffee table in deep contemplation, I noticed a recently opened letter from my cable provider.

Dear Valued Customer,

After multiple attempts to contact you with no response, we do NOT regret to inform you that your cable will be terminated effective immediately due to multiple unpaid bills. This is great for our company because we are going to take even more money out of your pocket when you decide to turn your cable back on. Yay us!

Sincerely,
The Biggest Piece-of-Shit Cable Provider Ever

I may have paraphrased a bit, but that was the gist of it. I had no immediate plans to deal with my bill, but it did give me an idea for my tweet. So I tried again:

Dear Girls Above Me,

I'm sorry that Chad isn't responding to your text, but honestly, can you blame him?

I pondered it for a few moments. Not my best work, but it felt impersonally personal enough to publish into the world. "Tweet," I clicked. And with that, I had written my first letter to the girls above me.

THE GIRLS ON FASHION

Dear Girls Above Me,

"I saw a terrorist at Forever 21 today!" What?! "She was wearing sandals with socks!" A fashion terrorist. I should've known.

Dear Girls Above Me,

"If I don't get a coat from Chanel's winter collection I'm honestly going to kill myself." Am I supposed to report this?

Dear Girls Above Me,

"Isn't it weird that we use the same word for the devil as we do for the most fab fabric?" Are you talking about Satan and satin?

Dear Girls Above Me,

(screaming) "J. Lo, if you're out there, what eyeliner do you use!?" It's times like these I wish I had a sassy Latina accent.

Dear Girls Above Me,

"She's wearing 5" heels tonight? That bitch! Time to bust out my 5 3/4" stilettos!" Shit just got real.

Dear Girls Above Me,

"If that bitch talks shit about me one more time, I'm gonna wear a white dress to her wedding." Men use fists, women use fabric.

Dear Girls Above Me,

"This week I'm only going to talk to guys who have
the same name as my favorite designers." Say hi to
Helmut from me.

CHAPTER FOUR

I woke up the next morning at the crack of dawn to the vibration of Michael Jackson's "Dirty Diana." At first I thought it was coming from the girls above me. Do they ever fall asleep? I wondered. Where do they get all this energy from? Drugs seemed like the only logical explanation.

But as the song's melody continued and I slowly became more awake, I realized the sounds weren't coming from above me; they were coming from inside my apartment. Unless a burglar with really good taste in music had broken into my living room and decided just to hang out and play some tunes, this could only have been coming from one person . . . my roommate, Pat.

I met Pat while we were both getting our undergraduate degrees at Chapman University. I was accepted into the film program, but Pat had gone to obtain his bachelor's degree in "leadership." His academic path seemed to follow along the same lines as that of people who majored in communications, otherwise known as the "I have no fucking clue what I want to do with my life" degree. I constantly made fun of Pat for choosing such a bullshit area of study, to which he would reply, "You mock me now, but when you're in need of a leader, I won't be there to show you the way." I decided to take my chances.

Pat and I have lived together for almost three years now. The plan was for him to temporarily stay in my spare room/office while he looked for a permanent place to live. He didn't know many people in Los Angeles, so I felt the need to help him make a smooth transition from his hometown, Mukilteo, Washington, to the annoyingly bright lights of Hollywood. After a month had gone by with Pat, I noticed that my apartment had become quite a bit cleaner, the aroma had improved tremendously, and I would often find little sticky notes that would lead to other little sticky notes that would lead to fresh-squeezed orange juice with a tiny umbrella sticking out of it. A small umbrella in your morning drink is something that people would consider a luxury, but it's also something you can't really accessorize by yourself without feeling totally pathetic. I realized I had found the perfect roommate. Finally, a man who would umbrella my drink for me. So I invited him to stay permanently (assuming the umbrellas would continue).

In college, Pat was my resident advisor, which was basically a semifancy way of saying that he was the person I went to if I clogged my toilet. He was certainly a leader in all things plunger related. But with this title, he also had the authority to fine me for things like lighting candles and/or farts, skateboarding in front of the dormitories, and playing the trumpet outside Jenny O'Brien's window. Luckily for me I quickly realized that Pat was much too nice of a guy to use his authority over me. Any time he would start to fumble his words, I knew I could easily talk him out of any disciplinary action, which for me is the sign of a potential best friend.

To this day, I believe I still hold the record for the most farts lit on fire (sixteen) in a public area without getting into trouble. I owe this crowning achievement to Pat, because Tyler Trautman was right on my tail (fourteen) and was really getting into a solid rhythm just before Pat busted him. Tyler was very confused as to why he suffered from disciplinary action over lighting farts while I did not. Later on, Pat was freaking out, thinking that Tyler was going to take this issue to a higher power: the school's board. I told Pat he needed to "calm the fuck down" and find a place to lie low for a bit. He sat on his large beanbag chair in his dorm room for a week, while I brought him tater tots every morning until things cooled off. Tyler never ended up filing a report. Maybe he was too embarrassed about having to admit he lost to me in a fart-lighting contest, or maybe he was scared by the life-threatening handwritten note I left on his pillow. It's unclear. Regardless, that little incident brought Pat and me closer.

So much for memory lane. I was groggy and sleep deprived as I made my way into the living room. It was seven thirty A.M. and Pat was playing a Wii video game called *Michael Jackson: The Experience.* The music was blaring at full volume as he danced along to the beat. If my apartment wasn't in a black hole from which no sound can escape, someone might've complained about the noise. He maneuvered his body perfectly in between our two La-Z-Boy recliners and gripped a remote in his hand as if it were a microphone, which for the record was absolutely pointless, because the game calculated his dance moves and had nothing to do with his singing.

"Dirty Diana, no. Dirty Diana, no. It's Dia . . . aa . . . aa . . . ana!" Pat sang with enough passion to raise Michael out of his "Thriller" grave.

"Good morning," I said quietly in order not to disturb his concentration.

"Charlie, I'm on my way to reaching eighty thousand points for the first time. Watch me get dirty with Diana."

Pat climbed up onto our coffee table and began thrusting his pelvis into a nonexistent woman. He was completely oblivious to everything he was knocking over and crushing on the table. The OCD boy living inside me almost passed out from sensory overload.

"Pat, come on, you just knocked over a glass of water—"

"Ssh . . . Dirty Diana, no!" I couldn't believe it; he'd actually shushed me. I absolutely hate it when people shush me. But then I remembered that MJ makes odd vocal noises during his songs and assumed Pat was just singing "Sha'mone," which is MJ-speak for "come on."

"You're not even looking at the video game anymore. Now you're just dry-humping our table," I said. But Pat was in his own world and nothing could stop him. As I watched Pat take our poor table's virginity, I couldn't help but wonder whom he pictured underneath him. He sang with such strong emotion and intensity that he couldn't have been thinking about just anybody. He must've been imagining someone he really cared about. Someone with whom he shared a real human connection. Someone who challenged him to be a better person. Someone with whom he had dreamed of breathing his last living breath. Someone with, possibly, a penis.

You see, I had this little theory that Pat was gay, though he would never ever admit it. Most people in my life believed that this was not a theory, but indeed 100 percent fact. Even my mom said, "Charlie, I've never met a young man as gay as Pat. And if you can't see that, then maybe I have a gay son." I'm not quite sure about her logic there, but I did begin to question whether or not I had grown so accustomed to Pat's "gayness" that I didn't even notice it anymore.

I should mention that I am not a homophobe. I'm extremely comfortable with and supportive of anyone who identifies as gay, straight, or bi. This was only an issue for me because I wanted Pat to live the life that made sense for him, and if he was in fact gay, I wanted him to be openly so. But at the time, my findings were not yet conclusive. It was possible, after all, that Pat was not gay but simply fabulous. It's easy to mistake fabulous for gay, so I decided to make a list of things that Pat had said or done that might possibly come across as even a tad bit gay. Upon completion of the list, I would have enough facts to make my final assessment. Here's the list I had so far:

COULD PAT BE GAY?

In seventh grade, Pat ran the number one Spice Girls fan page in America, called *Pat's Spicy Page.*

He often describes having good sex as "kick-ass intercourse."

He wants to marry Kylie Minogue so that she can sing to him "all day long."

He owns every color of American Apparel tighty whities, even the sea-foam green ones.

He's seen the musical *Wicked* thirty-two times.

"I never really liked Spider-Man. I was more of a Pinocchio kind of kid."

He read all four *Twilight* books in less than two days.

When I took him to a Lakers game, he said, "This is where Taylor Swift plays!"

He has described Nair as his "best friend" on multiple occasions.

So, as you can see, Pat was a super-fabulous guy. But was he gay? I still wasn't sure.

"Eighty-one thousand points, baby! Suck it, dead Michael Jackson!" Pat finally got off of our violated coffee table.

"Maybe next time you could play the game when it's not in the early hours of the morning?" Why did I even have to ask this?

"Shit, I'm so sorry! I'll make it up to you by squeezing you some extra orange juice. But I need to buy some more umbrellas."

"Don't worry about it. I just barely got any sleep; those girls who live above us kept me up most of the night—"

"Oh my God, me too. How good was that conversation about baby Cruise's little shirt? I found the picture online, they were so right. She looked adorable."

I made a mental note to add this to the "Could Pat Be Gay?" list.

"I'm sure Suri looked great, but I can't keep living my life listening to these idiotic girls yap to each other."

"Tell me about it. Hey, maybe we should just go knock on their door and see if they'd be down for a foursome. You know, just 'cause it would be an awesome story to tell," Pat blurted out with what I believed to be sincerity.

"Umm, I was thinking more along the lines of filing a noise complaint," I said.

"Totally. That's a great way to handle it too."

Before Pat left for work, he hand-squeezed me another glass of orange juice with a makeshift umbrella, even though I begged him not to. He said, "It's no problem at all. Who wouldn't want to squeeze something that feels just like titties?" This statement made me consider a new list. Could Pat be an alien?

THE GIRLS' KNOWLEDGE

Dear Girls Above Me,

"How do I spell . . . this word?" Unfortunately, I don't have a visual, but aren't you pointing to it?

Dear Girls Above Me,

"How does Google work? Is someone hired to look up your search and send it back to you?" Yes, and they search for it on Google.

Dear Girls Above Me,

"School was forever ago! I don't remember what a stupid adjective means!" Ironic that the adjective you just used was "stupid."

Dear Girls Above Me,

"I'm blanking, who discovered the world was round again? I mean flat—wait, did he think—yeah, flat—wait—" Christopher Columbus.

Dear Girls Above Me,

"She's kinda pathetic, spending years studying just to work at a bar." Does this "bar" happen to be called "the Bar"?

Dear Girls Above Me,

"He kept saying his name instead of using 'I.' What's that called again? Same person? Talking person?" 3rd person (Charlie sighs).

Dear Girls Above Me,

"All I want in life is a strand of Justin Timberlake's hair so I can make his babies." DNA doesn't produce children.

Dear Girls Above Me,

"Okay, I honestly just noticed that keyboards aren't in alphabetical order." This is a quote from you and my two year old cousin.

CHAPTER FIVE

I mapped out my course of action. The strategy was to deliver my rent check and then casually, while I happened to be there, file a noise complaint against the girls above me. I'm the king of the "Oh, by the way." As I walked down the long dark hallway to Mr. Molever's apartment, I heard a familiar clanking sound. My immediate reaction to this particular noise was to gag, find the nearest hiding spot, and wait for as long as it took till this noise went away. The source of said racket came from Penny's collar; she's a toy poodle who lives in my building and is my least-favorite dog on the planet. Her owner, Tania, isn't much better. Tania thinks that Penny and my dog Marvin are "lovers." Therefore, she believes they must see each other at least once a day to keep their spirits and sexual drive fulfilled. "A relationship is a partnership, which is why they both end in '-ship.'" I don't know what that even means. "So my Penny can't keep giving and giving emotionally while your Marvin is taking and taking." What a lunatic. By the way, Marvin *hates* Penny. Interacting with Penny is Marvin's "surgical neuter" . . . and he'd been surgically neutered.

They live on the other side of the building, 4F, but will often make trips by my apartment for reasons beyond comprehension. I know this because sometimes I spy on them through the peephole. Tania will pretend she's on the phone, just casually hanging out directly in front of my door. One time she was having a "hilarious" conversation with a friend on the phone, when all of a sudden I watched as her cell phone rang. She was so surprised and stunned by the loud ring in her ear that she let go of her phone and accidentally kicked Penny a good few feet down the hallway. She quickly turned and looked directly into my peephole, as if she sensed I was staring at her. She then sniffed around a little bit, which I found remarkably unsettling. The point is, I'm a grown man and I won't allow myself to be reduced to a childish fear all because of a scary lady named Tania.

So as I was frantically trying to find a hiding place to avoid Tania, Penny's collar was becoming more and more audible. Where should I go? I wasn't able to pinpoint the direction they were coming from, so turning back was just as risky as trekking forward. I was screwed. So, for whatever freakish reason, I got down on the floor and curled up into a lopsided ball. I guess I figured the hallway was dark enough that Tania might not even realize there was a person there. Or maybe I was unconsciously re-creating some traumatic experience I had suffered in the womb? Either way, even if she did spot me, maybe she'd think I was a pile of clothes or a sleeping zombie who should undoubtedly be left alone.

What I didn't take into account was Penny's bionic nose. Out of nowhere she trotted up to me, took one sniff, and began barking directly into my ear. It was truly the most annoying sound I had ever heard. I had a violent vision of swiftly grabbing Penny by the collar and, with the ease of Chuck Norris (but without the homophobia), snapping her bony poodle neck. But I had committed myself to this position and believed I still had a chance to stay invisible to Tania.

"Charlie? Is that you down there?"

"Huh? What?" I didn't quite know how else to respond.

"What are you doing? Are you hiding from me?" Tania asked.

"What? No. I was just—ducking and covering—from the earthquake."

"Umm, what earthquake?" She was onto me.

"You didn't just feel that tremor?"

"No."

"I can't believe you didn't feel it! You should probably go back inside your apartment and check the news for updates. Inside your apartment. The news. Inside."

"I didn't feel anything. Neither did Penny. So, where's our little Romeo?" Tania asked in a cutesy way that made me want to vomit.

"Oh, Marvin? The poor little guy is feeling under the weather. He's been resting."

"Aww, sweet sweet Marv. Well, I know what he needs."

"Yeah, rest," I reiterated.

"Nope. He needs the warmth of his lover."

"I'm pretty sure he just needs to rest."

But I was too late. Tania headed toward my door with Penny trotting at her feet. I thought about turning myself into a hallway barricade, making it more difficult for her to barge into my apartment, but I couldn't muster up the energy. Without any warning, my poor little Marvin was about to get pounced on by a freakishly energetic poodle. In a last attempt to save Marvin's life, I yelled, "My door's locked!" But Tania paid less attention to me than she did to the earthquake I had invented. She easily opened my unlocked door and called, "Romeo? Where art thou, Romeo?"

I left a good pug behind that day.

Mr. Molever came to his doorway dressed in striped baby-blue silk pajamas. Not that it would look normal on anyone, but he looked especially ridiculous. He gave me an "it's about time" glance, which then morphed into an "I'm disappointed in you" downward head nod, which finally transformed into an "I'm reminding you of your mother" glare because of his slightly squinting stare of indignation and subsequent silent judgment. But that might have been me bringing some of my own baggage to this exchange. After what felt like three hours of awkward silence and repressed childhood memories, I handed him my rent check.

"Thank you. I don't normally bend the rules for tardy tenants, but since I can see by your appearance that you've had a rough morning, I won't charge you the late penalty," Mr. Molever said to me. I felt like punching him in the testicles, or at least ripping off his terrible pajamas, but that would ultimately have punished me. I had to just grin and bear it, because I needed his authority in order to shut up the girls above me and bring some much-needed peace and quiet into my life.

"Oh, by the way . . ." I explained to Mr. Molever my unbearable living situation.

Who: The girls above me.

What: I can hear everything they say.

Where: In my apartment.

When: All hours of the day and night.

I went on to list specific examples of my noisy situation. I could tell Mr. Molever was intrigued by these girls more than anything and showed no signs of sympathy. He walked away for a moment and returned holding a large binder with a sticker on the side that read OFFICIAL COMPLAINT DOCUMENTS.

"Here, fill these out. Assuming there are no spelling mishaps or grammatical errors, I will give you the next set of documents you'll need to complete." He handed me the binder, which weighed about as much as a grown-up bowling ball.

"Can't you just go tell them to keep it down?" I pleaded.

"Theoretically, yes. Legally, no. Not until the proper paperwork has been filed."

My fists clenched. Although I'm not sure why, since I've never physically fought anyone before. If I ever do, Mr. Molever will definitely be the first person on my list, especially if he's wearing silk that day. I took a deep breath.

"I don't understand what you're complaining about," Mr. Molever blurted.

"Excuse me?" I asked, stunned by his boldness. I was quickly running out of fists to clench.

"A couple of attractive young gals talking locker room? Isn't that every guy's dream?"

Every guy's dream? What guy wants to hear about the latest dieting craze, called "the Tic Tac and edamame diet"? What guy do you know who wants to hear in great detail the cause of "toxic shock syndrome"? Can you find me one, just one, guy who wants this version of "Little Bunny Foo Foo" stuck in his head: "Little Bunny Foo Foo, hopping through the forest, jerking off the field mice and giving lots of head"? You should've seen the looks I got at the DMV when I accidentally sang that song out loud.

Mr. Molever, not surprisingly, was of no help. I was a thousand dollars poorer and my maddening situation was still very much in existence. I reluctantly took his "I'm never getting laid" binder of building incident reports and complaint forms, then headed down the hallway with my tail between my legs. Speaking of tails, I hoped Marvin was protecting his. If Tania was still playing Cupid at my apartment, forcing our dogs to make love to each other, I might possibly have been having the worst day of anyone's life. Except for maybe poor Marvin's. "You can always just go knock on their door yourself," Mr. Molever yelled out after me. What an idiot. The whole point of filing a noise complaint against your neighbor is so that they don't know which person ratted them out. If I showed my identity to these girls, I'd practically be handing myself over on a silver platter. Up until this point they had been noisy without even trying. Could you imagine the racket these girls would cause if they found out the snitch lived directly below them?

APARTMENT LIFE

Dear Girls Above Me,

I apologize for the Chewbacca greeting in the parking lot, I was eating a banana.

Dear Girls Above Me,

Our building doesn't have a ghost "trapped in
the walls on Thursday and Friday." It's just street
cleaning.

Dear Girls Above Me,

Sometimes when you're having sex, I play you in
Jenga. Right now I'm winning 3 games to 2.

Dear Girls Above Me,

"I wish my bad date could've been in dog years so it
ended faster." I'm so thankful your lease is in human
years.

Dear Girls Above Me,

"So, I gave him two options, breakfast in bed or a
blow job. Guess what he picked?" Well I didn't smell
burnt toast, so . . .

Dear Girls Above Me,

I changed my wireless Internet name to
"JohnStamosCondo" in hopes that it might confuse
and excite you. It did.

Dear Girls Above Me,

"The cleaning lady canceled! Okay, go to YouTube
and look for a video on how to use a washing
machine." Remember *lots* of bleach.

Dear Girls Above Me,

I know you're going crazy but stop Googling
"someone who kills birds, Los Angeles." Try replacing
the battery in your smoke alarm.

Dear Girls Above Me,

"We still have no electricity! Wow, the wind really
fucked us last night." Is "the wind" code for the guy
with the French accent?

CHAPTER SIX

Most people talk themselves into doing something gutsy. I much prefer talking myself *out* of doing something gutsy. Who needs gutsy? To me, gutsy is ordering double toasted at Quiznos. Unfortunately, before I was able to talk myself out of it, I found myself standing in front of the girls' front door. I could hear muffled "Valley girl" conversations on the other side, so they were home. All I had to do was knock on their door and politely ask them to never speak again, and I could finally get enough peace and quiet to get my life back in order. But why was I so afraid? I'm sure a therapist would have told me it comes from an incident in my childhood when my family neglected me. Most likely this fear comes from the time I took part in a local jump-rope competition at my middle school. Neither my parents nor my sisters showed up to watch me take home the gold . . . jump rope. I remember looking out into the crowd during my awe-inspiring grand finale, and there were the cliché empty seats where my family was supposed to be. To be fair, there were about forty empty seats. In fact, there were only two people sitting down, and they were both the grandparents of the student in charge of holding the stopwatch. Regardless, I prefer to blame most of my unique and challenging problems on this particular incident.

Intimacy issues . . . The jump rope competition.

Fear of rabbits . . . The jump rope competition.

Attention deficit disorder . . . The jump rope competition.

Annoying way of phrasing words . . . The jump rope competish.

Motion sickness . . . The jump rope competition.

Inability to walk in a straight line (even while I'm sober) . . . The jump rope competition.

"Come on, Charlie. Be strong." Yes, I whispered those words out loud to myself. I needed some extra motivation to actually go through with knocking, so why not act like a crazy person? As I slowly got closer and closer, roars of laughter from what sounded like three hundred females echoed through their door. I was petrified. I'm not going to lie, I almost turned back. But since I had already accepted that in my lifetime I would never reach the summit (or the base camp, for that matter) of Mount Kilimanjaro, this would be my version of a treacherous trek.

So, I went for it. I raised my fist, which was conveniently still clenched from my previous encounter with the landlord, and I pounded on the door. Well, I pretended to pound. In reality I timidly knocked in the pathetic hope that they wouldn't hear it and I could proudly walk back to my apartment, all while telling myself, "At least you tried, killer." But then suddenly, the door opened before I could walk away. I froze. A young twentysomething girl stood in front of me, but she wasn't one of the girls above me. She looked me up and down and couldn't have hidden her disappointment even if she tried. Which she didn't. "If I'd looked through the peephole before answering, I never would've opened the door," she said. The jump rope competish all over again. "Ugh, we're totally not interested in changing religions."

"Okay. Good to know," I said, having no clue what she was talking about.

"That's why you're here, right?" She stared at Mr. Molever's binder, clearly mistaking it for some kind of religious recruiting book. "You want to convert us to whatevs your religion is."

"No. I'm just a guy with a beard." Thankfully I wasn't wearing a black tie, otherwise things could've gotten really awkward. "Actually, I'm the neighbor who lives below."

"Oh, okay . . . It's just . . . your beard. It really threw me off." I could hear my mother saying, "See!" From her makeup and platinum-blond hair, I stereotyped her as a friend of Cathy and Claire. She was pretty enough, in an amateur-porn-star sort of way; like "I'll make a sex tape and just conveniently leave it around and when someone finds it I'll act like I'm outraged but really I'll be flattered." You know the type. This is not a girl you bring home to mom, unless you want to send mom into severe emotional trauma. Either her lips had been recently stung by an entire beehive, or she had made friends with a Beverly Hills doctor who had enormous plans for her, and even bigger plans for her prodigious mouth. Just then, from the other room, I heard a familiar voice call out, "Bridget, is someone at the door?"

A harem suddenly gathered around Bridget to see what the

commotion was all about. They studied me as if I were a chimpan-
zee who had just awakened from an unsuccessful scientific experi-
ment. Silent farts and dog whistles are heard in this kind of awkward
silence. Cathy and Claire were there, but I could tell by their unsettling faces that they didn't recognize me as someone who lived in
the building.

"Umm, hi. I'm your downstairs neighbor," I said in a voice that
a jerk liar might describe as a tremble. All of the girls let out an
impressively timed group sigh.

"Oh my God, come in! Come in!" they said at the same high-
frequency pitch. I immediately tried to explain my reason for stopping by, but no one was letting me get a word in. Eight girls guided
me into the apartment like an octopus's tentacles luring its prey.
There was nowhere for me to go except deeper and deeper into their
cave.

Due to the abundance of females, there was a moment where I
wondered whether the girls above me were involved in some sort of
cult. But from my understanding, cults mostly consisted of people
who don't get around to showering very much and who wear one-
piece clothing accompanied by all-black Velcro shoes. The prerequi-
sites for this particular cult would have been: at least a C-cup, modest
IQ, Christian Louboutin heels, and memorizing the Bible. And by
"Bible" I of course mean *Fifty Shades of Grey*.

As I walked in, I realized that their apartment had the same exact
layout as mine. I had just figured that the main difference would be
everything else. In retrospect I'm not sure what I was expecting. Actually, I'm exactly sure what I was expecting. Given the wide range of
conversations I was able to overhear, I thought there'd be an Edward
Cullen shrine between the kitchen and living room. Maybe some tiny
wall space reserved for Team Jacob. (That Claire is a real bandwagon

jumper and her "team" allegiances tend to shift just as frequently as Bella's.) But there was no *Twilight* memorabilia. I assumed that no matter where you looked, you'd see pink—pink carpet, pink pillows, pink toaster, pink Brita water filter—and I even assumed they'd be listening to the artist Pink. But again, their color choices were normal, dare I say even pleasant. I assumed that I must have interrupted one of their many FMK (F@#k, Marry, Kill) hypothetical conversations. That imaginary game was always a pleasure to hear at four in the morning, especially when you take into account how each scenario always managed to end with their choosing "f@#k" for *all three people*. I'm not kidding. Even though it's a theoretical game, impossible to play wrong, they'd manage to play wrong. Every. Time. Always. But alas, no such conversation was taking place. Normal-looking apartment, no *Twilight* shrine, and no FMK game being played incorrectly. That's when I realized something. . . .

The girls above me behave differently behind closed doors, in their own personal space, than they do in front of other people in their own personal living room. Just when I thought I had them figured out, a curveball. Their little social inconsistencies were twisting my brain like a pretzel. Who were they? In a matter of moments, I went from annoyed to intrigued.

As I was trying to put this puzzle together, the girls ushered me onto what I'd once overheard them call their "gossip couch." Then they offered me a fancy kind of wine called "Pinot Grigio," which I politely declined. "So, what's your name?" Claire asked.

"My name? Oh, it's Charlie."

In unison, all of the girls let out an adoring "aww." How was their timing so impeccable? They weren't just finishing each other's sentences, they *were* each other's sentences. Maybe my first instinct was right; this *was* a cult.

"Well, I'm Cathy, and this is Claire. We both live here. And these are some of our sorority sisters from our college days." All I could think about was how far Darwinism would be set back if these girls were all actually blood related. I also found it strange that after being out of college for a couple of years adults would still refer to their friends as "sisters." I don't go around telling people that the guy who makes my coffee every morning at Starbucks is my brother. And I guarantee that Alejandro and I have a much tighter bond than these girls could ever have.

Over the course of the next few minutes I was catching glimpses of the girls I'd been overhearing every night. For example, hints of their vocal fry (a way of talking in the lowest vocal register, making the words sound like a creaky vibration; think Kardashian-speak). As well as the unintended "ah" after a word. Such as "Thank you-ah." Or "Nooo-ah." This way of talking would sneak its way into the flow of the conversation like Anthony Hopkins's British accent whenever he plays an American. Also, at one point, Claire wondered if some businesses were closed on 4/20. There were the girls I knew. They popped out from time to time.

I became so enamored that I forgot to even mention what I was doing there in the first place. It was evident that they just assumed I was a new neighbor introducing myself to the tenants. My God, do people actually do that? Sounds exhausting. Anyway, I was debating bringing up the noise complaint when one of their "sisters" looked over at Claire and said, "You think Charlie would wanna play?" I was just hoping it wasn't another round of FMK, or in their case, FFF.

"Oh my God, do you want to play the texting game with us?" Claire blurted out.

"Umm, I'm not familiar with that game," I regrettably said out loud.

They began explaining it to me, as if I were five years old. The idea was one of them would come up with a random text message for me to send out. It could really be anything, but their example to me was, "Ugh, I want a baby!" I would then start scrolling through my cell phone contacts, until someone yelled *"stop."* I would then have to send that text message to whomever I landed on. The girls admitted to me they had been routinely playing this game since college and that "It's literally the best game since Alex Trebek invented *Wheel of Fortune!*" I could think of at least fifty games off the top of my head that were better than this one. Like *Jeopardy!,* for example. But if there's anything I learned from growing up with three sisters, it's that you never argue with a pack of girls. With one girl, you might win an argument every so often, but you shouldn't expect favorable results. With two girls, chances are very slim. Only a few men have ever pulled that off. With three girls, forget about it. Zero chance. I don't care how slick or good-looking you are, no man has pulled off a dispute against three or more women. No matter what, the women are right.

Cathy and Claire begged me to play. Perhaps I said yes because I was severely outnumbered, but before I knew it, my cell phone was out. I also realized another problem that might occur: The more I bonded with these two, the harder it would become to discuss the noise issue.

"Okay, here's your text message. Are you ready?" Claire asked.

I thought about quickly deleting a few numbers from my contacts list, but I didn't want to get penalized before I even started. So I anxiously nodded.

"You have to text . . . 'I'm stuck on the toilet; can you bring me some toilet paper?'" All the girls erupted in giddy laughter. If they thought I was going to send that text message to any of the people in my contact list, they were bat-shit crazy.

"I can't send that out. I have many colleagues' numbers in my phone," I informed them.

"Colleagues? What are you, friends with my dad or something?" I did not believe I was friends with their dad. Also, it's hard to have colleagues when you're unemployed, but I was grasping at straws.

"You have to send the text! That's the game!" The game? That's not a game. Pictionary, Taboo, Scrabble, Words with Friends—these are games. But I knew I wasn't going anywhere until I sent out that text message. So, I began scrolling through my contacts. The girls cheered and clapped as if I were doing something of much more importance. Oddly enough, I got a bit of an adrenaline rush from the anticipation of who I was going to land on. Please don't be my cable guy, please don't be my cable guy.

"And . . . *stop!*" Cathy yelled out. I lifted my thumb off of my Black-Berry and prayed for a landline or any other non-textable number. I looked down.

"Aunt Nancy," I said out loud. By the reactions I got from the girls, Aunt Nancy seemed to be quite a good pull. I was dreading having to send her a text about needing some toilet paper. I definitely didn't have a "poo-talking relationship" with my aunt. Plus, she lives almost two thousand miles away in Arkansas, and knowing her, she would probably do everything in her power to get me some toilet paper. But without putting any more thought into it, I typed out the sentence and pressed SEND. A couple of the girls gallivanted their way over to me, giving me multiple high fives. Bridget even wrapped her arms around me like a boa constrictor, not giving me the opportunity to breathe. Is this what it's like to be a girl? I wondered. When

I'm with my guy friends, we pretty much stay in our own quadrants and only communicate with one another through inaudible grunts. I was happy "the guys" couldn't see me now.

My cell phone buzzed. It was a text back from my aunt already.

I read the message out loud: "Honey, I'm in Arkansas, but don't worry! I'm gonna call my friend Sherry who lives an hour from you and see if she can help out. Sit tight." The girls fell on the floor laughing. I must admit, I found it rather funny myself. I couldn't help but let out a chuckle in an Ebenezer Scrooge sort of way. The texting game was marvelously immature, but because all the girls found it so amusing, I found a soft spot for it.

"Do it again! Do it again!" The girls egged me on. Luckily, I was immune to peer pressure. I had already made it through the tyranny of high school and college having never smoked a cigarette or done drugs; this was going to be a piece of cake.

I shook my head. "Nope, I'm done."

"Oh, come on! But you're *so* good at it. Like honestly the best player ever," Claire said to me.

All right, fine. Why not? I was practically a pro at this point. I whipped out my phone and began scrolling.

"Okay, the text is . . . 'Are you as sweaty as I am right now?' And . . . *stop*," they called out. *Bam!* Phil Salazar, my old violin teacher to whom I hadn't spoken in at least eight years. No problem. And *sent*. I was on a roll.

"Next," I barked out.

"'Do you consider me a limber person?'" Claire said off the top of her head. "And, *stop*." Jen Keeler. The hot mom who cuts my hair and sometimes trims my unibrow. I didn't even hesitate. Boom. SEND. I was Michael Jordan and this was game six.

"Oh, I know! Text someone 'I love you,'" Bridget said, challenging me. I'll do that; no problem, I thought to myself. What's the worst that can happen? If I land on someone I barely know, they will probably just think it was meant for someone else, and if I happen to land on my mother then it will make her entire month. A win-win situation. Weirdly enough, this was the most fun I had had in quite a while. So, I shuffled through the contacts once more until someone told me to stop. I let my thumb off of the scroller and looked down to see my next victim. Finally it settled.

My ex-girlfriend.

A powerful wave of sadness ran throughout my body. I could feel it in my fingers, my toes, my ankles, even my thigh muscles, pretty much anywhere that experiences feeling in the human body. The energy in the room shifted, and the girls could sense something was wrong. They didn't pry or ask questions. We all just sat there in silence. It was beginning to get a bit awkward, considering I had only just met these girls. But somehow they could sense how uncomfortable I felt, again showing an acute awareness that was a stark contrast to who these girls turn into after midnight. But at this particular moment I had bigger fish to fry.

"You don't have to send it. It's just a silly game we play," Claire said to make me feel better. And she did. But at this point I had become a devout player of the texting game and decided it was only right for me to be gallant and play by the rules we had established. I typed those three little words and felt the mechanical ball roll beneath my thumb. I pushed it. Message sent. In my head I tracked its journey into space, watched it very briefly ricochet off a satellite, then make its way back down to our planet and into her phone. I wondered where she was at that very moment. Did she look the same? Was she still wearing that moisturizer that I didn't like the smell of at first but grew to love? Maybe her new boyfriend was smelling it right now. Was she happy? I hoped not.

"I don't remember your name, but I want you to know that you're totally hot," Bridget interjected in order to break up the pathetic reminiscing in my head. Clearly she had gotten past the sandals.

"Yeah, but you'd be way hotter if you shaved your beard," Cathy said, weighing in with her two cents. The rest of them nodded, agreeing with her. So did the manifestation of my mother. I didn't want to get into a discussion with strangers about my facial hair choices, so I just grinned.

"Thank you for an interesting afternoon. I'm sure I'll see you around the apartment building," I said to them as I headed for the door.

"Wait. We're having a party tomorrow night, you should totally come!"

My brain frantically searched for the perfect excuse, but the pressure of sixteen eyes focused on me longingly made it difficult to assemble one. I started speaking before I had any idea what I was going to say. "Tomorrow night . . . is a night . . . and the weather is going to be . . . good . . . so . . . I'll be there." Damn it. Maybe I wasn't as good at dodging peer pressure as I thought.

"And just so you know, the theme of the party is pastel-colored shirts, so wear your favorite one," Claire said in full-on vocal-fry mode, which could only have been a result of the three bottles of Pinot they'd all drunk to kick off "Sunday Funday." "We got the idea from US Weekly. Ryan Gosling has been wearing them a lot lately," Cathy announced. Yup, the wine had turned them into the girls I knew them to be. Or maybe it was my Hall of Fame–worthy skills at the texting game. I won't give the wine all the credit.

On my way out, I was reminded of the real reason I was there in the first place. Funny enough, Claire herself reminded me:

"Hey, are we ever too loud? Like you can't hear us talking, can you?"

They couldn't have made it any easier for me. It was as if they were psychic. They lobbed me the perfect pitch, and all I had to do was smack it out of the park. Now it was just like telling an old friend to politely keep it down. Every high-heeled stomp, sleepless night, mind-numbing pointless conversation, gone forever if I wanted them to be. All I had to do was say yes.

"No," I replied.

Maybe I felt sorry and didn't want to embarrass them? Maybe I was self-destructive and this was my form of "cutting." Or maybe there was a smidgen of a possibility that I actually wanted to keep listening to the girls' conversations. . . . Uh, doubt it. Regardless of my nonsensical reasoning, there was one thing that was for sure: At first, I'd entered the dragon's den as a knight intending to behead the fire-breathing beast, but I may have left looking like the dragon's gay bestie. Regardless of how you want to describe it, my new "roommates" were here to stay, and I had better get used to it.

THE GIRLS ON MOVIES

Dear Girls Above Me,

"Seeing *The Girl With the Dragon Tattoo* has made me wanna get a badass tattoo." The Girl With the Star on Her Foot isn't "badass."

Dear Girls Above Me,

(Watching the *Hunger Games* trailer) "I play very different hunger games." Yes, but anorexia doesn't make for good cinema.

Dear Girls Above Me,

"There are these billboards everywhere saying the world's coming to an end on Friday!" Does Harry Potter happen to be on them?

Dear Girls Above Me,

"No! The 'which *Sex and the City* girl are you' survey I took said I'm Samantha. I'm so a Carrie!" Don't beat yourself up, I got Miranda.

Dear Girls Above Me,

"How do I vote for Best Actor? If Bieber doesn't win for *Never Say Never,* I'm done with movies." Oh God, please be done with movies.

Dear Girls Above Me,

Thanks for leaving on the DVD menu to *27 Dresses*
while you're out of town. I've been meaning to listen
to that loop 5,473 times.

Dear Girls Above Me,

I know you "like seriously love black people movies,"
but that doesn't make you "practically besties with
Precious."

THEY WATCH SHARK WEEK

Dear Girls Above Me,

"Shark Week is over!? But it was only on for like a
week! Oh, wait a minute—" Nope, you already said it
out loud!

Dear Girls Above Me,

"It's Shark Week *and* the gays can finally get
married?! Best. Week. Ever." I'm glad you got your
priorities in order.

CHAPTER SEVEN

As I approached the door to my apartment with much trepidation, a hideous image flashed before my eyes. It was of Tania lying on my bed in the nude with Marvin and Penny by her side. In this fantasy nightmare from hell she looked at me and, in an awkwardly forced seductive whisper, said, "How about we show these pups who the real lovers are?" The imagery alone made me want to throw up a little bit in my mouth, but the audio I heard in my mind's ear made me want to projectile-vomit. I listened for the chime of Penny's collar but heard nothing. I knew I was in the clear.

I opened the door and found my sweet little Marvin standing eerily frozen directly in front of me, not even a wag of his curly tail. He looked up at me with his watery eyes with such sorrow. I couldn't tell if he had been hysterically crying or if his eyes were just glossed over like those of a prison inmate who just got a new three-hundred-pound cell mate.

I distracted him with a treat, and he instantly forgave me. I wish humans would react as easily to such rewards. Can you imagine if you were in a spousal quarrel, on the verge of splitting up with your partner forever, and all you had to do was pull out a Snausage? It would be incredible. Any pent-up anger would be forgotten and all focus would be put into the glorious Milk-Bone or Greenie. And once the treat had proven successful in domestic partnerships, the military would want to get in on it as well. The Israelis could lob Dentley's Meaty Whole Femur Bones over the Palestine border, and the Palestinians could shoot Jakks Pets Wrizzles across Israel's border, and *bam*, I just gave peace to the Middle East. Perhaps I should've been an army general. But I have a deviated septum, so, you know, boot camp would be a problem.

I sat down at my desk in hopes of actually getting some writing done. It's just hard when the Internet has so many enticing pop-up ads, such as "Top Celebrity Beach Bods." Even though I knew I shouldn't click, I just got so much joy out of confirming that Matthew McConaughey was still number one. There are certain constants in life you don't want to ever see change because you find them so refreshing. I just hope to be long in my grave the dark day he's replaced by Channing Tatum.

But before I even allowed myself the chance to get Internet-distracted, I realized I was already reality-distracted. I looked down at my phone and was immediately reminded of the mortifying text I sent to my ex-girlfriend after falling victim to the girls above me's texting game. I was curious if she was going to respond. And every second that ticked away lowered the likelihood that she'd text me back. Just like how the police say that after a kidnapping you have a two-day window to get your child back, and then each passing moment after increases the likelihood that you'll never see your kid again. . . . Well, actually, I'm not sure if police say that; I'm just quoting Delroy Lindo from the movie *Ransom*. Regardless, she had yet to respond to my text, and I wasn't surprised in the slightest. She was the type of girl who never looked back once her mind had been made up. I wished I had known that a few weeks ago, before I had come up with the ingenious idea to write her this e-mail:

Subject: Food for thought . . .

I have emotionally accepted that we are over (although I still cradle hope); however, we should have sex a couple times a week to smooth out the transition, don't you agree?

Her response:

Subject: RE: Food for thought . . .

Call a therapist, Charlie.

The worst part about the whole thing was I did end up consulting with a therapist, and was charged a hundred and fifty dollars for a diagnosis of "You shouldn't have done that." Then the therapist started blabbering on about how my act of desperation came from an unresolved experience I had during my youth, which most likely involved my parents or the jump rope. I wasn't sure how asking my ex-girlfriend to have sex with me had something to do with my family, so I decided to take a break from professional healing for a while.

The time was six P.M. and I felt guilty for the wasted day. Then I started thinking about starving kids in Africa and felt guilty for feeling guilty. Then I thought about how I routinely put money in the Save Our African Children donation jar at Whole Foods and felt guilty for feeling guilty about feeling guilty. The liberal guilt went on for a while until I felt a vibration from my phone buzzing. Followed by a double beep. An alert, not a ring. The *beep-beep* of an incoming text, for some reason, is more exciting than an actual call. I guess maybe it's because our minds revel in all the thrilling possibilities of who it could be. Maybe it's my ex? Does she still care enough to take the time to physically type out her thoughts on a smartphone? Hope . . .

Nope. It was from Phil Salazar, my old violin teacher. For a moment I wondered why in the world he was texting me, but then I remembered I had landed on him during the texting game and was forced to send, "Are you as sweaty as I am right now?" His response was, "Just got done restringing a viola, so, uh yeah, I believe that question answers itself. Any interest in playing again?" Playing again? I would hardly consider my violin career a success. Pretty much the only thing I learned was how to hold the violin under my chin without making myself look fat. And I'm already thin! What an appalling instrument. I politely told him no thanks because I'd taken up the gong.

I received another text message, this one from Pat, asking whether or not it would be cool if he had a few friends come by and hang out. When you have a roommate who invites friends over that you don't know and you're going to be home at the same time, there are two options: hang out and be social or lock yourself in your room, waiting out the hang-out session for as long as it takes, even if it means peeing into a discarded Gatorade bottle. (I've only had to do that disgusting act once. The other five times don't count.) I quickly had to weigh out all of my potential responses.

POTENTIAL RESPONSES

1. Say that I normally wouldn't mind but tonight I'd really like to be productive and get some creative writing done. But then I stared at a shirtless Matthew McConaughey, still enjoying his reign as number one beach bod. Who was I kidding? Productivity wasn't in my future that night. Also, I'm not the kind of person who would tell my roommate that he can't have people over. I'm not Adolf Hitler.

2. Tell Pat sure. Then hide away in the safe confines of my bedroom. Only problem with that was the confines of my bedroom weren't exactly safe anymore. I knew the girls above me would no doubt be loud as hell with their "sisters from different misters" spending the night while consuming numerous bottles of "Pinot Greege." Then I thought, hey, if one of them mentions me, that would be pretty cool. But soon I got to thinking that if they *didn't* mention me, or even worse, *did* mention me but said something negative, it would set me back a solid week emotionally. So that left me only one possibility. . . .

3. Hang out with Pat and a few of his friends whom I'd never met before. And I was fine with that. If there's one thing you can say about Pat, it's that the guy knows how to have a good time. He lets everyone do their own thing. He's not strict or limiting.

"The rule is simple: Absolutely *no* talking while Gaga is singing." Pat said this to all of us with a look in his eye that I've never quite seen before. A look in his eye that said, "It appears that I'm talking to everybody right now, but I'm really just talking to *you*, Charlie

McDowell." I may have even gulped. And before long, the Lady Gaga concert DVD was delicately placed into our player and my living room was as quiet as a library packed with mutes. A library that, for some strange reason, blared Lady Gaga.

I found myself in the middle of what used to be my spacious L-shaped couch. There were a few other guys I'd never met before, overpopulating my living room, enjoying "Born This Way" with the thousands of other "Little Monsters" attending the actual concert playing on my TV. Pat and his friends took this concert seriously. Needless to say, they weren't thrilled when I held a lighter in the air and swayed back and forth. I felt like reminding Pat that he wasn't exactly watching *Death of a Salesman*. But I guess there are just certain men out there who don't have a sense of humor when it comes to Gaga. Finally, after Lady Gaga's fifth encore, the concert ended. Or so I thought. . . . It turned out that my good friend Pat had an encore of his own.

Pat stood up and addressed the crowd, some of whom were still riding their Gaga high with no signs of coming down. "Okay, so I have an amazing surprise, something even better than the concert we all just experienced." (You don't watch a Gaga concert, you experience it.) One of his friends wondered what could possibly be better than the concert. I remember thinking, Anything?

"Well, since I work at the most amazing company in the world, Disney, I'm happy to announce"—his speech was painfully rehearsed—"that due to an office raffle that yours truly won, all of us are going to be spending the weekend . . . at . . ." The suspense wasn't the thing killing me. "Disneyland!" It was the payoff.

The room permeated with positive energy and genuine excitement; it was like Richard Simmons getting a blow job on ecstasy. "First Gaga, now Disney," one of them exclaimed. Then they proceeded to stand up and high-five one another in an incredibly masculine way that seemed to contradict their previous exclamation.

"Charlie, did you not hear me? We are spending the weekend at Disneyland!" Pat reiterated.

"Yeah, I heard you."

"Well, then why aren't you getting all excited with us?" Pat asked.

Pat was right. They were excited. If ten minutes ago my living room had turned into a library, it had now morphed into the reopening of Studio 54. "I'm sorry, but I'm just not going to be able to make it," I said out loud. Everyone went quiet. They looked at me with such disappointment. Studio 54 closed its doors again that night, and this time it was my fault.

"But why?" They were begging for an answer. Even though they were glaring at me with their perfectly plucked raised eyebrows, I still didn't flinch. I didn't have the strength to clarify; it was all much too painful for me. It still is, my hatred for "the happiest place on earth."

THE GIRLS ON DREAMS

Dear Girls Above Me,

"I had a nightmare that I was getting raped but he couldn't get it up. It was scary but super offensive."
I wanna feel bad for you.

Dear Girls Above Me,

"If I got a dime for every sex dream a guy's had of me, I'd have like 500 dollars and 75 cents." Dimes can't make that number.

THEY WRITE POETRY

Dear Girls Above Me,

"I think it's 'roses are red, violets are blue, things . . . I see . . . are . . . I know . . . is true.' Just type that." What the hell was *that*?

THE GIRLS ON WISDOM

Dear Girls Above Me,

"Let's just say she's not the sharpest pool in the shed." To be fair you're not exactly the sharpest wife in the drawer either.

LIFE REALIZATIONS

Dear Girls Above Me,

"It kinda makes me sad that I can never be a teen mom, like that's not even an option anymore." Aww, all grown up.

THEY INVENT STUFF FOR DOGS

Dear Girls Above Me,

"I finally came up with a gazillion dollar idea. Ready?" No. "Friendship bracelets for dogs!" That's only a billion dollar idea.

Dear Girls Above Me,

"It's time we get a dog!" *Please, do not get a—* "But we should invent wireless leashes first." Oh okay, I'm good.

CHAPTER EIGHT

"Why are you so against Disneyland?" She whisper-asked it, but I could still hear everything from my bed.

"Because I'm handing over hundreds of dollars to stand around getting all hot and sweaty."

"I think they have other things there," I responded, to myself.

"Also, there's a lack of consistency to the characters." I had no idea what that meant; good thing the voice elaborated: "Pluto is a dog who can't speak, yet we're supposed to believe that Goofy, also a dog, miraculously can? That's preposterous."

"I live under a lunatic," I recall groaning.

"When I was a boy in England, I didn't need a park for amusement. I played with garbage in the streets," he argued.

Other than this being the night before the most traumatizing experience of my childhood existence, this night also marked the first time I was blessed (or cursed) with the ability to overhear people who shouldn't be overheard.

I was five years old, and through the right combination of opened

windows and doors, a sound tunnel was created from my parents'
room that allowed me to hear everything. But there are some things
that no five-year-old should hear. . . . No, I'm not talking about *that*—
well yes, that too. Only I'd rather have heard my parents do *that* than
heard them denigrate the most magical place on earth.

It started just like any other day. My sister Lilly and I were both
drawing in our Strawberry Shortcake coloring books. As a kid, pretty
much anything my sister did, I wanted to do as well. Particularly, I
was enamored with the Strawberry Shortcake scent. If Lilly wanted
to wear a pink tutu out to dinner, I wanted to wear a pink tutu out
to dinner. I was completely oblivious to any social norms and was
happily living my life as a little girl. Of course, this all changed on
my first day of elementary school when Jeremy Powell made fun of
me for having a purple headband in my hair.

As we continued coloring, I distinctly remember Lilly criticizing
my Strawberry Shortcake palette: "I just don't get what you're trying to do." I know how Fellini must've felt; clearly I was ahead of my
time. Before I was able to defend my delightful pinkish hue, a television commercial for Disneyland appeared before my eyes. I was
transfixed. I had never experienced anything so magical through a
TV set in my entire life. It was a warm summer night in 1988; I was
five years old, and in that moment I made it my life's mission to go
to this heavenly place.

"If you haven't been to Disneyland lately, you and your family have
a lot to catch up on," the man from the commercial said directly to
me. As he spoke, images of kids whirling around in life-sized tea-
cups, a humongous delighted mouse, an enormous wooden log sailing down a waterfall into a refreshing pool of water, and even a scary
pirate steering a ship flashed onto the screen, taunting me. A life I'd

never known; I was Stevie Wonder now able to see. My sister and I both shared a look—the kid version of "WTF." "Disneyland, where the magic begins. Come now and discover the perfect family vacation. Located in beautiful Southern California." Then it vanished; I was blind once again. I turned off the TV, for what good is television to a blind kid? Without any spoken words, my sister and I jumped up and bolted toward our parents' room.

"We wanna go to Disneyland!" We stood there with our mouths wide open, catching our breath, awaiting our life-altering fate. My parents looked at each other with eyes that said, "Code red! Code red!" They had clearly tried keeping this incredible land from us for as long as possible, but did they really expect we would never find it? The name Mickey Mouse made so much more sense to me now. And he was clearly not the mascot for a pest-control service, as my dad previously claimed.

My sister and I didn't budge. We had them in the hot seat, in desperate need of answers before a hissy fit would ensue. My mom gave a nod to my dad, which I assumed meant "This is your department." My dad reluctantly got out of bed and carefully approached his fiendish children.

"Disneyland is closed on the weekends and you start school next week, so we'll plan a trip to go there next summer," my dad said with his cheeky British accent.

This was bullshit. I knew it then as I know it now. "Why would it be closed on the weekends? Isn't that when mommies and daddies don't have to go to work?" I could tell my sister really wanted to give me a high five for decoding that one. "Perhaps next time you'll think before critiquing my crayon choices," I remember wanting to say.

My dad glanced at my mother. He was in need of some major help, but she kept her head buried in her book. Smart move. The poor guy was walking a tightrope without a net. I sort of felt bad for him, but I kept my sympathetic thoughts in check. Disneyland was the priority. I was ready to knock him down.

"We want to go to Disneyland tomorrow," I said in a calm yet firm tone. My mom dropped *The Mists of Avalon* and hid under the covers. Lilly was proud to be my sister. And my dad had no fight left in him.

"Disneyland it is," he said with such defeat. My sister jumped up and down. Pretty soon it would be she who dressed like me; the student had become the teacher. I stood, anchored solidly to the ground in my Velcro shoes with my chest puffed out, showing my family who was really running things.

It was later that night, through the right sequence of windows and doors left open, that I was able to hear my father's true feelings about Disney. But as long as I was going, I couldn't have given a shit how he really felt about it. We were set to leave at seven in the morning and that was all that mattered.

I was up at four thirty because you'd have to be out of your mind to sleep in on a Disney day. I gathered the necessary essentials for my impending adventure. Luckily, I had a neon-green fanny pack my uncle Arthur had given me for my five-and-three-quarters birthday. These were the objects I placed inside:

Half-eaten Jawbreaker.

Strand of my dog Lucy's hair in case she died while we were gone.

Bag of Fruit Gushers.

My entire collection of Garbage Pail Kids trading cards.

Thirty-seven cents in case my parents forgot their wallets.

I was ready. The problem was the only people with official driver's licenses were fast asleep. Fortunately for me, not them, I was much more effective than an alarm clock. As I leapt up and down on their bed, muffled sounds of agony came from their pillows.

"Charlie, Disneyland isn't open for another five hours. Go back to sleep!" my mom said in her most irritated tone. How were they not as excited as me? The commercial said it was the perfect family vacation. Were we not a perfect family? All I could do was imagine a happy *Leave It to Beaver*–like family piling into a minivan with the parents calling out, "Hurry up, children! We wanna be the first ones there so we can go on every single ride!" My dad was half-asleep with a line of drool running down his chin.

After a few agonizing hours, we made it into our Volvo station wagon, finally on our way to Disneyland. "Are we there yet?" my sister asked. Good thing too, because I had been wondering the same thing. We had been driving for at least an hour, so we must've been getting close.

"We've only been driving for seven minutes," my dad barked at us from the driver's seat. His apathetic attitude toward the most magical place in all the world was beginning to make me lose respect for the guy. Who is this pod person, and what has he done with my real father? I wondered. After another hour went by, I chimed in with, "I think it's the next exit."

"We have been driving for thirty minutes and are nowhere near our insufferable destination." I could tell my dad's irritation level was reaching its peak. Luckily, I knew just what to do to mellow him out while simultaneously lifting his spirits. . . .

"It's a small world, after all. It's a small world, after all. It's a small world, after all. It's a small, small world." I nailed it pitch-perfect, a future *American Idol* winner. My sister soon joined in, effectively turning my solo into a duet. We managed to harmonize on a song that had no harmony.

My father stared me down in the rearview mirror. His reflection wasn't even half as intimidating as it would have been had our eyes locked directly. So I continued on, this time a smidgen louder. And Lilly followed my lead. I opened my mouth as wide as I could and sang my little heart out at the top of my reverberating lungs. Eventually, I felt as though the lyrics to "It's a Small World" had run their course, so I began making up my own verses on the spot:

"Disneyland is so much fun. I can't wait to ride the rides. I hope there's a candy store in the snowy mountain. I'm going to touch Mickey Mouse's tail." To this day, I believe I'd achieve great success as an underground battle rapper; my ability to make up lyrics on the spot remains unmatched. I'm talking to you, Eminem.

I guess our duet was so loud, I couldn't hear the car phone ring, but my dad violently picked it up and asked who was there. I lowered my voice a little bit but had no intention of stopping until my parents believed in the magical place just as my sister and I did.

"Wait, so this is Mickey Mouse? Why are you calling me?" my dad asked in a loud voice.

The singing stopped immediately. Umm, why was Mickey Mouse calling my father?!

"Give it to me, I wanna talk to him!" My sister desperately reached for the phone, but my father shushed her. Something was seriously wrong. I was so nervous I felt as if I was going to pee my pants, which is the ultimate betrayal of a five-year-old's body, because at that age, you've only just recently stopped using diapers.

"I understand. Well, I'm sorry, Mickey. Be safe. Take care now." My dad hung up the phone. All eyes were on him, including my mother's. She seemed just as shocked as we were. We awaited the verdict.

"I have an announcement to make." My dad paused to collect his thoughts, while a little bit of pee ran down my leg. "I hate to be the one to tell you this . . . but . . . it's official. Disneyland has burned down."

"Nooooooooooooooo!"

THREE MONTHS LATER . . .

I sat at a picnic table under a large oak tree with my best friend, Duncan Winecoff. I was enjoying *his* peanut butter and jelly sandwich as he scarfed down *my* ham and cheese. Lunchtime at elementary school is basically the NBA draft of packed brown bags, except much more intense. The strategy that went into planning my lunch for the week qualified me to be the GM of a professional sports team. I remember convincing my mom to make things I had no intention of eating, days in advance, just because I knew the trading leverage I'd acquire. People still talk about November 23, 1994, or as it's been immortalized, "Thank-Charlie's Day." The day before Thanksgiving I was able to trade my Fruit Roll-Up for a half-drunk can of Dr Pepper. No big deal, you say? Well, I forgot to mention that the trade was with a *teacher*. Nuff said.

Out of nowhere, into the snacking area walked the infamous Teddy Long. I had never seen a second grader wander into our quarters before. What was the purpose of his visit? Did some lucky bastard have Bubble Tape? I could only imagine the trouble that was brewing on the horizon. It soon became apparent that Teddy had his eyes set on one thing and one thing only: Annie Greynold.

Annie Greynold was the Paris Hilton of kindergarten. Which meant she was smarter than Paris Hilton, but you get the idea. He approached Annie as if she were just another one of his AYSO soccer trophies. I noticed Teddy was wearing an odd-looking hat, but as he got closer, the outline of it became more clear. Two felt black circles protruding from the top. . . . Very similar to a certain mouse.

Through my extensive research, I knew the only place to purchase one of these hats was at a kiosk at the late great Disneyland. I had seen Teddy get dropped off at school every single day, but not once had I seen him sporting a Mickey Mouse hat. Where did it come from? I needed answers.

I have no idea where I mustered up the courage, but out of nowhere I stood up, Velcroed my shoes a little snugger, and headed off into the land of cooler kids. Duncan remained seated, mouth open in disbelief, with pieces of my mom's ham and cheese sandwich still on his lips. As I got closer to Teddy, my knees began to quiver. Not only was I going to converse with a second grader, but Annie was going to hear me speak for the first time. I cleared my throat, making sure no hidden saliva would send my vocal cords into an even more girl-like pitch than normal. I swiped my hand along the ground, collecting dirt to rub on my shirt to match Teddy's casual grunge. As I got closer, I felt the eyes of other kids staring at me. I could tell they all thought I was on a suicide mission. Maybe I was, but I had thought about Disneyland every single day since it had burned to the ground, and Teddy was the only hope I had for some answers.

"Teddy?" My voice seemed to echo off of every single lunch box in the snacking area. He turned around, not pleased by my interruption. "Umm, where'd you get that hat?" I had felt somewhat self-assured, until I saw Annie's "Are you fucking crazy-ah?" face. I looked up at Teddy, who weighed in at an impressive four foot five and fifty-seven pounds, ready to kill me at any moment.

"Who wants to know?" he grunted.

"Me," I said while instinctively raising my hand. I quickly put it down, realizing we weren't in Mrs. Shanel's classroom.

"Well, if you must know, I got it at Disneyland over the weekend."

"You're lying."

"No I'm not."

"Yes you are."

"No I'm not."

"Yeah-huh."

"Nuh-uh."

"Yeah-huh, yeah-huh."

"Nuh-uh, nuh-uh."

"Disneyland burned down months ago," I shouted out for the entire snack-time-area population to hear. Everyone instantly erupted in laughter. I couldn't believe it; these morons had no clue. Was I the only one who was privy to this information? It was possible. I mean, Mickey Mouse did call my father directly.

"Whoever told you that is stupid. I went on Space Mountain yesterday. And it was awesome." Jealousy and rage took over for rational thought. He had not only called my dad stupid, but he had supposedly just ridden on the very ride that started the fire. What was going on? What the hell was going on!?

"I sat in the front cart on the Matterhorn and I didn't even close my eyes once," one kid yelled out.

"My older brother said he touched a ghost's wee-wee in the Haunted Mansion," another said.

"Yeah, I just went on the Jungle Cruise and I got out to feed the alligators. They're real."

I couldn't believe it. Had my dad completely fabricated a story about Disneyland burning to the ground just so he wouldn't have to go? If so, then I was living with a monster. (Not one of Gaga's.) How could I ever face that man again? Oh my God, and did that mean he wasn't actually friends with Mickey Mouse?!

I reluctantly glanced over at Annie. She had a look of empathy, which quickly dissolved into a look of repulsion. Then she got sucked into the vicious kindergarten peer pressure and laughed at me along with the rest of them.

"Your dad just got here," my after-school teacher informed me as I stood in a corner brooding.

Dad? What dad? I didn't have a dad. A dad is an honest man who gets excited about taking a family trip to Disneyland. The gentleman who referred to himself as my father was a lying son of a grandma named Edna. And I knew for a fact she would not approve of his deceitful behavior.

I entered his car (the scene of the crime) without speaking a word to him. I attempted to strap myself into the car seat. I admit I was having a bit of trouble as I was not confident enough to work this strange contraption on my own. My father tried to help.

"I can do it myself!" I roared. I knew I couldn't, but I was willing to live on the wild side for the seven-minute drive home. Plus, given the state I was in, my dad knew not to mess with me.

We drove in silence. I was so infuriated. Everything I saw out the window was stupid. Stupid hair salon. Stupid metal gate. Stupid orange tree. Stupid running creek. Stupid person putting change in a homeless man's stupid cup. The homeless man was the last straw; I couldn't take it anymore.

"Why did you lie to me about Disneyland!?" My high-pitched voice echoed off of every windowpane in the car. My dad was so startled by the noise that he swerved into the lane next to us, almost crashing into the stupid guy in the stupid Porsche.

"I did not lie to you," he turned around and said directly to my face.

"Yes you did! I know Disneyland didn't burn down!"

"Listen. Disneyland *did* burn down. But they recently rebuilt it!"

"Really? Well, can we go?"

"We can, although I heard it's not even close to as good since the reopening. They don't even have bathrooms anymore. Plus they had to replace the castle with a vegetable farm."

My father was very lucky that it was the eighties, 'cause if I'd had access to Google, I probably never would've spoken to him again. To this day, I've still never been to stupid Disneyland, nor do I have any desire to. . . .

Especially now that it sucks since they've rebuilt it.

THE GIRLS ON DIETING

Dear Girls Above Me,

"Oh I get it. It's called string cheese cause it comes off all stringy." Next week we'll tackle Push-Pops.

Dear Girls Above Me,

"If breakfast is the most important meal of the day, can I just skip the others?" That might be healthier than throwing them up.

Dear Girls Above Me,

"How much did that gluten stuff in food cost before they made it free?" Oh man, you don't even wanna know.

Dear Girls Above Me,

"I know this might sound stupid." Not again, please no— "But does air have any fat calories in it?" 9-1-1.

Dear Girls Above Me,

"OMG! I lost three pounds from food poisoning! We're so going back there." Finally you found a place that does the vomiting for you.

Dear Girls Above Me,

"He's taking me out to some restaurant in Koreatown. Oh great, I hate sushi!" Maybe they can whip you up some Korean food.

Dear Girls Above Me,

"If I eat half of the fries and then I bite those in half with only a little salt, will I get fat?" Your version of the SATs?

Dear Girls Above Me,

"I just realized it's March! You know what that means . . ." March Madness tournament? "Girl scout cookie diet month!" Oh . . . right.

CHAPTER NINE

I said my good riddance to the Disney boys, then reclaimed the living room couch as my own. I could hear murmurs coming from the ceiling, but the girls weren't speaking loudly enough for me to comprehend their topic of conversation. Normally, I would pray for this low decibel level, but I was bored and wanted someone to talk—I mean listen—to. I could hear the Jewish mother inside me saying, "You can't have your cake and eat it too. Oy vey. And while I'm on the subject, how come you never call anymore?" If I had a choice in the matter, I would want them to be silent for the rest of my existence, except at that very moment. That's not entirely unreasonable.

I cracked open a window, hoping to boost the volume. I now had the ability to make out certain words, but their sentences were still a little fuzzy. So I grabbed my computer and went on an adventure to find the most clear listening spots. My apartment is only about seven hundred square feet, so the trek wasn't that strenuous, but it took a while to pinpoint the perfect area to camp out. Here are my easy-listening results:

Living room: Decent. If they were excited, drunk, or in a fight, I could hear them well from there, but otherwise it's not ideal. Note: For reasons unknown, high heels are loudest here.

My bedroom: Solid. The acoustics are phenomenal. Coldplay could perform unplugged. Because both our apartments share the same layout, daytime does not experience a lot of activity in this spot. Nighttime is hopping, though.

Pat's bedroom: Unknown. He and I have boundaries.

Bathroom: Bad. Luckily for both parties, the bathroom remains private.

Breakfast nook: Promising. Once I get screens for the windows, this spot holds a lot of potential.

Kitchen: Good.

Kitchen sink: Best. This was the sweet spot.

I sat in the kitchen sink with my legs dangling. I attributed the optimized acoustics here to some quirk of our shared vent system. It was like a portal connecting our two very different worlds. "Hello?" I halfheartedly called out. I was curious about whether they were able to hear me through this particular vent, but at the same time, I didn't want to get caught. No response. I tried again, this time a tad louder. Still nothing. So, I just listened.

After a while I decided that I would write them another "letter." When I logged on to my Twitter account this time, I learned that I now had nine followers! Who were these mysterious people? I clicked on one of them. Dahlia Stone. I had never seen her in my life. Her profile picture was of an angry-looking teenage girl. Dark eye shadow, jet-black hair, and a T-shirt that read DON'T LOOK AT ME. As I scrolled down her timeline, I noticed she had written to me:

"I loathe girls who obsess over text messages. Post another letter or I'll kill you . . . kidding, but still do it."

I've always planned on dying of natural causes; not at the hands of an emo teenager who will most likely grow up to become a banker. So I posted my next letter for Dahlia and my other followers:

Dear Girls Above Me,

Talking about how it's raining for 37 minutes can be simplified to "Hey, it's raining outside."

And another.

Dear Girls Above Me,

Just because a guy looked at you funny on the street doesn't mean you're living in *The Truman Show*.

And another.

Dear Girls Above Me,

I'm sorry that you just came to realize there are no
spring breaks in "real life."

Why not quote them one more time?

Dear Girls Above Me,

"Did someone break in?! We didn't leave the TV
on CNN, right?" I've heard of these intelligent
news-watching burglars. Be careful.

By the time I was done posting my flurry of letters, I had gained
six new followers. I was now up to fifteen people. More of them
wrote to me:

"These girls are such morons! Hilarious."

"Your letters are seriously making my day!"

"How are you not chasing your brain out the door? I'd have gone
upstairs and brutally murdered those girls by now."

I was a little creeped out by that last guy, but everyone else had
given me a taste of what it must feel like to be a rock star. And I
wanted more. I had heard Ashton Kutcher was considered the king
of Twitter, so I looked up his profile to compare the number of followers we each had. I figured he couldn't possibly have many more
than me. Maybe just a few . . . *million*! Holy crap, I had a lot of letter
writing to do.

The next morning I awoke to Bon Jovi's "Shot Through the
Heart." I eliminated Pat as the cause of this racket, knowing that he
was at Disneyland, and also because the song didn't have a "sassy"

techno beat behind it. And as if I had cued the girls above me myself, they started singing along perfectly off-key. I tried burying my head in the pillows, but no amount of feathers could block their serenading. Half-asleep, I opened my computer and typed,

Dear Girls Above Me,

"Shot Through the Heart" at 7:25 A.M. is not allowed.

At this point, there was no hope of my sleeping any longer. The girls were excited for their party, which meant I was forced to be excited for their party, which made me even less excited for their party. On top of that, I needed to find a pastel-colored shirt to wear.

I opened up my closet to an underwhelming amount of pigment. I turned on a light to illuminate the shadows but discovered that the shadows were actually my colorless clothes. Blacks, grays, browns, dark greens; this was my wardrobe. The only item that stood out was a pair of orange Crocs I bought one day when I was feeling particularly jaunty. I had a special distaste for these shoes, because I was 76 percent sure that I was dumped as a result of once wearing them. I had never noticed how somber my clothes were until I imagined them next to a soft-hued color, much like the one I would be forced to wear later that night. If my closet were in an animated movie, this is where the wisecracking bat voiced by Chris Rock would live and admonish me: "Ya gotta get out and live ya life, but before ya do, how 'bout stopping at Macy's . . . JCPenney . . . the Gap. . . . Hell, I'll even settle for a stroll through the Salvation Army. That way you can at least tell a bitch you're wearing vintage; just please, I beg ya, buy some new shiiiiit." (Sorry for that digression. In retrospect, perhaps my Chris Rock impression doesn't translate to the written word, but vocalized it's *really* good. Trust me.) Anyway, I sure as hell wasn't going to find my costume in there.

So I headed over to Urban Outfitters in search of a color I had never worn before. As I walked into the store, I was overwhelmingly soothed by an entire section of SweeTart-colored shirts. I had no idea they were so "hip." I felt very bleak approaching such cheery colors, but I persevered. Even the names of these colors were cooler than I am. POWDER PINK, SEA FOAM, WEDGWOOD BLUE, MARIGOLD, CREAM-SICLE ORANGE—

"Sir, can I help you?" asked a skinny hipster whose dirty blond hair looked as if it were slapped across his forehead. His name tag read SUNSHINE.

"Umm, yes. Are these all of your pastel shirts or do you have more in another section?" In the moment, I felt this would make me sound more discerning and trendy. "Sure," he would undoubtedly respond as he ushered me into the special secret section of extra-super-cool pastels. "We like to keep this section closed off to all but our most discerning and trendy customers." Unfortunately, I read that wrong.

"No, I'm sorry, this is all we have in stock at the moment."

"Oh, bummer, well I guess I can make do with what's here." Sunshine looked at me like I was crazy.

"Is there a particular color you're interested in?"

I pictured myself in every single one of those shirts and quickly realized that I was not going to look good in any pastel color. My pale skin and hairy arms were meant to be covered up forever. But I hadn't come all this way to get another pair of Crocs. I thought back to my Crayola days and summoned the most interesting crayon shade I could think of to let Sunshine know I was not some color philistine.

"Do you have a salmon-colored shirt? Like something Ryan Gosling might wear?" Don't know why I threw that second part in. Sunshine stared at me through his fake prescription-less glasses.

"I'm not exactly sure of Ryan Gosling's color scheme, but we do have something similar to what you're describing, called Peachy." Well, his proclaimed ignorance of anything Gosling made him a liar, but he totally hooked me up, shirt-wise.

He handed me two of the peachiest shirts I had ever seen. Not even real peaches are this peach. One had a regular collar, the other a V-neck. I was beginning to sorely regret my decision to attend this party. When it comes to fashion, I'm about as clueless as they come, but I was starting to think that this color worked on Ryan Gosling simply because every color works on Ryan Gosling. I pictured myself walking in and hearing people say, "Hey, who let in the giant peach from *James and the Giant Peach*?"

Now I had a big decision ahead of me: Did I buy the regular shirt or did I go for the V-neck? My instinct was telling me to go with the regular shirt, but my newfound hipster friend was sporting a V-neck, and I may go as far as to say that he looked quite dashing in it. Feeling super confident from this successful foray into hipsterdom, I pushed my luck and attempted some knowing banter.

"Why do they call this a V-neck shirt anyway? Does the *V* stand for *vegan* or something?" Sunshine paused long enough for me to hear my words hanging in the air and feel our rapport shatter at my feet.

"I'm pretty sure the *V* stands for the shape that it is making," he responded, very slowly, for some reason. "Is there anything else I can help you with?"

I guess we weren't going to be best friends. "I'll just take the . . ."

He scrunched his forehead, staring me down to see if I was going to say it.

I mouthed the words *vegan-neck* followed by, ". . . T-shirt. Thank you." He rang me up in complete silence and I was out in record time with my new Peachy V.

I got home feeling slightly optimistic about my new shirt. I realized I should've probably tried it on before buying it, but I have a weird thing about putting on clothes outside the confines of my own bedroom, especially in store dressing rooms. I never really feel like there's enough room to actually figure out if I look good in what I'm trying on. Like, how would this shirt look if I was trampolining? There's no way to know. I also rush my dressing room experience because I have this paranoia that people will think I'm stealing clothes. I go as far as to make an exaggerated point of showing them everything I brought in as I'm on the way out. It's silly, I know, but ever since Winona Ryder got caught shoplifting, I have avoided dressing rooms like the plague.

Having said that, I definitely should've tried on the damned shirt. My prominent neck tan line and chest fro did not make for a good look. No wonder hipsters look so "fabulous" in V-neck shirts; they have perfectly spray-tanned skin and "fierce," hairless pectoral muscles. I hadn't exposed my chest to the sun since the summer of '92 and my pecs were about as toned as the queen of England's thigh muscles (and I'm being generous there). The question now was did I wear the shirt or did I forget about the theme and go up there looking like my usual Johnny Cash self?

Right around the time the party sounded as if it was starting, my good friend Luke showed up. I had specifically invited him knowing that I was more likely to meet a lot of women as a result of his outgoing personality. I've never seen anyone work a girl quite like Luke. The man experiences no shame. I rarely ask girls for their phone number, due to a fear of rejection. Just picturing a girl in the uncomfortable position of wondering how to say no to me is enough motivation for me to be single the rest of my life. And even if I know for sure that they want me to step up to the plate and ask them out, I still can't do it. The worst of these moments was when I was having a very flirty chat with a premed student I had met at a bar. At the end of the night, she stood there just waiting for me to make a move. But there was still that 0.001 percent chance that her elated smile was just politeness, which left me to say, "Well, hopefully, you'll be my doctor one day."

Luke, on the other hand, will strut up to a group of single ladies and blurt out, "Let me get all of your numbers in order of age, please." The most shocking part about this is they actually do it. His phone is like the Mecca of cellular devices, housing the names of thousands and thousands of girls, most of which he's only glanced at once.

"What are you wearing?" Luke asked in judging tones.

"What do you mean? It's a V-neck shirt."

"You look like the giant peach from *James and the Giant Peach*." Uh-oh.

"You do know this is a pastel-shirt-themed party, right?" I asked him.

"You do know that no one actually dresses up for themed parties, right?" I had been wondering why he was wearing a gray cardigan.

Luke curiously walked over to a vent hidden behind an old leather chair in my living room. After a few moments of examining, he opened it as if he were Sherlock Holmes at a crime scene. The conversations coming from the growing party upstairs grew louder. He sat back down on the couch cross-legged and slowly closed his eyes in a very Zen manner.

"So should we head on up there?" I asked the question as if I were an untrained Jedi speaking to Master Yoda.

"Not yet. Just listen we will," he responded without opening his eyes.

Unfortunately, one of my many compulsions is that I absolutely cannot be late for *anything*. It doesn't matter if I don't even want to be there; I have to be early. I think this comes from something my mom said to me as a child: "Charlie, always remember never to be late; otherwise people won't like you." What's completely absurd is that every single member of my family is late to everything, but for some reason I can't shake my mother's contradictory words of wisdom. Luckily for Luke, he had not listened to his mother growing up.

All I could do was fixate on the clock on my wall. With every tick, my anxiety grew stronger and stronger. Luke remained in a meditative state just listening. To distract myself, I wrote the girls a letter.

Dear Girls Above Me,

"I had the shittiest day, all I wanna do is get wasted." I remember you saying the same thing last week when having the best day.

After eavesdropping on a debate about the all-time-hottest movie ghost (Patrick Swayze narrowly edging out Beetlejuice), Luke finally opened his eyes. "I can't believe you listen to this all day."

"I know. It's horrific."

"Horrific? This is absolutely amazing."

"Why does everyone keep saying that?"

"This actually might be the greatest thing to ever happen to us."

"Us?"

"Dude, you're getting a sneak peek at the other team's playbook," Luke said.

"I think I'm going to come clean tonight. Tell them I can hear everything they say."

Before my optic nerve could transmit the visual information of his movement from my retina to my brain, Luke was inches away from my face with his hand around the back of my collarless neck, squeezing it tight. I was stunned and could find no way out of his grip, which was fine because, quite honestly, it felt like a really good deep-tissue massage. He came in real close and whispered, "You will not tell them a thing. Do you understand me?" I quickly nodded. "I'm doing this for your own good." I nodded again. It's not that I can't hold my own, but it would've been foolish to fight a guy who's a good six inches taller and has fifty pounds on me.

As if she knew I was in danger, Claire yelled from upstairs, "Oh my God, *Cosmo*'s new horoscope says I should hook up with a guy because the moon is waxing. I don't know what that means, but I'm totally gonna do it." This made Luke ease up on his kung-fu grip, prematurely ending my free massage.

"This vent doesn't lead to an apartment, Charlie. It leads to heaven. I must meet these angels, particularly the one confused by lunar phases." I took a deep sigh of relief. I guess it was time to party.

THE GIRLS ON DRINKING

Dear Girls Above Me,

"No joke, I'm never drinking again—Wait, is Jen's party tonight?! Next week I'm never drinking again." A quote from every Friday.

Dear Girls Above Me,

"You know the worst part about not having a job?" Not making your own income? "Being the only one getting drunk during the week."

Dear Girls Above Me,

"The worst part about these stupid antibiotics is I can't have any alcohol. I'd rather die." I'd rather be on stupid antibiotics.

Dear Girls Above Me,

"Here's the plan for tonight: we stay in, drink red wine, and do kegel exercises." Let me know if you guys need a spotter.

Dear Girls Above Me,

"If we wanna leave her party, say the words, *I'm super drunk.*" This might be confusing as you actually get "super drunk."

Dear Girls Above Me,

"My version of white water rafting is to down a bottle of chardonnay." My version of white water rafting is white water rafting.

Dear Girls Above Me,

"He only had beer! I mean, obviously I wanna get drunk, but I'm not gonna get fat while doing it." So beer is what kept you sober?

CHAPTER TEN

I stood in a packed room that, to my left, stank of alcohol and marijuana, which had been steadily wafting in from the balcony. To my right, a lethal mixture of Prada perfume and Hugo Boss cologne enveloped the living room. For the record, I prefer the alcohol and marijuana.

The more people behaved foolishly around me, trying desperately to look like extras in a Captain Morgan commercial, the more I missed my ex and the ease with which we had a good time. Everyone says they love the "honeymoon" period. For me the "honeymoon" period is nothing but a series of contrived feel-good moments, plucked from those tedious ensemble holiday rom-coms. I'm a strong advocate of living my life in the "comfortable" period. Who wants to wear a suit when you can wear pajamas? But that's probably the very thing that broke us up. She never did like my bedtime flannels.

As far as I could tell, every single girl in the room was wearing a pastel-colored shirt. Some went with the traditional Palm Beach country club look, while others altered this convention (with scissors) to go for more of the "conservative slut" look. And there I was, one of only two guys who actually dressed up to suit the theme of the party. The other guy wore a chartreuse Lacoste shirt and matching suede shoes, which all went horribly with his naturally orange hair. He stood all alone in the corner of the room, bobbing his head off-beat to the music. When he became aware of my arrival, he raised his glass of Pinot, toasting me, and yelled out, "We've got ourselves a party!" I wasn't exactly sure why two men in delicate-colored T-shirts were the linchpin of a great party, but I had no interest in finding out.

"The name's Wyatt," he yelled out to me over a sea of gyrating people.

"Cool." I had to give him something, but it sure as hell wasn't going to be my name.

"We should totally chill all night 'cause we're in these shirts, you know?" This made me want to change my shirt immediately. Thankfully, all I had to do was walk down a flight of stairs.

I bolted for the exit. Luke was already mingling with multiple female contenders, so I felt zero remorse leaving him alone for a moment. As I approached the door that would lead me out of my current nightmare, a couple of familiar voices held me back.

"Hey, you can't leave yet!" Claire called to me in a drunken lilt.

"Yeah, you aren't allowed to leave for like three hundred hours," Cathy added.

I slowly turned around, hoping they were talking to someone else. They weren't. "Hey, you guys."

"You guys? You're the guy! Hi, my name's Claire."

Was I that unmemorable? Did I look that much different in a pastel shirt? I had literally sat on her couch and almost started sobbing in front of her when I landed on my ex-girlfriend in the texting game only twenty-four hours ago. How did she not remember me? Surely Cathy was bound to know who I was.

"Claire, you idiot. You know him. That's Stephanie's new lawyer boyfriend!"

"Oh my God, that's you! Now I remember!" Claire's eyes lit up.

I tried reasoning with them. "Wait, what? No, I can assure you that's not me—"

"Of course that's you! You're all smart, using lawyer words like *assure*." They had a point; I did use that word.

"I'm pretty certain that's a common word in the English language," I said, unsure why.

"Uh-huh. *Certain, common,* you can't even pretend not to be all smart," Cathy shouted.

"And you're wearing such a cute shirt," Claire said to me in her forever-whining voice. Shirt-ah.

"I was actually thinking about putting on something else. The men here don't seem to be participating in the theme."

"Don't change! That's so Lamesville, USA! Hey, where's Stephanie?"

"She's on her way." I guess I'm officially someone who is defeated easily by females. Not only did I accept my role as the boyfriend of Stephanie, a girl whom I'd never met, but I was also somehow persuaded to stay in my Peachy V. Looked like it was going to be a "Charlie and Wyatt" night.

As Cathy and Claire prepared celebratory shots, I directed my attention over at Luke, who seemed to be deep in conversation with Bridget. I could only imagine the rehearsed bullshit he was feeding her. This is how their conversation went in my head:

BRIDGET: And that's when I realized I was destined to save the beluga whales.

LUKE: You're an incredible human being. You know that, right?

BRIDGET: You think so? It's just, they can't fight the fight on their own.

LUKE: I know, I know. So . . . speaking of beluga whales—

BRIDGET: Yeah, I'll totally suck your dick.

Mistaking my daydreaming for gazing longingly at Bridget, Claire leaned into me and said, "I won't tell Stephanie you want Bridget."

"Oh, no, no. I don't want her at all."

"Oh my God, are you gay?"

"No, it's just that I'm in a relationship with . . . Stephanie. And I care about her very much." Who had I become, Mr. Ripley?

She leaned in even closer. "I may be drunk, but I can tell you're lying. I know you don't really love Stephanie." Well, at least she was right about something.

I had no idea how to respond to her. I was living this lie too hard to remind Claire that I was her downstairs neighbor.

"Come on, go talk to her. She's way easier than she looks." And with those eloquent words of wisdom, Claire shoved me in the direction of Bridget and Luke. I faintly heard Claire say to Cathy, "A V-neck does not suit Stephanie's boyfriend at all." In my head, I immediately started composing a letter:

Dear Urban Outfitters,

> I recently patronized your establishment and was
> helped with my purchase by a bespectacled man named
> Sunshine. I would like to bring it to your attention
> that he let me buy a new Peachy with the V-neck, even
> though I obviously would have looked better in the
> regular collar. There were also thoughts in his head
> comparing me to a giant peach from a clay animation
> feature film for children. I have no hard evidence of
> this but strongly suspect it to be true. Is this the kind
> of customer service you're comfortable providing?
> Enclosed, please find my address, where you can send
> my full refund and a photo of Sunshine being fired.

As I came nearer to the chattering couple, I bookmarked my mental letter. Luke stared me down with widened eyes, as if he were trying to tell me something. I paused, not understanding our form of communication. I mouthed a *what,* hoping for a clearer signal, but all I got were larger eyes and a raised upper lip. Did he want me to save him from this conversation with Bridget or was he telling me to leave him alone? I tried using a few on-the-cuff hand signals, hoping that might clarify things a bit. It didn't. Bridget, of course, had no idea any of this was going on as she rambled on. . . . Wait, did I just hear her say *beluga?*

Luke mouthed back at me, "Ticktock," I believed.

Ticktock? Well, that could have meant any number of things. Maybe he was making a reference to the amount of time he was wasting talking to Bridget and wanted me to get him the hell out of there? Or maybe he was signaling me to tell the DJ to play the Ke$ha song "Tik Tok"? Or maybe he was sweetly informing me of a bomb he had planted and was allowing me the opportunity to get out of Dodge? So many possibilities, each of them equally likely. But after he aggressively mouthed *ticktock* a few more times and pointed to Bridget with his eyes, I decoded that he needed me for my saving skills.

"Hey, guys," I said to the floundering couple. At least Bridget seemed to know me as someone other than Stephanie's boyfriend.

"What are you doing here?" Luke replied in what sounded like a combative tone. I guess he was playing along as if he didn't need my services, so that Bridget wouldn't suspect anything. This made me out to be the bad guy, but sometimes those are the sacrifices that need to be made for a friend in need.

"Luke, I'm gonna need you to come with me to the foyer," I said with the utmost confidence.

"Wait, why?" Bridget asked me. I don't blame her. The poor girl must have really felt as if they were making a connection.

"Sorry, Bridget. Just need to chat with my compadre here. I got an emergency call from one of his family members." And with that I whisked him away, leaving Bridget alone with no one to talk to for a few seconds until the next guy approached her.

Meanwhile, Luke was giving an impressively concerned performance.

"What the fuck happened? Is everyone okay?"

"Luke, you can stop now. She's not even looking over here."

"What the hell are you talking about!?"

Hmm . . . Could there be a slight smidgen of a possibility that Luke and I had gotten lost in translation somewhere? Would that mean that I not only yanked him away from a girl guaranteed to give him a great blow job, but that I also guided him to believe a family tragedy had occurred? Don't feel too bad; this is Luke we're talking about. He'd have been more distressed over the missed blow-job opportunity than the dead relative.

"Charlie, tell me what's going on."

"Ticktock? Now, what exactly did you mean by that?" I was still having a hard time figuring out if Luke was really committed to making our interaction believable or if he was just upset.

"*Ticktock? Cock block,* you idiot! I saw you coming over and was calling you a cock block." Daniel Day-Lewis Luke is not.

"Oh, cock block. They're very similar when being mouthed, you know." Speaking of cock blocks, I decided to protect mine with my hands in case he was considering seeking some below-the-belt revenge.

"Sorry about that. Look, it's not too late. . . ." I began to say, but then realized it was. Bridget had already found herself a new suitor. The douchiest one of them all—the Con-Man. Without even glancing over at Luke, I could tell he was furious with me.

"Will you let me go talk to sluts without getting in the way?" Luke calmly asked. And I was grateful for the new tone.

"Yes. I will let you talk to sluts." "That's What Friends Are For" was written for moments like this.

"Will you be okay alone?"

"Of course," I assured him.

"Now, will you kindly point me in the direction of the girls above you?"

I showed him the way, which consisted of my calling attention to a few girls huddled around a keg. He was still agitated but thankful for the new possibilities. As he ventured off into the land of perfume and high heels, I stood there by myself. I felt companionless in an ever-growing room of connection, even if it was cheap and alcohol induced.

"Stop moping. You're always moping," I imagined my ex saying to me, like she did when we were together.

"I do not mope," I responded in a mopey tone in my mind.

"You're at a party and single. Will you go talk to a girl already?"

I was a little saddened by the fact that even in my own hallucination, my ex wanted me to meet someone else. Did she not even feel an ounce of jealousy? Maybe jealousy doesn't carry over into the illusory world. If I ever got the opportunity to be a figment of her imagination, I would tell her she should live a solitary life, free of all affection and passion, unless she wanted to take me back. Then my imaginary self wouldn't have a problem with her having those things.

But maybe she was right. Why did she always have to be right? Believe it or not, there once was a time when I had no issues wooing a member of the female gender. Not only that, but I was actually pretty good at it. Just a few years back I had gotten two different girls' numbers while driving on the 405 freeway and both happened on the same commute! There was a bit of traffic, but still, you try plucking numbers all the way from the carpool lane. It was a dangerous feat, but in the end the nickname I acquired from my friends, "the Freeway Pimp," was well worth the risk. I campaigned hard for Carpool-Lane Cutie, but you can't always get what you want.

My main problem in approaching women is that I'm not the right mixture of vulgar and nice. Some girls are into the bad-boy type, while others are more attracted to sensitivity and romance. Unfortunately for me, I fall directly in the middle of the spectrum. No-man's-land. Very few girls like to hang out in this area. And the ones who do are generally unstable. I'm looking at you, Patricia Sobel from seventh-grade chemistry. It may have been the name of the class, but no chemistry was had that year.

Much like in seventh grade, my chances of finding love at this party felt quite slim. Yet, the possibility of scoring a one-night stand seemed almost unfairly favorable. But was I ready? I figured there was only one way to find out.

So I checked my breath by blowing into my hand (which, by the way, has never worked for anyone, but we as humans continue to do this generation after generation). I put my hand under my armpit to see whether moisture was creating an incredibly unattractive pit stain, and thankfully it wasn't. Then I gently lifted my right leg and squeezed out a fart that would've been deafening in a library but was completely soundless in the spot where I was standing, next to the DJ's table. It was time for me to get back into the game. Here's how my series of conversations went:

CHARLIE: Hi.

NOSE JOB GIRL: Hi.

CHARLIE: Hi [now with a made-up accent].

NOSE JOB GIRL: Umm, hi.

CHARLIE: Hi [very quickly].

NOSE JOB GIRL: You already said—

CHARLIE: Hi [in an even more made-up accent].

NOT THE FUTURE MOTHER OF MY CHILD: Last week was my Tic Tac–only diet, this week it's edamame, next week I might try and only eat gluten.

CHARLIE: I think I've heard of this diet before.

NOT THE FUTURE MOTHER OF MY CHILD: So, what kind of stuff do you like to eat?

CHARLIE: Oh, you know, just normal stuff.

NOT THE FUTURE MOTHER OF MY CHILD: [poltergeist voice] Are you saying I'm not normal?

CHARLIE: What? No. I know plenty of people doing the whole Tic Tac thing. I'm very supportive of it.

NOT THE FUTURE MOTHER OF MY CHILD: Hmm. I'm not sure yet, but I think I like you.

SIZE MATTERS GIRL: I miss my ex-boyfriend's cock.

CHARLIE: Oh, wow. I'm sorry to hear that.

SIZE MATTERS GIRL: It's just so big, you know? Like way bigger than yours probably.

CHARLIE: That seems unfairly presumptuous.

SIZE MATTERS GIRL: Not really. Guys with big dicks don't use words like *presumptuous*.

CHARLIE: What if I showed you with my hands how big mine is? Would you compare the two honestly?

SIZE MATTERS GIRL: Yeah, sure.

CHARLIE: [showing my approximate size plus five inches] There it is.

SIZE MATTERS GIRL: Hmm. His is way bigger.

CHARLIE: Oh come on!

———————————————

CHARLIE: So, what is it you do?

GIRL WHO WHISTLES WHEN SHE TALKS: Oh, I'm a dog trainer.

CHARLIE: Really?! Don't they ever get confused?

GIRL WHO WHISTLES WHEN SHE TALKS: By what?

———————————————

CHARLIE: What's your name?

GIRL NOT NAMED "DRUNK": Drunk.

CHARLIE: Oh yeah? Is that a first or last name?

GIRL NOT NAMED "DRUNK": First and last. My middle name too.

CHARLIE: Well, it's a pleasure to meet you, Drunk Drunk Drunk.

GIRL NOT NAMED "DRUNK": You too, asshole.

SOMEONE WHO JUST MOVED TO LOS ANGELES: I don't like to tell many people this, but I'm an actress.

CHARLIE: Oh, cool. What kind of stuff do you do?

SOMEONE WHO JUST MOVED TO LOS ANGELES: I'm so embarrassed to even be saying this out loud, but like mostly quirky comedy and period-piece stuff.

CHARLIE: That's really great. Anything I may have seen?

SOMEONE WHO JUST MOVED TO LOS ANGELES: Oh my God, maybe. I'm blushing just from talking about it. Maybe we should change the subject?

CHARLIE: Okay. No worries. So listen . . . would you ever be interested in going—

SOMEONE WHO JUST MOVED TO LOS ANGELES: Hey, do you know if there are any agents here tonight?

So maybe I was a bit rusty; I think when my previous relationship started, people were still using CD-ROMs. But, even so, was this what dating was like nowadays? Perhaps I had some brushing up to do. I was better off in my apartment, where it didn't feel quite so dim.

"Enjoy the party, Wyatt," I said to the poor bastard on my way out.

"But we didn't even take drunken pictures in our shirts," he slurred. "It would've been hilarious, man."

"That's very true. Maybe some other time."

"Wait, what's your name, bro?"

As I walked out the door, I turned back and responded over my shoulder, "Drunk."

THE GIRLS ON BLOW JOBS

Dear Girls Above Me,

"When he said he didn't want a blow job, it made me wanna give him one!" Do not make me chicken marsala. You hear me, DO NOT.

Dear Girls Above Me,

"At college I learned to make the guy go down on you first: otherwise, you won't get shit back." Sounds like community college to me.

Dear Girls Above Me,

"I'd never kiss a guy if he got me something from Kay.
But jewelry from Tiffany, blow job fo sho." I'd like to
see that commercial.

Dear Girls Above Me,

"I so would've given Prince William carriage-head
during that long ride to Buckingham Palace." And
that's why you'll never be a princess.

Dear Girls Above Me,

"The best blow job I ever gave was when I wrapped
a guy's thingy in a Fruit Roll Up." I got some dried
apricots down here . . .

Dear Girls Above Me,

"Jen went down on Tom while he played a video
game. Gross!" Was it *Mario Kart*? That would be the
Nintendo equivalent to road head.

Dear Girls Above Me,

"I think we should start like a movement to bring back the hand job. It's soooooo much easier than giving a blow job." Good luck with your endeavors.

THE GIRLS ON PENISES

Dear Girls Above Me,

"I don't care how big his cock is, Claire, he still uses Myspace!" But an average size penis on Facebook is okay, right? Phew.

Dear Girls Above Me,

"I really want a penis just for a day. All I would do is flop it around." Sorry, did you say something? Was busy slapping my dick.

CHAPTER ELEVEN

NOTE TO SELF: Find the architect who designed my building and kill him.

SUBCATEGORY OF THE NOTE: If the architect has a wife and child, do not kill them. They must live to pass on the cautionary tale, and it would be dishonorable to take the life of a woman or child. Unless a woman or child designed the building, then it's okay to kill them.

The reverberations coming from the party above seemed to be even louder from the comfort of my own apartment. How was that even possible?! But instead of the normal two girls chattering aimlessly, I was under attack by a horde of mind-numbing conversations. I felt like the Grinch on Christmas Eve, forced to listen to the city of Whoville . . . if the citizens of Whoville spoke like this: "Give me my tequila back, or I'll shove my stiletto up your ass." Whoever that was, she was no Dr. Seuss.

I fought back with earplugs, two different types of sound machines, a rickety old fan, and the opening scene to *Saving Private Ryan* at full blast, but the party, full of intoxicated Whos, roared louder. There was no stopping them. The techno music was not music to my ears and was decreasing the size of my heart with every beat played. I've heard the old saying "If you can't beat 'em, join 'em." Of course, nobody came up with that saying after having taken the time to join 'em and failing miserably. I'm going to coin a new phrase.

Dear *Bartlett's Familiar Quotations,*

I would like to come forward as the author of the latest hot phrase to hit the streets:

"If you can't beat 'em, and you didn't do a very good job of joining 'em, then accept that you've been defeated and distract yourself by purchasing a new pair of Nikes or something."

No doubt this variation on the old proverb has made its way to you already, as it improves a tired old phrase and updates it for the new millennium. Please direct all credit to Charles McDowell, and forward all royalties accordingly.

Unfortunately, I couldn't even follow my freshly coined advice, because it was two A.M. already and Niketown was almost definitely closed. I stood in my living room wearing the maroon Snuggie my aunt Nancy had recently sent me for my birthday. Underneath my especially comfortable blanket with sleeves, I was in the nude. I apologized to Marvin profusely for the view of my backside, where there was no cloth covering. He didn't seem to mind, although long-term effects are still to be determined. But that's one of the many benefits of being single. You can wear whatever you want, whenever you want, and in any position you want. For instance, if I wanted to put my legs behind my head in a pretzel position while naked and wearing the Snuggie, I could. No one would be there to judge me. Apart from God and Marvin . . . in that order.

A LIST OF BENEFITS TO BEING SINGLE

I don't have to watch all of the *Real Housewives* series (including Atlanta) unless I want to. (I want to, it just feels nice not *having* to.)

I can play Fantasy Football without sneaking off to the hallway closet.

I can play with myself without sneaking off to the hallway closet.

I don't have to eat only kale salads and drink coconut water.

I can wear Patagonia, even in public.

I don't have to lie about wanting to go to Las Vegas "just to see Cirque du Soleil's *O*."

I can gain a pound or two and not be reminded of it. Actually, scratch this one. Mr. Molever can be quite passive-aggressive.

To better "focus my organizational skills" I'm not constantly pressured to "make lists" anymore—oh. . . . Shit.

As I sipped a cup of hot water with freshly squeezed lemon juice (my nighttime drink), I reveled in the possibilities of my newfound freedom. There was no one there to dictate the parameters of my life. Suddenly, I was overwhelmed with a desire to express the ownership of my freedom. I could continue sitting there, drinking my nighttime drink. I could trash the whole apartment like a punk rocker (and then carefully clean it before Pat returned from his trip). I could do most anything. . . .

I began bobbing my head to the rhythm of the party music. Slowly, I introduced a couple of leg movements into my routine. A few pelvic thrusts later, I had placed my hot drink down in order to prevent any more spillage. With the extra free hand, I was able to incorporate finger snaps and knee lifts into my number. I paused for a moment, wondering if this was the beginning of my path to insanity or a career with Debbie Allen. But my shimmying hips had a mind of their own.

Marvin got up from his very comfy position on the top of the couch and went into my bedroom. The poor bastard had seen enough. In retrospect, it was probably a good thing that he wasn't there to witness my attempt to ride a bicycle around the coffee table. No animal needs to see that.

I had broken into a sweat from all the movement, which felt like my cue to get some much-needed sleep. The party was slowly starting to die down, thank God. I figured it would remain somewhat active as long as Luke was still there, but the volume was low enough that I could probably go to sleep with just two white-noise machines tonight.

I finally crawled into my place of rest at three fifteen A.M. And as I lay in bed, I was able to hear Luke and Claire in deep conversation. Since I knew Claire's room was directly above mine, I figured Luke was well on his way to a night of copulation with my neighbor. This was the conversation:

CLAIRE: As you can see, I got the bigger room because Cathy pays less rent.

LUKE: It's really nice. I like the color of the walls. Gray, but with a hint of purple.

CLAIRE: Elephant's Breath! That's what the color's called. I did it myself—well, I mean I didn't actually paint the walls myself, Mexicans did that, but I chose the color.

LUKE: It's really great.

CLAIRE: Thanks.

(a moment of silence)

LUKE: Hey, you, get over here.

CLAIRE: Who? Me?

LUKE: Yeah, you. Come next to me. I feel like you're a million miles away.

CLAIRE: Yeah, I guess I am kinda far.

(high heels)

LUKE: Can I be brutally honest with you about something?

CLAIRE: For sure, honesty is like my favorite.

LUKE: Okay. Look, I could be making a complete fool out of myself right now, but you know what, I'm totally cool with that. When I saw you for the first time, over by that keg stand, I couldn't take—

CLAIRE: Oh my God, I'm so sorry. But I have to tell you, just now when you were talking to me, you rubbed your eye like you were a little kid and it was honestly the cutest thing ever!

LUKE: Oh, really? I had no idea.

I couldn't believe it. He'd told me all about this "move." I didn't think in a million years any girl would actually fall for it, but in this instance I was happy to be wrong. I could only imagine the smile he must've had on his face knowing that I was probably listening to their conversation. Clearly I was witnessing a true master at work.

CLAIRE: I'm sorry. What were you saying?

LUKE: I seem to have lost my train of thought. . . .

CLAIRE: You were talking about noticing me for the first time.

LUKE: Oh, right. How could I forget? [probably another eye rub]
    Baby, you took my breath away.

CLAIRE: Reeeaaallly?

LUKE: Really.

CLAIRE: Well, I'll admit I was pretty jealous when I saw you
    laughing it up with Bridget.

LUKE: Who?

CLAIRE: [laughing] You're so funny.

I could tell he actually had no idea which girl she was talking
about. In fact, chances were very high that he didn't even know
Claire's name.

LUKE: Do you mind if I just hang out in here for a little while to
    sober up?

CLAIRE: Do you mind if I don't even hesitate to answer that
    question?

LUKE: Do you mind if I turn my phone off because there's no one
    in the world I'd rather be talking to?

CLAIRE: Do you mind if I slip into something a little bit sexier?

LUKE: Do you mind if I kiss the nape of your neck first?

Do you both mind if I throw up a little in my mouth?

CLAIRE: Do you mind if I . . . Okay, I can't think of another one, so
      let's just make out now.

LUKE: Bring that nape on over here. . . .

I didn't even know where the nape is! Was it located in the front just below the Adam's apple? Or around back near the top of the spine? The sides of the neck didn't feel very napelike to me, so I wasn't even considering that. This is the sort of stuff you're supposed to learn in grade school. Once you're an adult, you can't say to a girl, "Um, can you point out the nape of your neck, please?" You might as well ask her what that crevasse between her legs is.

I turned my noise machines at full volume to the appropriately selected "jungle sounds." I figured orangutans, kookaburras, and howler monkeys were my best bet for drowning out the animal noises that were about to take place upstairs. I shut my eyes tight, forcing myself to fall asleep as quickly as possible, knowing that when the bed frame knocking against the wall started up, no animal in the entire kingdom could overpower the uproar. Sadly, trying to coerce myself into falling asleep quicker was only keeping me awake. The expectation of listening to Luke and Claire have sex outweighed the desire to not want to listen to Luke and Claire having sex.

Out of nowhere I heard a single *ding*. At first I wondered if it was merely my imagination stepping in to save me like the stories you hear about people claiming to see the Virgin Mary right before experiencing something traumatic. But just as there were no literal virgins upstairs, there was no divine Virgin downstairs, and I became conscious of the fact that someone was at my front door.

Who the hell could possibly be ringing my doorbell at two A.M.? I thought. There was no way it could have been Mr. Molever; rent wasn't due for a few more weeks. Tania wouldn't have dared stop by for a doggie date at this hour, would she? I was hoping it was the FedEx guy delivering my new multipurpose juicer, but that didn't seem very likely either. The girls above me forgot who I was thirteen and a half seconds after meeting me, so it couldn't have been them. . . . Could it?

I didn't feel like putting on any clothes for this unwelcome guest. So I slipped back into my Snuggie, which would at least shelter my front side and give me the opportunity to send them packing. As I came nearer to the door, I could make out pitiful whimpers coming from a sullen person on the other side. I stopped myself, realizing that no one was making me open the door. There was no reason I couldn't just pretend as if I were an extremely deep sleeper and didn't hear a peep. Or what if I was out of town? Then I wouldn't even be there. . . .

"I can see your shadow under the door. Open up!" the mysterious voice cried out.

Stupid shadow. If I could have just one superhero power, being shadowless would definitely be my choice. Who wants a black empty figure following them around at all times of the day and night? Not me. Maybe if I let myself get vampired. I know vampires don't have reflections, but do they have shadows? Something to look into. *Ding! Ding! Ding!* Oh right, the door.

As I cracked open the door, standing right in front of me was Bridget. She looked quite a bit more disheveled than when I had seen her earlier in the night. This may have been the result of all the crying she had been doing, which it didn't take a rocket scientist to notice due to the mascara stains running down to her chin. Or maybe her drunken stupor was making her look especially unkempt. Regardless, she was much worse off than I.

"I'm drunk. Can I come in?"

All men have soft spots for moderately attractive women who are drunk with vulnerability and who are, you know, drunk literally. It's built into our consciousness. So, Mother Nature took over and opened the door for me.

Bridget plopped down on my couch and let out a huge sigh of anything but relief. She was visibly distressed about something, and her sitting position made me feel as though I was about to play therapist until the sun came up, which has to be the one thing worse than the friend zone. . . . The shrink zone. After a few moments of childlike exaggerated pouting, she looked up at me. Her eyes were bloodshot from either crying or smoking pot, but they still had a uniquely round beauty to them.

"Are you wearing a Snuggie?" she said as her eyes shifted into a judging squint.

"I wasn't expecting company." (Who the hell does this girl think she is judging my Snuggie?) "Can I get you something to drink?" I offered.

"A bottle of Pinot Grigio?"

"Oh, no, I just meant a Dr Pepper or something. I could also do a hot water with lemon. I don't have any alcohol."

"Why the hell not? Are you Amish or something?"

Clearly I have functioning electricity. I thought that, I didn't say it. Shrinks don't make snide judgments during the first session.

Despite her drunken disappointment, I decided to fix her my nighttime drink anyway. As I turned to walk into the kitchen, I had completely forgotten that I was wearing nothing under my Snuggie; therefore, my entire backside was exposed for her amusement. She gasped. I had no idea if it was a pleasant sudden breath or a horrified gasp, but I kept walking in silence, hoping that the situation would just fix itself. I put on the kettle and cut up some fresh lemon. Thankfully, her groaning subsided.

"Are you still alive?" I called out. I had a terrible vision of being blamed for her death and getting thrown in prison with my backside exposed.

"Sort of."

I prepared the lemon water faster, knowing full well she was probably just showing off her wit, but, then again, you can never be too careful. As a thoughtful finishing touch, I added a drink umbrella to my concoction but immediately took it out upon further thought. I was already a guy in a blanket with sleeves at four A.M. boiling hot water and fresh-squeezed lemon for a girl I barely knew. An umbrella seemed a little too fabulous.

When I delivered her the warm mug, she gave me an honest smile, much like the one I had seen her give Luke earlier in the night. At that moment, I was half-glad I had opened the door for her.

"You have a cute butt," she announced to me and Marvin, who was snoring next to her. I was about to thank her, but I didn't want to sound full of myself. Like, oh, I agree that my butt is cute. So I decided to, very slightly, turn on the self-deprecation.

"Really? Don't you think it's all hairy and gross?" Whoops. Too much.

"I didn't notice too much hair. Let me look again." And with that she reached over and tried to roll me over to my exposed side. My immediate reaction was to keep her away from my Sherwood Forest, so I playfully grabbed her arms and held her back. She burst into tears.

"I'm so sorry. I shouldn't have done that!" I released my burly grip.

"It's not you. I actually kinda like being held down." She pulled out an already soggy tissue from her pocket and blew her nose. "It's just that I've had the worst night of my entire life."

Why do girls, specifically the ones who lived above me and their associates, constantly feel the need to construct such exaggerating statements? It makes it harder for me to trust them.

RECORD OF OVERHEARD EXAGGERATIONS

"If he doesn't text me back within half an hour I'm never going to eat again." Compliments of Cathy.

"I have the worst hangover of all time. Watch, I'm done with drinking forever." Another Cathy statement.

"Did you just say Nick Lachey's name? He's like one of my best friends in the whole world," Claire said two weeks after standing behind him in line at Jamba Juice.

"The movie *Bring It On* is the greatest thing to ever happen to me." I believe both Cathy and Claire have said this before.

Women exaggerate literally 125 percent of the time. And what they don't seem to understand is that these extreme overstatements make men doubt their credibility. Like how about "I haven't had a worse night since April of '08." If Bridget had said something specific and to the point like that, I would have wholeheartedly believed her. Not only that, I would've actually wanted to know what went down in the springtime of 2008.

Bridget stared at me as if she wanted me to say something. I ignored the expectant question that hung in the air for as long as I could, but the awkward silence was too much. Once Marvin opened his eyes and joined in, it was too much for me to handle. "All right, tell me what happened."

"You don't want me to talk about it. I can tell." At this point I couldn't figure out if she was pouting or if it was just her lip collagen acting up. Either way she was totally right, but my mom raised me to be a "good listener."

"You've read me completely wrong. I'm dying to know what happened." Men don't exaggerate. We lie.

"Okay, fine."

Bridget then launched into one of the most unimportant testimonials I have ever listened to in my entire life—I mean, since the freezing winter of 2010. The details of her story were fuzzy because I was only giving her half of my attention. But it had something to do with Luke's flirting with her, which made Claire want to flirt with Luke, which made Luke want to start flirting with Claire, which made Bridget want to "never speak to Claire ever again." Something of that nature. As I said, the details were a little fuzzy.

The other half of me was tackling something of much more importance. I was trying to work out in my head if I had enough macaroni and cheese in the fridge for lunch the next day or if I needed to open a new box. I was leaning toward having to open a new box but hadn't fully committed myself to any decisions yet. I find that when contemplating the quantity of macaroni and cheese one has in one's fridge, it's best to sleep on it and come to a conclusion after a good night's rest. . . .

She rudely interrupted my train of thought. "So, will you talk to Luke for me? See if he's still interested?"

"I would, but he's currently having sex with Claire above my bed."

"*What!?*" She leapt up from the couch and bolted into my bedroom. "That whore!"

I guess I should've paid more attention to her story. I probably would have left the words "but he's currently having sex with Claire" out of my response. But then I would've just responded with "I would above my bed." I think that still would have been better.

In my room Bridget gasped—and I could tell this was not a pleased gasp—at the romping sounds that were seeping through my ceiling. Claire was undoubtedly having a grand time, and Luke was sweetly making sure of it: "You like that? You like when I spank you hard?"

I honestly felt bad for Bridget, regardless of the fact that she had only just met Luke that night and probably couldn't even recall the color of his "fuck scarf."

> **fuck scarf** *(noun)* A scarf of Luke's that when worn has
> always resulted in sexual intercourse.

For the record, I do not own a fuck scarf. That doesn't mean I don't believe in the fuck scarf. It's just that I look funny wearing one, thus making the "fucking" aspect a difficult transition. On a side note, I do own a pair of fuck mittens that have about a 75 percent approval rating. Might have to do with the fact that they're a special kind of cashmere. Unfortunately, this is Southern California and I only get like two opportunities a year to lace up my fuck mittens. That unquestionably hurts the statistical approval rating.

"So, you wanna talk about it or something?" I offered my services to Bridget. But she just stood there in silence listening to her friend scream in ecstasy. I could tell she was either on the verge of hysterically crying or plotting a murder-suicide. Either way, I didn't want to be a witness.

"I'm gonna be your electric blanket all night long!" Luke responded to the throes of Claire's passion.

"Oh come on, Bridget. Do you really like a guy who describes himself as an electric blanket?" Regardless of my friendship with the guy, someone needed to say it, even if she didn't want to hear it.

"I'm cold, so, yeah." And with that, she broke down into a pitiful wail. I was pretty sure I had a real electric blanket somewhere in my closet, but I pieced together that she was speaking in metaphor.

I couldn't tell if I genuinely wanted to make her feel better or if I was just trying to shut her up, but out of nowhere I let slip a groan that even surprised myself: "Oooohhhh yyyeaaaahhh." She looked up at me from across the room with frightened eyes, clearly not understanding where I was going with my apparent Tourette's. So I made it a little bit more obvious: "Oh yeah, Bridge. Ride me like a child on a roller coaster!" This made her even more confused and genuinely frightened. I'll admit, it wasn't my best line. I watched as she nonchalantly made her way to the door, most likely to run for safety. But before I could let her go, I tried once again. And this time I screamed as loud as I possibly could up at the ceiling. "You like that, Bridget? You like it when we have sex? Please tell me you like it!"

Her concerned expression transformed into a delighted smirk. We were finally on the same page.

"Do I like it? I love it—sorry, what's your name again?" she whispered.

"It's Charlie."

"Oh, Charlie! Do me harder! Ahhhhh, ooohhhh yeahhhh!"

This was the first time I had ever consummated pretend sex before. It didn't quite bring the same enjoyment as normal sex, but it was fun in a different kind of way, and I didn't have to wear mittens in ninety-degree weather either. Also, I think I was pretty solid in the pretend sack, especially with coming up with believable and creatively dirty sentences. My favorite: "Do you, Bridget, take me to be your lawfully fuckable sex mate?"

"Yesssssssssssss."

I don't know if it was the magic of Pastel Party Night or something to do with geomagnetic storms beyond my understanding, but that night, my one-way connection upstairs became a two-way wormhole, and the noises from my room could be heard upstairs. I haven't been able to replicate these circumstances since. Maybe I should consult a *Farmers' Almanac*.

Luke and Claire quieted down from having real sex to listen to our wild pretend sex. We felt the thrill of what it must be like to be understudies performing onstage for the first time. We were perfectly in sync with each other, which was sure to bring jealousy to our rival couple. Little did they know we were yards away from even touching each other.

Typical male competition kicked in, and from upstairs, the headboard banging began. Luke was giving Claire all he had, which didn't sound all that pleasurable. Bridget and I looked at each other and, without saying a word, grabbed either end of my bed and started driving it repeatedly into my wall. At this point we were knee-deep in a sex-off.

For a brief moment, I questioned why we weren't just having actual sex, instead of needing to force the issue. But once I looked over at Bridget, who was belting out imitation orgasms while ramming my bed into the wall, all with a huge smile on her face, I decided that this was even better. . . . Well, probably not better, but it was late and sometimes even a guy has to fake it when he needs some sleep.

As Luke and Claire grew louder, so did we. Every move they made, we responded with twice as much might. I could tell Bridget really wanted this win. And I was going to do everything in my power to get it for her. I thrust my bed that much harder into the wall.

"I never even knew what a Reverse Frog Squat was until this very second. It's fantastic!" I yelled out.

At this point we had made two indentation marks in the drywall. The lanterns above my bed were crooked and just a few pushes away from crashing to the ground. My side tables were actually on their sides. And poor Marvin was trembling in the corner. Bridget took note of all of the destruction.

"Hey, maybe we should stop. We've done enough damage as it is," she whispered, so as not to let our opponents hear.

"But we haven't finished simultaneously yet," I slyly said with such a confident smirk.

"You're right. Bring it home." She pretend-moaned with an arousing combination of intensity and hope. I could immediately recognize that she'd never ever been fake-fucked like this before. I fake-performed like a champ, so much so that afterward she should've considered lighting up a fake cigarette, and the next day she'd have been well advised to buy a fake morning-after pill.

It got quiet. Such is post–fake coitus. We weren't sure if they had actually finished or if they just didn't have enough endurance to keep up with us. It didn't matter either way. Silence meant the white flag had been raised. We were victorious.

Well, I guess that all of this fraudulent sex inadvertently got Bridget in the mood, because out of nowhere she leapt across the bed, grabbed my Snuggie, and kissed me. I was not at all prepared for this ninjalike move but was more than happy to roll with the punches.

"Thank you for tonight," she whispered.

"No problem. Was it the fake best you've ever had?"

"Yes," she said with a grin on her face. "What about you?"

"I've had better."

And then she kissed me again. Eventually, she pulled away, but not before leaving an eyelash on my retina as a souvenir. I was one second into rubbing her eyelash out of my eye when I heard: "Oh my God, the way you just rubbed your eye? It was so adorable. Especially in those PJs." I smiled. Tonight had turned out to be pretty good.

By the time I had gone to the bathroom and come back with throat lozenges for our sore orgasmed throats, she was fast asleep sideways on my bed. I tried moving her the proper way and under the covers, but a drunk girl's weight is much heavier than I anticipated. There's a scientific formula for it. Something about Earth's gravitational pull increasing exponentially with every ounce of alcohol imbibed. I was too exhausted to care. So I gently curled up sideways next to her and closed my eyes. Just as I was about to enter into a dreamlike state, I heard my good friend's muffled voice through the ceiling.

"Well played, Charlie. Well played . . ."

Then, after a slight pause, I also heard: "Uhhh, my name's Claire, asshole. Who the hell's Charlie?"

THE GIRLS ON FACEBOOK

Dear Girls Above Me,

(Reading her Facebook wall) "Who is this Rip Lewis everyone's talking about?" I'm sorry but I think your friend Lewis died.

Dear Girls Above Me,

"Screw you, Claire. The only reason you have more Facebook friends is because you accept everyone." Subtext: You're a whore.

Dear Girls Above Me,

"I've had a horrible day and now I gotta learn this new Facebook timeline?! Life is out to get me!" Apparently so is the Internet.

Dear Girls Above Me,

"He totally drunk friend requested me at 3 am! Should I reject it and sober add him tomorrow?" Don't, he'll hangover ignore you.

Dear Girls Above Me,

"It's official, I deleted my Facebook." Nice, I have
a lot of respect—"Luke and Sara went to Cancun!?
Reactivate!" 14 seconds.

Dear Girls Above Me,

"I don't even want a boyfriend, I just wanna be 'in a
relationship' with someone on Facebook." My teenage
cousin is looking . . .

Dear Girls Above Me,

"I had to leave the gym early to detag a photo Jess
posted of me where I look fat!" Maybe if you worked
out more . . .

CHAPTER TWELVE

I awoke the next morning, dangling sideways off my bed, to the thunderous sound of somebody snoring behind me. For a moment I believed I was living my worst nightmare: a burly burglar had broken into my apartment to steal my television but decided to just lie with me instead. Once my brain began functioning properly, I remembered that a girl had actually spent the night (that makes it sound way cooler than it was). The fact that Bridget, a girl so petite, could produce that much nasal noise was more impressive than annoying. I then wondered what might happen when Bridget awakened. There's nothing more awkward than waking up in the sunlight to a stranger in your bed after a fake night romp. As I rolled over and pretended to cough in order to wake her up, I was taken aback by the fact that she wasn't there. The source of the heavy breathing was Marvin, who lay horizontally against me, fast asleep on Bridget's sweater.

I cleared my throat of morning mucus. "Bridget?" I called out.

This woke Marvin, but I got no human response. My room was

eerily silent; not even the girls above could be heard. It finally hit me that Bridget had taken off. So, not only had I not had sex with her, and I'm talking about real sex here, but she also had left me in the wee hours of the morning without saying good-bye. Had I been fake-used? What a real bitch!

I checked my phone and found a text message from Luke that read, "I went to breakfast with the girls above you. It's weird, I remember Cathy's name but can't remember the name of the girl I fucked. Help!" I didn't find this weird. I could tell from listening to him last night that he never knew her name, especially when they were having sex and she was yelling at him, "Say my name, bitch!" to which he responded, "You're the bitch, bitch!" And for whatever twisted reason, this turned her on even more. Luke clearly had many skills. Nothing practical that could, say, land him a job, but he knew some stuff.

I began typing out Claire's name but decided to delete it after I pictured Luke trying to figure it out on his own. I started to wonder why Bridget had left her sweater. Was this done on purpose or was she so regretful of the fake one-night stand that she left it in a hurry? My thoughts on most things in the past had always been very straightforward. For example, if I had seen a sweater at my apartment that didn't belong to me, then I would've thought that someone had left it by accident. Now, with the recent addition of the girls above me, I'd started to become more of a conspiracy theorist. Apparently not everything is what it seems. . . .

"When I left Will's house, I *so* wasn't looking my cutest and I was afraid he'd never want to see me again. So, when he wasn't paying attention, I snuck his cell into my purse and said good-bye. Then I came home, ran a bath, changed into cute clothes, and put makeup on. By the time he contacted me to see if I had accidentally taken it,

I was looking all hot and ready to see him again." Cathy, a master-mind, had said this to Claire a few weeks prior.

I had no idea that brains could even function this way. No girl had ever "accidentally" taken my cell phone before, but was Bridget's sweater her version of this? If so, I decided I should probably get it dry-cleaned; Marvin had slept on it. I figured I would just have to wait and see if she contacted me about it. Then I remembered she never got my number, nor did I have hers. Huh, she really did use me, didn't she? And it wasn't even for something that benefited me. Instead, it was to make another girl jealous. Which isn't the worst thing, as it does make me an object of lust used to manu-facture mental trauma in an unsuspecting recipient. That's almost like sex.

Regardless of the morning's outcome, I had a bit of pep in my step. There was a slight possibility it was a cramp in my foot, but for the purposes of my self-worth I was going to stick with my being in high spirits. The last girl to have lain down in my bed was my ex, so at the very least, I was moving in the right direction. It was time for me to make something of my day. I pulled the curtains open to greet the world, and the world welcomed me back with . . . pouring rain.

Before I could take the day by storm in my Wellington rain boots, the events of last night inspired me to do a little Facebook-profile renovation. I had been dreading this moment for quite a while, but it was time to make the big change from "in a relationship" to "single." The only problem with this momentous decision was the baggage that came with it. Clicking "single" on your status was just another way of saying "I got dumped and I'm letting you know in the most pathetic way humanly possible." And on top of that, I knew my en-tire Facebook "family" would have something to say about it. I could hear the responses now. . . .

What happened?! Do I need to kill her? You know I will.
I'm not afraid.
> —*Aunt Nancy*

Saweeeeeeeeet.
> —*Childhood male friend*

OMG :(:(:~).
> —*My teenage cousin*

Want a hooker? My treat.
> —*My dad's friend (has been arrested)*

I'm really sorry, Charlie.
> —*An ex-girlfriend who isn't sorry*

I guess that's another year I don't have to buy baby
clothes for grandchildren.
> —*My mother*

Click. I did it. I was officially single and letting the world know
about it. My plan now: Wait ninety seconds and then hit the REFRESH
button to see the flood of digital responses to my relationship (or
lack thereof) status. I got a little excited, partly because waiting for
anything causes some form of exhilaration, but mostly because I had
jotted down a few "fun" retorts to people's comments. My favorite
being "She died horribly. I'm okay."

Only ten seconds had gone by. The anticipation was killing me.
I needed to stay active. Here's what I did in the remaining eighty
seconds:

Snapped at Marvin for snoring even though he wasn't anymore.

Stuck a thumbtack in my wooden desk (three times).

Ignored two phone calls from my mother, plus a text
(something about grandchildren).

Bam. REFRESH. What?! No one? Really? Nobody had any thoughts,
concerns, or pity about my sudden loss of relationship? I guess I
didn't know my "Facebook family" as well as I thought I did. *Or,*
everyone was at lunch . . . at 10:23 A.M. Okay, fine, I accepted the fact
that people weren't as interested in my life's crumbling to pieces as
I was. That may have been true. But I refused to believe that none
of my friends cared. I hit REFRESH again, believing that I had possibly
not given everyone an acceptable amount of time. I clicked it again.
   A response.
   Success.
   Sort of . . .
   It came from my eleventh-grade English teacher, Mrs. Kelley. Not
the worst news in the world; it could've come from Mr. Olyer, my
Intro to Greek professor (a cold shiver ran down my spine). Let's
see what Mrs. Kelley had to say: "APPLE Inc. is giving FREE 64 GB
APPLE iPAD's to ALL the US fans." So not only did my one response
come from my high school English teacher, but since she'd clearly
been hacked, it was *spam.*
   I checked my new friend requests. There were five people awaiting my approval. Two of them had no mutual friends in common
with me, so that was an easy NOT NOW. NOT NOW. (Not never.) One of
them was from my stalker, Star Epple, whom I reject every day but

like clockwork attempts to become a part of my Facebook family again the next day. NOT NOW, see you again tomorrow, Star. Another request was from my estranged uncle, whom I hadn't seen since I was a young boy. In fact, it took me a few times of saying his name out loud to even remember who he was. I called my dad to ask him if I needed to accept his request, to which he replied, "Yes, you do. But make sure not to give him any of my contact information. Just tell him I keep changing it and it's hard to keep up." My dad, Mary Poppins. CONFIRM.

The final request was from a young gentleman I went to high school with, Graham King. I was never really good friends with Graham, but not enemies either. He was undoubtedly considered our "class clown," and not only because he was humorous, but also because he actually looked like a clown. He would often wear jeans you could fit another person into, shoes that must've been a couple sizes too big, a red and white *Where's Waldo?*–looking T-shirt, and a black bowler cap. This everyday outfit would complement his portly body to perfection. People would often laugh at his jokes, but I always wondered if we were just laughing at *him*.

By the looks of his profile picture, no one would have found Graham funny anymore. He now wore a tight Duran Duran T-shirt, skinny black jeans, and long stallion-like hair, and posed as if he were a Calvin Klein model. I guess that's what almost ten years and escaping the brutal high school hierarchy will do to you. And, CONFIRM.

That got me thinking about how my fellow high school classmates would describe my current appearance. More attractive? Less attractive? The same? From my wallet I pulled out my first-ever driver's license. Holy crap, I had a lot of hair! A sun-kissed golden color with naturally curled locks, and now . . . not so much. I don't get it, why does hair just stop growing in certain places? Who knew hair was suicidal? I wish I could sit my hair down and have a real heart-to-heart discussion:

> To my community of Hair: This exodus must end.
> Entirely too many of you are fleeing the top headlands
> and seeking refuge in the back and buttock regions.
> I assure you, there is no reason to evacuate. Things
> are good on the top of the head. Maybe I have been
> too neglectful. I promise that in the future, I will use
> overpriced product at least once a week, and we can
> talk about why the Frosted Tips incident of '99 will not
> happen again.

After finally convincing myself that I looked "the same-ish" as I did in high school, I started to think about the most beautiful girls from my class. But there was one UGGs wearer who stood out from the rest (or at least for the purposes of this story), and her name was Katie Rosenfeld. She was in a league of her own and completely embodied all aspects of the "perfect girl" cliché: not that smart, unwittingly funny, institutionally crazy—okay, wait, maybe she wasn't the definition of the "perfect girl," but she was for sure the hottest girl I had ever seen. Sandy blond hair, humongous blue eyes, and a set of pearly whites you'd normally only see on a piano.

So I did a search for Katie Rosenfeld, mostly out of curiosity, but also to please the sixteen-year-old Charlie's hormones. And . . . ENTER.

Great. There were twenty-two Katie Rosenfelds in my network. And to make matters worse, twenty of them had privacy settings, so stalking—I mean, reacquainting myself with—her was going to be somewhat difficult. But I had desperation and determination on my side. I made myself a bowl of Quaker Oatmeal with fresh blueberries, as fuel for the hunt. "Okay, let's do this." I actually said those words out loud.

I decided to use an old tactic I learned in the schoolyard, called "the process of elimination." Even though it had a negative connotation for me, meaning I had always been eliminated from everything, it still felt like the best way to identify Katie's profile. So, I started with the cities. Athens, Georgia; Bloomington, Illinois; Raleigh, North Carolina; Casper, Wyoming—none of these places felt very "Katie" to me. I figured the best bet was that she'd stayed in the greater Los Angeles area, as most wealthy spoiled kids from my school did, including me. Up next, eliminate any girls I knew weren't Katie, based on their profile pictures.

I went out on a limb and assumed that the Katie of today did not have jet-black hair and had probably not grown about a foot and a half since high school, nor was she *really* into snakes (that picture still haunts me). I was now down to four. I noticed that one of the Katie Rosenfelds lived in Burbank. I distinctly remembered overhearing my Katie discussing Burbank with one of her friends senior year: "The party's in the Valley? Only crackheads live over there." I was relying on the presumption that Katie did not become a crackhead. So, I crossed Burbank crackhead Katie off the list. Down to three. Okay, now things got a little more difficult. One of the profiles had a picture of a pig with a baby monkey on its back (quite cute), another was a painting of the late/great Tupac Shakur (RIP), and the last one didn't have a picture at all (lame). I decided that no attractive girl would have a Facebook account without posting a visual to at least hint at the fact that she's hot. So I said my good-byes to No Picture Katie: "I wish you the best of luck. Hope you find the right JPG one day."

And then there were two. Baby monkey on a pig or Tupac . . .

Tricky? Perhaps to someone of below-average intelligence. You see, I came up with the ingenious idea to send the same message to both girls. One of them was bound to be the "real" Katie, and I was sure the "fake" Katie would feel so sorry for me that she'd probably just avoid the message altogether. It went a little something like this:

> Katie,
>
> Hola, como estas? It's Charlie McDowell from AP Spanish class! How the hell are you? I think the last time we saw each other was on grad night when an ambulance whisked you away to get your stomach pumped. Still have a hangover? Just kidding! Anyway, you popped into my head the other day, so I thought I'd send a hello and see how you're doing. Hello. I'm sure you're still turning the heads of every guy you pass. I still have neck pains! Hope you're well.
>
> Ciao (I'm speaking Italian now),
> Charlie

And . . . SEND. There was no turning back. My precious message was now in the hands of the Facebook gods; unfortunately, it wasn't long before I realized that I was a strict Facebook atheist.

"You've got mail."

Wait. Shit, did I just admit to still using AOL e-mail as my primary account? This book is now a tell-all.

Anyway, I saw my e-mail: "Facebook notification message from Katie Rosenfeld." It worked! It was a message from Baby Monkey on a Pig Katie:

Charlie,

Hola, como estas too (whatever that means). I took
French in high school. I believe you're looking for
someone else. Good luck in your mission to get laid.

Sincerely,
Katie

I was a quarter of the way done with cursing the fates when the
computer sang again: "You've got mail." I froze. "Facebook notification message from Katie Rosenfeld." I was cautiously excited. I opened
up my Facebook, only to discover a message from the Tupac Katie:

Charlie!

What a pleasant surprise! Thank God my hangover is
gone from that night! I do hope that's not how you
remember me. It wasn't one of my finer moments, but
I'm happy to report no more trips to the emergency
room since, or Disney for that matter.

(Something we both had in common. Back to her letter.)

Where are you living? I would love to see you
sometime . . . As for the head turning, I don't remember
you even glancing at me. Trust me, I would've noticed
that . . . Hope to hear from you soon . . .

Ciao bella,
Katie R.

What an incredible turn of events. Many thoughts were smashing up against my head. Like the fact that the most beautiful thing ever to grace the halls of my high school not only recalled my insignificant presence but actually wanted to see the "all-grown-up" me. Was she still the same? Did she expect me to be the same? And on what number date would it be appropriate for me to question her thought process behind the oddly chosen Tupac profile picture without running the risk of offending her?

More important than all of those questions, I couldn't help but realize that reaching out to Katie was something I wouldn't have dreamed of doing yesterday at this time. For a brief moment, I was curious as to what inspired this great change in me. . . . But then Marvin peed on Bridget's sweater and now I actually did have to go and get it dry-cleaned.

THE GIRLS KNOW THEIR CURRENT EVENTS

Dear Girls Above Me,

"I don't get it, why do all these people want to live on Wall Street? Soho is such a better area." You're right. Occupy Soho!

Dear Girls Above Me,

"I'm so sad. I couldn't live a day without my iPhone. Rest in peace Bill Gates." Let me lend a hand, rest in peace Steve Jobs.

Dear Girls Above Me,

"So I guess they found Obama Bin Laden pretty much dead at a house in Iraq." Literally nothing in that sentence was correct.

Dear Girls Above Me,

"Doesn't global warming just mean more warm weather vacation spots?" You're sounding an awful lot like President Bush.

Dear Girls Above Me,

"So I missed that eclipse thingy last night. I'll just catch it next year." The previous solstice lunar eclipse occurred in 1638.

Dear Girls Above Me,

"It's Wear Purple Day? Now I have an excuse to match my new bra and panties!" Putting an end to teen bullying one thong at a time.

Dear Girls Above Me,

"Did you hear that all these kids were rescued in
Chile after being trapped in some mountain?" Miners,
not minors.

Dear Girls Above Me,

"What oil spill? I thought I heard there was a flood
somewhere." Current events must feel like a Rubik's
Cube to you.

Dear Girls Above Me,

"Did you see that Schwarzenegger's in a new movie?
Is he allowed to do that when he's Mayor?" Only if
Governor Obama OK's it.

CHAPTER THIRTEEN

One of the many annoying parts of living in an old apartment building is the constant surprise maintenance. If one person clogs a toilet with a tampon or someone's pilot light blows out or someone loads an outlet with too many plugs, Mr. Molever hangs up freshly laminated signs that announce "emergency water shutoffs," "gas deactivation tests," and "electricity drills." Of course, I rarely pay attention to these notices, which often comes back to bite me in the butt. Especially the water-shutoff ones.

One day I was enjoying a perfectly satisfying morning poo, and when I flushed the toilet . . . silence. The metal handle jiggled but yielded no water. I went to the lobby to get some answers and found a warning sign that read TODAY WE CELEBRATE OUR "FIXING A BURST WATER PIPE DAY." PROPER WATER CIRCULATION WILL RESUME LATER TONIGHT. Pat must've used the one bonus courtesy flush you get after they shut off the water. You know, for a guy who's constantly leaving me little notes that I don't care about, a Post-it in this case might've been a good idea. Well, fortunately, I was dressed and ready to take on the world because there was absolutely no chance I was going to spend the entire day in my apartment with that floater lurking in the bathroom.

The biggest (non-girl-above-me) problem with my apartment is the shower. I feel comfortable admitting that bathroom upkeep has not always been my top priority. I mean, it's not a frat house lavatory, but it ain't the Four Seasons either. However, one of the luxuries I've become rather accustomed to in my life is hot water. Recently, that comfort has been taken from me and replaced with a stream of pure glacier water piped directly from the Arctic. Even prison inmates get hot water. They may get gang-raped while trying to wash their hair, but the water raining on their violated bodies when it's over is always nice and warm.

I asked Pat, who was on a much later showering schedule than I, whether he was experiencing a similar problem. He responded, "My showers are as steamy as an episode of *Gossip Girl*."

"Is that . . . hot?"

"Ohhhhhh yeah."

The gentleman I needed to speak to concerning this predicament was the one they call Stanley. He heads all of the maintenance for the building and is also the biggest weirdo on the property. I don't know much about him personally, but I have a sneaking suspicion that he illegally dwells in the janitor closet that happens to be on the same floor as my apartment. One day I was walking Marvin, and I happened to peek into Stanley's maintenance room. The door was ajar, just enough for me to see him lying on a fold-out cot, staring up at the ceiling humming the Britney Spears song "Circus." I felt as if I were trapped in a second-rate horror flick. Thankfully, he didn't notice me; otherwise I'm pretty sure he would've chopped me up and worn my reconstructed skin as a costume, or worse, started a conversation with me.

Stanley has a bizarre connection to the apartment building. I'm convinced he can feel what the building is feeling. I have often found him with his ear up against the wall in the hallway as if he were communicating with the building. I've tried listening myself, but all I hear is Pat watching *Judge Judy*. I can't imagine the pain he must endure during an earthquake. But as long as the building is still standing, I'm sure Stanley will be as well.

I stood in my foyer, mentally preparing myself for this awkward interaction. Ever since my breakup, I'd found it much harder to chat with people I don't know, something I used to be able to do with ease. I don't know if my confidence had been adjusted since my ex had ended things or whether my overall outlook on life had become much more pessimistic. Either way, at that moment, having to ask Stanley to fix my water heater was not high on my list of dream activities.

CHARLIE'S LIST OF DREAM ACTIVITIES

1. Being the official sunscreen applier for a *Baywatch* reunion movie.
2. Being the official taste tester at Krispy Kreme headquarters.
3. Being the official sex therapist for the Pitt-Jolie household.
4. Being the official test driver every time Batman gets a new Batmobile.
5. Not having to ask Stanley to fix anything or whatever.

But it needed to be done, as ice-cold showers were beginning to give me a permanently high-pitched voice, which hampered my ability to effectively sing along with my Barry White records.

As I opened the front door, leaving my quiet room behind (the girls were shopping in Beverly Hills), standing directly in front of me, as if he were psychic, was Stanley. I was taken aback to see him so soon, although he did not seem to be startled in the slightest. It was as if he knew I was on my way to pay him a visit. The building must've told him.

"I haven't been getting any hot water in the morning," I said.

"I know," he responded.

"How did you know?"

"Come with me."

Stanley turned around and walked with his bowlegged strut down the underlit hallway. I gave Marvin one last pat on the head and off I went, to either find out about my shower or get murdered by my handyman.

When we reached Stanley's janitorial closet, he pulled from his pocket a chain of what must have been fifty keys. All of the keys looked the same; none had any distinct markings or colors. He intuitively knew which one opened the door to his room without even looking. I stood behind him, not sure if he wanted me following him into his private area or not. He disappeared into the dark closet. I heard the sound of a striking match, accompanied by the faint aroma of a candle that smelled like pumpkin. He popped his head out and motioned for me to enter.

His rectangular closet felt more lived-in than my own apartment. From what I could see in the candlelight, he had a vintage army cot for a bed that was folded up and propped against the wall. I assumed he did that every morning when he woke, giving himself enough room to move around during the day. He had a few workman jumpsuits hanging from a plumbing pipe that ran from one wall to the other. Besides that, he had mostly tools, rusting appliances, some mops, and a couple of mysterious contraptions that were in the middle of restoration at a small table in the corner.

"I don't have any electricity," he said in a gruff voice.

"I'm sorry."

"Why? It's not your fault."

"I know, but I still wish for you to have it," I responded.

"I could rig it if I wanted to, but I don't. Okay?" he said as he began searching for something.

"Okay," I said, wondering which steel pipe would afford me the best chance at getting a clear shot to the head. I knew I would eventually be overpowered, but if I could leave a big enough mark, someone in the building might discover the location of my body within the next year or so.

"I found it." Stanley pulled out a worn blueprint from his stack of papers, breaking my concentration. He handed me a thin document. I stared at it, puzzled for a few moments. It just looked like a series of carefully sketched lines. Some sort of map.

"I'm sorry, but I've never been a fan of cartography. If you could just show me how to fix the water issue, I'll get out of your hair." Oops, he was balding. I hoped he didn't take offense to that statement. I had so wanted my death to be painless.

Stanley leaned in close to me, wanting to show me something on his map. "Right there. That's your problem."

His finger pointed to a line that ran from one complicated-looking square to another. I was confused by all the lines and numbers, but after a while I began to realize that he was showing me a blueprint of our building.

"Is that my apartment?" I asked. I was starting to feel just like Lisbeth Salander putting together all the loose ends of a high-profile case, the only difference being that I was missing a dragon tattoo, nipple piercings, trained combat skills, and computer-hacking capabilities.

"Your problem is that you share a water heater with someone else in the building," Stanley announced.

"Who?" I asked.

"This apartment, right here." His dirtied fingernail pointed to the unit above me. The girls.

I should've known that it was Cathy and Claire who had been stealing my hot water. For as long as I'd heard them, their showering habits had been ridiculous. Some days I would note a combined two hours of bathing. I'm someone who gets bored in the shower after just a few minutes. I had even made the switch to Pantene Pro-V's 2-in-1 Shampoo and Conditioner, just so I could get it done all at once. Get in, rub-a-dub-dub, and get out. I guess men and women have different showering habits. But honestly, what could the girls have been doing in there that would possibly take up so much time? I had my theories. . . .

Shaving their legs and other sundry parts (I've heard all about the red-bump irritation).

Practicing for *American Idol* (there's no way Cathy's making it to Hollywood Week).

Generating steam for nude re-creations of their favorite noir films (not likely, but my favorite theory so far).

Pooping (covering up bowel sounds from each other with running water. Didn't work on me, though).

eBaying (I believe Claire pretended to be in the shower but secretly outbid Cathy on a cashmere sweater).

Hangover nap time (how else could they explain the morning of April 17, 2011, when the water ran for five hours straight?).

I said my good-byes to Stanley, and he responded with some sort of good-bye grunt that was a cross between "See ya later" and "I'll be killing you later." Now I had someone other than the girls keeping me up at night in fear.

On the way back to my apartment, it hit me. I found that the only feasible explanation for my recent hot water shortage was that the girls were all of a sudden waking up earlier than I was and using it all up. I have always considered myself to be an early riser. Those days, I couldn't sleep much later than eight A.M. And the first thing I did to start my day was take a shower. The girls above me, on the other hand, could sleep later than Lindsay Lohan on a bottle of Ambien. I'd even clocked them rising as late as three in the afternoon. So why the abrupt change in schedule? It's not like they all of a sudden had nine-to-five jobs or anything. Was it possible that my two familiar voices had actually found a line of work other than selling used clothes on eBay?

I decided to cancel dinner plans with an actor friend of mine who wanted notes on his reel (the only note I had written so far was "Give up!") and awaited a conversation from the girls that would shed some light on this quagmire. Unfortunately, they weren't giving me what I wanted. So I waited. . . .

"He's really hot but sometimes in public he acts so premature. Grow up!" You're not even remotely using that word correctly.

And waited . . .

"Do you think I could ever win an Emmy for just loving *Grey's Anatomy* so much?" No I don't.

And waited . . .

"What does it mean to be Lacoste Intolerant again?" The inability to wear a preppy shirt.

I was losing brain cells by the second. When were these girls going to spill the beans as to why they were waking up so early? Finally, while I was in the middle of making myself a peanut butter and jelly sandwich, accompanied by some Top Ramen noodles, they filled me in on the secret.

"You know I don't even like Pilates, right?" Cathy said.

"Yeah, neither do I," Claire replied.

"But the instructor is just so hot."

"I know, it's like offensive how hot he is. I would so rub up against his calves if he let me."

I looked down at my own legs and became fairly certain that no girl had ever yearned for them. I flexed my calves, hoping they might transform into something more attractive. They didn't.

"It sucks that he only teaches morning classes," Cathy admitted.

"And we have to wake up so early to make ourselves look all sexy and stuff. The things a girl will do for an Australian."

Aha. I knew there was no chance they had become employed. I should've known that this sudden behavioral shift was all because of a beautiful Australian man. As usual.

After continuing my eavesdropping for a while longer, I found out that the Pilates class they were taking started at eight A.M., which meant that their showering began at six thirty A.M. Since Cathy and Claire shared a bathroom, one of them would take the first showering shift, which lasted about thirty minutes, and then the other would get in. This meant that hot water poured out of their faucet nonstop for over an hour. No wonder I had been bathing in icicles.

So I decided to beat the girls at their own game. I switched my regularly scheduled BlackBerry alarm from 8:01 A.M. to 6:01 A.M. This way I would be the first resident to use the freshly heated water in the morning, ensuring a successful cleansing experience. What I didn't plan for was how exhausted I would get after I finished. There was really no reason for me to be awake at such an early hour, so after a while I found myself waking up at the crack of dawn, showering, and then going right back to sleep. My entire day would get thrown off schedule. I was eating breakfast at lunch, lunch at afternoon teatime, and tea for dinner. And then, to make matters worse, the girls were beginning to catch on to my little scheme.

"My shower was lukewarm at best," Claire whined.

"I know, mine too."

"I think the bearded guy below us is using up all of our hot water." No matter how many times I gave them my name, I was still just a face with lots of plush luxurious hair on it.

"Good thing the Australian hottie teaches a seven A.M. class. Let's just wake up earlier!" Cathy said with enough enthusiasm to make me want to vomit.

I switched my newly scheduled BlackBerry alarm from 6:01 A.M. to 5:01 A.M. I was knee-deep in a hot-water battle with the girls above me, and there was no way I was going to lose, not this one. So now I was waking up while it was completely pitch-black outside. I would stumble into the shower as if I were a drunken zombie. Something that had once been such an enjoyable and refreshing part of my morning was starting to become a horrible chore. When the water hit my body, I would wince, and when I applied facial cleanser, the grimace got even worse. Nothing was pleasant to me that early in the morning. Even Marvin, who associates waking up with "food, food, food," was not on board with my shenanigans. But I stayed strong in my fight for heated water.

The early-morning Water Battle of the Sexes lasted for about a week. In the end the girls surrendered to their Anthropologie-quilted beds. They had fought a good fight, but the stronger, or quite possibly the more pathetic, survived. Looked like Cathy and Claire would have to go back to getting their kicks from *Crocodile Dundee in Los Angeles* on DVD.

As my Dear Girls Above Me Twitter following grew, so did my guilt and anxiety. Each day, more and more people were discovering my "letters" to the girls, and I felt as if it was only a matter of time before they stumbled across it. How would they react to a Twitter feed dedicated to their uncensored conversations? Probably not too favorably, unless they possessed a perverse attraction to Peeping Toms, or in this case an "Attentive Charlie." Was it possible they would happen upon it and not even realize it was them? Based on the level of discourse that typically dripped through my ceiling, I believed I had a shot.

My main focus was trying to find a way to tame my paranoia. Whenever I would hear a knock at my door, my instinct was to hide in the large cupboard in my kitchen. I moved pots and pans and even my George Foreman Grill from this area, just to give myself enough room to conceal my entire body.

"I've got a package here for Charlie McDowell," the FedEx guy called out, completely exposing my identity for anyone who might have been lurking in the hallway.

"Just leave it by the door," I said from the depths of the cupboard.

"I need a signature," he shouted back.

What if the girls had discovered my blog and hired a gentleman disguised as a deliveryman to survey my apartment as part of a planned attack later in the week? Because of this likely possibility, I considered not opening the door, but then I remembered I was waiting on a shipment of Wild Harvest oatmeal. I needed that fucking oatmeal.

I cracked my front door open. A man dressed in black shorts and a matching FedEx shirt and hat stood before me. His outfit appeared to be authentic enough, although a knockoff didn't seem that complicated to piece together. He handed me my package, and I could tell from its weight and size that it was indeed my oatmeal (thank you, God). As I was signing the FedEx slip I watched as his eyes peered into my apartment. Did he see anything?! How much were the girls paying him? Should I offer him double? I swiftly shut my door until there was just enough space for my arm to hang out and finish up my John Hancock. I tossed his pen to the ground, diverting his attention and giving myself enough time to reel my arm into safety. Sorry, ladies, but you gotta get up pretty early in the morning. And we know that's not your thing.

This paranoia even began to carry over into my sleep. One night I dreamed that I came home and the girls were in my kitchen cooking, dressed in matching aprons. They appeared so cheerful when they saw me . . . a little too cheerful. When I asked them how they had gotten into my apartment, they opened their mouths and started talking with cartoonlike enthusiasm, but no sound was coming out. For the first time, I could see them but not hear them. And to make matters worse, when Claire took the top off a pot on my stove, inside, sitting in some heavily seasoned broth, was Marvin. They were boiling my faithful dog alive, and the sickest part of all was that he seemed to be enjoying it. I feverishly woke up looking as if I had participated in a wet T-shirt contest. I checked on Marvin, who was fast asleep in his bed, far away from the kitchen stove.

I was hoping that my girls-above-me nightmare was a one-time thing, but the very next night I had another one. This time I was alone on vacation in the Bahamas, escaping any conversations from above me (I even requested a room on the top floor just in case). After an incredibly relaxing week, filled with sunbathing, scuba diving, a badminton tournament, and intense karaoke nights, I decided to ride a horse (bareback) to the other side of the island on my last day there. It was an exquisite jaunt, and I was feeling quite good about myself . . . that is, until I happened upon a cove where Cathy and Claire were making sand angels . . . with my mother. Much like Marvin in the stew, my mom was having a wonderful time with Cathy and Claire. They had all sorts of inside jokes and were even hand-feeding each other freshly cut pineapple. I watched all of this from behind a palm tree. All of a sudden my mom cried out, "I love this Club Med vacation with my soul sistas!" What the hell was going on? My mother hates Club Med!

There was definitely a moment when I contemplated abandoning writing the "letters" altogether and deleting any evidence that might expose me to Cathy and Claire. This was a big decision to make and it wasn't easy. Was this supposed to be a quick and harmless way to vent my frustrations, or was it my duty to transcribe these discussions for thousands of people's enjoyment? I was at a crossroads.

I pulled up Google and typed, "What to do at a crossroads?" I clicked the very first link that popped up, which was a quote from Taylor Swift. She said, "Everybody has that point in their life where you hit a crossroads and you've had a bunch of bad days and there's different ways you can deal with it and the way I dealt with it was I just turned completely to music." Wow. What a sage singer/

songwriter. I could totally draw a parallel to my own life. You see, "bad days" for me represented the difficult breakup I had gone through, but then I "dealt" with it by "turning," or in my case being forced to listen, to the conversations of the girls above me. Cathy and Claire were my "music." Also, instead of giving interviews about it to music journalists, I had nightmares about the girls partying with my loved ones while I watched in horror.

It was partly thanks to Taylor's wisdom that I decided to continue on, but it mainly had to do with the overwhelmingly positive responses I got each day from people who read my letters. I can only assume that my readers felt sympathy for me instead of finding me thoroughly creepy, although there were a few of those people too. But over time I actually started acquiring "fans." These people would show up every day and comment on my Twitter posts, Facebook status, and website. This didn't exactly put me into John Lennon status, but I did feel as though I was at least Ringo Starr. Okay, okay, I was a Monkee. But for the first time in my life I was adored by people other than the members of my own family. From a self-worth perspective this made me feel very good about myself. Here are a few of my favorite supporters:

Alexis—This high schooler visited the website's message board often to write a haiku that had to do with whatever the girls talked about on that particular day. Most of them were quite good. "Girls Above Charlie / so easy on the eyes, yet / so hard on the ears."

Kevin—My right-hand man. He was always the very first person to comment on Facebook and was extremely good at making sure any naysayers never returned. From his profile

picture, I figured him to be about twenty years old . . .
in 1970.

Maddy—Every evening, at six o'clock PST, Maddy would
confess to me that she wanted to "comb my beard." When
I finally acknowledged her presence with "All right, Maddy,
I'll let you comb it," I never heard from her again. Maddy, if
you're out there, does the offer still stand? Or did I ruin the
whole thing by being into it? I guess no one likes to comb a
willing beard.

Sunny—One day I received a message that said, "I just
wanted to tell you that I met my fiancée when we were both
reading 'Dear Girls Above Me' in a coffee shop and laughed
at the same time. Thank you." My suffering was responsible
for a romantic pairing? If this couple procreated, theirs
would be a child of my pain.

Carl—This young man offered me five cases of peach
Snapple if I let him come over and listen to the girls.
Unfortunately, I had to decline, because I already had some
peach Snapple, and also I'm not a psycho.

Rebi—She always wanted to know if both of the girls above
me were blondes. When I finally wrote back to inform her
that one of them was in fact a brunette, she said, "Goodbye
forever." Huh? I miss you, Rebi!

Angela, Sarah, and Lena—One day, all three of these girls
asked for my hand in marriage. When I clicked on their

profiles I noticed that two of them were in middle school and the other was already married with two kids, but a proposal is a proposal. I let all of them know that they needed to get my mom's approval before we could begin planning any legally binding ceremony. My mom said I should go for it with Angela because she was president of her school's debate team.

Once I had decided to make letter-writing a full-time job, I realized that I needed to prepare myself for the worst-case scenario—the girls above discovering my secret identity. I needed a blueprint that I could throw into action at a moment's notice, kind of like Macaulay Culkin in *Home Alone*. But instead of two desperate criminals invading my house, I would be facing two prima donnas with expensive handbags and a serious attitude problem. A far worse scenario.

THE GIRLS ARE WORLD TRAVELERS

Dear Girls Above Me,

"Claire! I just met this Asian guy who had a British accent! How is that even possible?" Let me ask my white South African friend.

Dear Girls Above Me,

"I think I wanna learn a new language. Maybe a little parle vu espanol, por favors?" I'm not sure which Rosetta Stone to get you.

Dear Girls Above Me,

"He's going on a family vacation to Amazon? To like
the headquarters or something?" More likely than that
measly rainforest.

Dear Girls Above Me,

"He said he was French Canadian? Wait, France and
Canada aren't even near each other!" Wait, neither
are Africa and America!

Dear Girls Above Me,

"He said he was Spanish but not a Mexican. What the
hell, that doesn't even make sense!" It does to the
entire country of Spain.

Dear Girls Above Me,

"Her wedding is in Costa Rica?! Wait, don't Americans
get kidnapped in Mexico all the time?" Good thing
you're not going there.

THEY LOVE THEIR CELEBRITY MEN

Dear Girls Above Me,

"Umm, Bradley Cooper is not the Sexiest Man Alive.
What about Gos, Effy, Chan, Laut, and Gylly?" Oh no,
I totally understood that.

Dear Girls Above Me,

"Hey Olympic website, stop being so annoying and
just tell me when David Beckham is swimming!" I
think you're confusing your abs.

Dear Girls Above Me,

"I hate to say this but even if Ryan Gosling proposed
to me with a Zales ring, I would say no." Because it's
Ryan Gosling, right?

CHAPTER FOURTEEN

My previous relationship had lasted several years; the one before it lasted even longer. Even in my precollegiate days I never found myself between girlfriends for any meaningful period of time. I was the Green Bay Packers of relationships.

Here's what I mean by that: It's extremely rare for a football organization to have an elite franchise quarterback. And it's almost unheard of to go from one franchise quarterback to another within a season. Most organizations need many off-seasons to rebuild their team, and then, maybe if they're lucky, another golden QB strolls in and saves the day. Well, the Packers went from Brett Favre to Aaron Rodgers before there was enough time to even change jerseys.

My romantic life had been the relationship equivalent of that. From high school to college and then grad school, I was in three serious relationships. So if you think about it, I actually have the Packers beat. Brett Favre and Aaron Rodgers are amateur hour. I had *three* franchise relationships without having to ever suffer a lonely, miserable off-season.

Now, however, things were different. I was rebuilding. I didn't even have a draft pick. (Not sure what the equivalent of a draft pick would be for this analogy. Match.com maybe?) The point is, I'm a relationship guy. Dating is an entirely different ball game. And after a solid ten-year run of relationships, the prospect of dating seemed quite daunting. I mean, just think about all that'd happened in the span of years I'd been out of the dating game.

CULTURAL LANDMARKS THAT OCCURRED SINCE I WAS LAST ON THE DATING SCENE

Facebook was invented

The Kardashians were invented

Twitter was made

A Kardashian sex tape was made

Our first African-American president took the oath of office

Two Kardashians took the oath of marriage

A spacecraft passed through space, landing somewhere on Mars

Two babies passed through a Kardashian birth canal, landing somewhere in Calabasas

Basically, what I'm trying to say is, I had a few things to brush up on and I needed some sort of CliffsNotes crash course on today's dating landscape—

"Ugh, Chad just texted me 'Dinner tonight?' Doesn't he know that drinks are text-approved but dinner deserves a phone call?" Cathy adamantly asked.

Right. Thanks for reminding me, Cathy. That was another big change. Texting had become the primary way to communicate in the beginning stages of a new relationship. Some other helpful snippets overheard over the past few months:

"Ugh, he showed up with a condom. I so would've fucked him if he hadn't expected to fuck me."

"Never date a guy who doesn't routinely update his Facebook profile picture."

"I find it so sexy when he orders a drink for me, but when he orders my dinner it's like, whoa, getting a little aggressive there, OJ."

I had a week before drinks with Katie, and if this was what dating had turned into, I desperately needed to prepare. The girls above went from a nuisance to crucial in the amount of time it took Michael Phelps to re-up his Subway endorsement deal—er, I'm sorry, I meant the amount of time it took a Kardashian husband to be traded and signed to two different Los Angeles NBA teams.

The point being, I became a courtroom stenographer. Anything I overheard Cathy and Claire discuss in the dating realm was immediately transcribed and committed to memory. At this point I had grown quite adept at deciphering their lingo and breaking it down into human-speak. Yes, it was time to get back out there, and with each passing day, I was growing stronger. Not physically, of course—in fact, I think I may have put on a few pounds—but I was getting date strong.

That being said, there were a few hiccups along the way. Like the time I was transcribing a riveting conversation between Cathy and Claire about the mixed messages that "swallowing too early on in a relationship" might send. Their friend Becca had stormed in, interrupting the entire flow of this captivating discussion—

"So I stopped at Starbucks this morning and you're not gonna believe who I met and have been texting back and forth with all day!"

"A cast member from *Entourage*?" I groaned to myself.

"Turtle from *Entourage*!"

I mean, that'd been my go-to response after each overreaction to a celebrity sighting. It was bound to happen; I'd just been playing the same lottery numbers over and over until I won.

"He was totally hitting on me while he was waiting for his Very Berry Coffee Cake to get warmed up. And the best part is, he's not, like, fat anymore. I think we're gonna end up meeting for drinks! Can you believe it? Me and Turtle!"

Maybe I was irritated because Becca had barged in on my eavesdropping dating seminar. I mean, this was *my* time with Cathy and Claire. Didn't she know that? Or maybe I was just upset because I couldn't fathom anyone generating that level of excitement based on scoring a date with Turtle. When television's history book is finally written, I'm fairly confident that Turtle will have his spot securely immortalized two notches above Screech.

Then, suddenly, like most of the vapid conversations before it, this back-and-forth led to something quite troublesome that I hadn't previously considered. . . .

"I would never date Turtle," Cathy proudly declared as if she deserved some sort of medal for this bold proclamation.

"You're telling me you wouldn't have drinks with Turtle from *Entourage*?"

"No, I'd totally have drinks with him. But on the friend tip."

"But he'd go out for drinks with you thinking it was a date."

"Well, he'd find out very quickly that it wasn't."

Uh-oh. My brain was a computer that had just crashed. Was it conceivable that Katie assumed we were just two old friends reconnecting and catching up over drinks? I mean, was it actually possible that Katie didn't even consider Friday night a date?

I'd love to say that the idea of this horrific prospect's coming to fruition was a one-time concern, but it wasn't. It was a fear I was all too familiar with, an awkward dating trend I've been unfortunate enough to experience on every single first date I have ever been on. And that dating trend is:

> I never know if the girl I'm on a date with knows that
> she's also on a date.

By and large, all the relationships I've ever had blossomed into a romance *after* we were already friends. So there was never any need for a "first date." We already knew each other fairly well; I skipped right from friend to boyfriend. I said "by and large" because there were a few rare instances where I'd meet a girl and go out on what I hoped was a date. *Hoped* being the operative, italicized word . . .

I have yet to experience a first date where prior to it I was able to say with 100 percent certainty that it was in fact a date. Over the span of my three marathon relationships, there were times when a big fight would happen and we'd take a breather from the relationship. It usually never lasted more than a month or so, but on those rare relationship time-outs, sometimes I'd find myself going out with a girl I'd just met. It was always really tough for me to gauge whether or not the girl was interested in dating me, wanted to make a new friend, or wanted to network socially and make a new contact. This is L.A.; even people's pets meet for drinks at five for networking purposes.

Most of the time, on a first date, guys are trying to measure how well they're doing, gauging whether or not their date is responding favorably to them. Not me. I find myself in the unique position of dedicating my energy to figuring out if my date even knows she's on a date.

CLUES THAT MY DATE KNOWS SHE'S ON A DATE

She doesn't tell me that she's really pulling for me and my ex to patch things up

She doesn't *volunteer to help* me and my ex patch things up

She laughs at my Seinfeld impression

She doesn't laugh at my Seinfeld impression

She goes through the charade of pretending to reach for her purse to contribute money to the bill, but then lets me pay after reminding me that I don't have to

She has sex with me (this one is a big clue)

If I'm being conservative, I'd say that up to this point, 84 percent is the highest level of assurance I've ever felt going into a date that the person facing me knew she was also on a date. With Katie, though, this was a whole different situation. We'd known each other for years but had been out of touch for just as many years. I'd say I was 96 percent confident that she knew this was a date and understood that I wasn't just trying to build up contacts in my LinkedIn account. Just kidding. I'm not a douche. I don't have a LinkedIn account.

LIFE'S IMPORTANT QUESTIONS

Dear Girls Above Me,

"What do you think happened first, tea bagging or like actual tea bags?" Is this your version of the chicken and the egg?

Dear Girls Above Me,

"This might be a stupid question—" Girls, there's no such thing as a— "Do fish, like, drink water?" Never mind, stupid question.

Dear Girls Above Me,

"You know what I really wanna know?" How
Stonehenge was formed? "Do ladybugs get jet lag?"
Oh right, that mystery.

Dear Girls Above Me,

"What if the world actually did end and we're painting
our nails in heaven right now?" Then I'm the devil
sitting on a toilet.

Dear Girls Above Me,

"Do guys actually circle jerk? Can you imagine if girls
were like, come on over and we'll all touch ourselves."
Yes, I can imagine.

THE GIRLS ON THE CASEY ANTHONY TRIAL

Dear Girls Above Me,

"The verdict is not guilty!? (pause) So, is she going to
jail or no?" What's confusing you, the word "verdict"
or "not"?

THEY ARE GOOD SISTERS

Dear Girls Above Me,

"My little brother just called to find out the exact location of a girl's G-Spot. He's so cute!" Replace cute with *very creepy.*

CHAPTER FIFTEEN

"You really fucked me good, Claire."

Is it Thursday night already? I jokingly wondered.

"I can't believe you were dumb enough to tag me at 3rd Stop. I told Chad I had reading to catch up on and now he's gonna see on Facebook I was out happy-houring it with you!"

In Claire's defense, I'm not sure how strong of a landing the "catching up on some reading" excuse would have made. I knew that Cathy had finished the entire *Fifty Shades* series in less than a month, and if those late-night visits from Chad were any indication, he knew too. So unless she started reading Tolstoy, I think happy hour drinks at 3rd Stop was a pretty safe bet.

It used to be that a distrusting spouse, suspicious of infidelity, would reticently tail his potential cheating partner in the dreaded hope of confirming his fears. And if things really got desperate, one might consider hiring a third party to monitor and then take pictures in order to catch the cheater right in the act. Times are now different. We're all somehow connected, so there's no need for any type of surveillance. People catch themselves by . . .

1. Literally tagging themselves with the person they're cheating with (FYI, Becca, tagging yourself with Turtle is going to raise some eyebrows).

    Example—My friend Jennifer's status update . . . Friday night at 9 P.M.:

ROUND UP SPORTS BAR

$30 and you DRINK ANYTHING you want ALL NIGHT LONG!!

No one does it better than us!!!—with Jon Bergman and 3 others.

    My friend Jennifer's status update . . . That same Friday night at 1:30 A.M.:

DOUBLETREE HOTEL

ROOM 220 No one does it better than us . . . STILL!!!—with Jon Bergman

2. Using Foursquare to become the mayor of the motel that they frequent when cheating on their spouses. (I believe my friend Jennifer was the first female mayor of a DoubleTree hotel; she really broke through that glass ceiling.)
3. Accidentally Instagramming a naked pic they meant to send

to the dude they're secretly fucking ("accidentally" adding the Amaro filter might make one question whether or not the whole thing was intentional).

4. Or checking into a bed-and-breakfast (only to then @check-in to a bed-and-breakfast). Sometimes I think Jennifer was just crying for help.

People, this is how empires crumble, destroying themselves from within. We talk about the Internet killing the newspaper industry or Facebook rendering high school reunions irrelevant, but you know whom I really feel bad for? You know which group of individuals, by far, has taken the biggest hit since the social media boom?

Private eyes.

No group has been more negatively impacted by social media than those poor PIs. We cry for newspapers and magazines, but nobody has taken up the private investigator cause. Well, I'm here to speak on behalf of all the PIs out there who don't have the means to speak for themselves. (Incidentally, most are older men who don't know how to work a computer, let alone have social media accounts, so they literally don't have the means to speak for themselves.) You want to talk about job creation; these poor bastards are losing business because idiot twentysomethings (and a few politicians) are outing themselves as cheaters on social media platforms. Cathy, Claire, Anthony Weiner, and others of your ilk, stop putting PIs out of work by doing their job for them 140 characters at a time.

And now, mothers, a breed of the human species that *already* has carte blanche when it comes to invading privacy, have joined the ranks. Albeit, they don't understand what tagging actually is. Sometimes my mom tags me when she goes out to lunch with my sister because she wants me "there in spirit." Then, in an attempt to avoid confusion, I detag myself so people I evaded hanging out with in the first place can't be all like, "Charlie, you're not trampolining today, you're out with your mom and sister eating veggie burgers." Then my mom gets offended because I detagged myself from her post.

We were better off with beepers. You had a code number that you used to identify yourself (mine was 220) and different combinations of numbers translated to different things (45 56 meant good night, sweet dreams). This was a convenient, easy-to-decipher form of teenage correspondence. Moms couldn't pick up a beeper and decode the messages. It was paradise. Then we had to go and get all advanced and ruin everything. Oh, whatever.

220—45 56, private eyes.

"Would you keep dating a guy you really liked if he admitted to wanting to have sex with your mom?" Cathy fervently asked Claire during one of their impromptu one A.M. think-tank sessions.

"Hmm, that's a toughie" was Claire's inspired response, the two of them really spitballing now. "I guess I'd wanna know if he's masturbated to her or not. That's the million-dollar question."

"Chad told me he looked my mom up on Facebook and started going through her pictures. He thinks she's hot. Ugh, I wish my mom understood the meaning of privacy settings."

"I know. Facebook settings are *such* an invasion of privacy," Claire said sympathetically. Claire and Cathy continued complaining about Facebook's invading their privacy. This coming from two girls who never missed an opportunity to pose in front of a mirror and take a picture of their reflection while exposing their "toned tummies" right after yoga. You can't complain about Facebook privacy settings if your profile picture is a self-portrait of you with your shirt off and pouty lips.

Other than that one glaring hypocrisy, I totally empathized with Cathy's complaint about Chad wanting to bang her mother. No son or daughter should ever have to worry about that imagery. Trust me, the effects of something like that will ripple through the rest of your life.

We all casually throw the term *MILF* around like it's a football on Sunday morning. To hear Cathy complain about her MILF mom's exposed Facebook photo album was pure comedy compared to the hell I had to live through growing up.

Most people who suffer the burden of having an attractive mother don't also share the additional burden of that mother's being an Academy Award–winning actress. I come from a strong bloodline of actors. Both of my parents have individually made names for themselves working the last four decades in theater, film, and television. I was lucky enough to grow up in a household of people with immense talent and determination to live out almost every single goal they had ever set for themselves.

The first question I inevitably get asked when meeting someone for the first time is "What's it like growing up with a famous parent?" That I can handle. Their wanting to have sex with that parent, I can't.

And it's not just strangers I have to deal with. Just the other day, during a routine checkup, my family doctor said, "So your mom came in for some flu shots last week. She's a MILF that just keeps looking younger, isn't she? Okay, now cough again for me, please. Sorry, my hands are a little cold."

Did Dr. Romoff just tell me that he would like to have sex with my mother, while in the very same breath cupping my testicles? There's an illusory familiarity people believe they have with my mom because they saw her on a movie screen, and they think this artificial familiarity gives them the go-ahead to say whatever filth comes to their mind.

The traumatizing experience that irrevocably changed the course of my early teenage life forever occurred one Friday afternoon, during a sleepover at a friend's house. Specifically, my best friend's house. His name was Alex Israel, and his dad kept a hidden stash of *Playboy* magazines in a box that would have survived a nuclear holocaust. Or so we thought. You see, Alex's dad got crafty. He knew the game we were playing, and he didn't want us to be any part of that world. So he relocated his pornographic treasure trove to an undisclosed location.

For hours, we scoured the entire house looking for the magazines. The search went on into the late evening, to no avail. Rome was built in the amount of time we dedicated to finding a box of porn. After a disappointing night of frustration with no arousal, we decided to hit the hay. I made myself comfortable in my Ninja Turtle sleeping bag, which I'd outgrown but couldn't find the strength to part with.

I closed my eyes. And just as I was about to welcome REM into my night, I was attacked by a sudden burst of noise and flash of light. I opened my eyes. The TV was on.

"Israel, what are you doing?" I said with an annoyed tone.

"I'm looking for some porn on the TV. Go to sleep," he replied. Back in those days, once you scrolled all the way up to the scrambled channels, sometimes, if you got lucky, the astrological gods would smile down on you. If the right sequence of satellite signals bounced back and forth at precise congruent angles, they'd form a perfect synchronized alignment that beamed directly to your TV. And when that happened, you were able to see part of a scrambled boob with fuzzy lines going through it. In other words, heaven for a thirteen-year-old boy. But tonight, Alex was determined to scroll through the channels and find the real thing. It was in his eyes. I saw it.

"Are you going to jerk off while I'm sleeping in the same room?" That was an important question, not to be overlooked.

"Just go to sleep!" Israel said after one too many beats of silence.

"Go to sleep? Are you crazy? How do you expect me to go to sleep knowing what you're about to do?"

He continued to browse through the TV guide, looking for any title with even a slightly pornographic name. I watched as he paused on *Dirty Harry* for a moment, read the description, oddly contemplated keeping it on, but then thankfully changed the channel.

"You're tired. That's all that should matter," he said to me.

"My friend masturbating a few feet from me while I sleep is something that matters to me very much." Did he really expect me to fall asleep at this point?

I rolled over, facing the wall, and wrapped my pillow around my ears, which ended up being uncomfortably pointless. I could still hear an indistinct hullabaloo coming from the television. Every few seconds a whole new set of voices could be heard as Israel feverishly changed to the next channel. My only hope was that with each failed channel, his horniness would lose steam.

After a few more minutes had passed in this great hunt for pornography, Israel finally settled on a station. "All right, here we go. I finally found some good shit."

The sexually aroused teenage boy in me wanted to turn around to catch a glimpse of a woman's naked body, but I was equally exhausted and didn't want to give Israel the satisfaction of being interested in what he had found. So I continued to stare at the wall as projections of light danced and mocked my stubborn decision. What if he had come across something really great? It would be a disservice to me, and mankind, to not even look and see the type of porn Israel had discovered. Maybe just a peek?

As I turned my body over and locked eyes with the television, I realized I was looking directly at my absolute worst nightmare. . . .

My own mother, naked on-screen.

It was the movie *Melvin and Howard,* which she won an Oscar for, but it would now become infamously renowned as the movie that caused the death of her only son. A medley of so many horribly disturbing emotions took over my dumbfounded body. I was like a deer in the headlights; the only difference was that I was begging for the TV to drive off the wall and put me out of my misery. Not to mention the most appalling part of all of this was that my best friend was on the floor aroused, with no idea that the figure arousing him was my mother at the innocent age of twenty-seven.

"Israel!?"

"I knew you'd be thanking me," he said coyly, which only made me want to direct the vomit that was seconds away from projecting out of my mouth on his stupid face.

"That's my mom!"

He slowed down his stroking movements in disbelief. "What— that's not—wait, how is that—okay, is that your mom?"

"Yes! Stop masturbating to her!" Tears began to stream.

It took me a while to fall asleep that night. The image-that-must-not-be-named was still burning up my mind like the Chicago fire. So when I tell you I chuckled at Cathy's complaining about Chad's looking at pictures of her mom taken during a family cruise, you now understand why I think such a concern is a joke. Try walking a mile in my Ninja Turtle sleeping bag.

THE GIRLS ON THE KARDASHIANS

Dear Girls Above Me,

"Oh thank God, for a second I thought I read Kim Kardashian died!" Nope, just an evil dictator that sort of looks like her mom.

Dear Girls Above Me,

"Ahhhhhh!" What? "Ahhhhhh!" What? "Ahhhhhh!" What!? "Kim Kardashian is getting a divorce!" Thanks for wasting my whats.

Dear Girls Above Me,

"The Kardashian Wedding was totally our Royal Wedding." And just like that an empire falls.

THE GIRLS ON ADDICTIONS

Dear Girls Above Me,

"I wish I had hotter addictions like heroin and cocaine. Nasal spray isn't sexy enough." Don't underestimate medicated nose water.

THE HORRIBLE WEEK REBECCA BLACK WAS INTRODUCED INTO OUR LIVES

Dear Girls Above Me,

"Hey Claire, what day is it?" Oh no, please don't sing—"It's Friday, Friday, gotta get down on Friday." It's Thursday!

CHAPTER SIXTEEN

"I don't think we can be friends with Kayla anymore?" Cathy half proclaimed, half asked. It was an odd speaking habit that I noticed the girls had recently adopted.

"What happened now?" Claire asked. "Is it because she hooked up with Steve? I mean, who hasn't. . . . I hooked up with Ryan, who hooked up with Jenny. And Jenny used to date Steve. So in a weird way, I hooked up with Steve too." If Steve ended up hooking up with Kevin Bacon, I think they may have stumbled upon a new idea for a "degrees of separation" game.

"No, that's not it. It's because she broke up with Tom. We were only friends with Kayla because she and Tom were dating. Without Tom in the picture, what the hell are we supposed to talk about?"

This was something that I could relate to. I'd lost my fair share of friends as collateral damage due to my former relationship's imploding. I used to have a ton of friends. Before my relationship I'd had at least three of them. But what tends to happen during a serious relationship is you lose touch. It's inevitable, it's shitty, it happens.

Now, as a couple, you meet new people, but these are "couple friends." In other words, they're shared. But more importantly, you only exist to them as one-half of a relationship. The very nature of a friendship with couple friends hinges upon the concept that you're the other half of a whole. And when you're part of a social circle that has only existed for as long as you've been in a relationship, you run the risk of those friends only being able to see you in that particular light. Which is a huge problem once your relationship ends. It's the friendship equivalent of the "Successful Sitcom Curse."

> **Successful Sitcom Curse** *(noun)* After a megahit sitcom has its run, the main actor has difficulty finding other roles because he or she is so identified with the iconic character portrayed in the show.

Well, when a megahit relationship ends, it's no different. As far as my group of couple friends was concerned, I was viewed as my ex's boyfriend. And now that our relationship was over, they couldn't see me as anything else.

I'm like Matthew Perry in every fall season's inevitable attempt at a post-*Friends* TV show. My couple friends give me a chance, they have a few chuckles because I'm still the same guy, but something seems a little off. The dynamic isn't quite the same. They can't put their finger on it; it just *feels* different. . . .

Soon they come to the conclusion that even though I'm Matthew Perry, I'm no longer Chandler Bing. I may look like Bing. I may act like him. But I'm no longer must-see TV. So my social circle stops calling me until eventually we're no longer Friends.

As my date with Katie approached, I couldn't help but wonder if she was the right type of girl for me to see after my ex. "Beer before liquor, you'll never get sicker." Well, dating the wrong type of girl after a relationship ends could induce a similar kind of illness. Who you choose to date next should be an easy transition from whoever you dated previously. You can't go from the girl next door to an S & M dominatrix. Been there, done that.

Going back to my successful-sitcom analogy, after the show has its run, the actor having trouble getting work may try a new sitcom. But this new sitcom will be somewhat similar in tone to the show they're best known for, this strategy being an attempt to slowly wean the audience off their preconceived expectations while still remaining familiar. "I may not be playing George Costanza anymore, but my new role is still a comedic weasel who's manipulative."

Did this mean that post-breakup I should date someone similar to my ex? Hmm . . . Do you remember the show that Jason Alexander did after *Seinfeld* ended called *Bob Patterson*? Don't worry, neither does Jason Alexander.

The other, and more extreme, route to go would be to shed the very image that's holding you hostage. Meaning, if I was the wacky next-door neighbor on a sitcom, my next role should be a drug addict who teaches at an elementary school full of inner-city children in a gritty indie film. Did I look for a girl who was the polar opposite of my ex?

I wasn't quite sure where Katie would land on the fucked-up spectrum compared to my ex-girlfriend's personality. I wanted to find out. So I did the only logical thing I could think of. . . . Stalk her Facebook page. That's a dangerous game to play, because one's Facebook page is in no way indicative of who one really is. But at worst, you can always pick up a few context clues, right?

Katie's page gave me no context clues. I mean, this was a girl with a Tupac profile picture, for crying out loud. I was in no-man's-land. I was about to give up for the night when I noticed a comment on her wall. An "I miss you, sweetie, don't forget to check the air pressure in your tires" type of comment that could only have come from a parent. Yes, it was her mom. . . .

Click. Click. Click.

And like all moms before her, her page had absolutely zero privacy settings. Katie's entire family history was up for grabs. But first things first; I needed to check out the photo albums. . . .

Click. Click. Click.

That's when I hit the jackpot. Not just one picture, but multiple pics of Katie Rosenfeld spanning across numerous albums. Family vacations, mom-and-daughter spa day, Hunter's bar mitzvah, creepy Uncle Ed's sobriety birthday—it's like I was there for all of it. And any doubts I had about Katie's not being the flawless specimen I remembered her to be in high school were shattered. She was perfect. Thank God for moms and their love of and devotion to the "upload" button.

Speaking of moms, she looked pret-tay hot as well.

THE GIRLS ON DATING

Dear Girls Above Me,

"Wanna know what he said to me? 'You had me at hello.' He's so good at being romantic." He's so good at Netflixing *Jerry Maguire*.

Dear Girls Above Me,

"He was literally perfect! Except for when he asked me if it looks like his eyes have seen murder." Don't get caught up in details.

Dear Girls Above Me,

"That fucker had glitter in his beard, which means he was making out with some whore!" Maybe he's really into arts and crafts?

Dear Girls Above Me,

"We have a major situation on our hands: He's ungoogleable! I don't date anyone I can't stalk first." Thank God we're not dating.

Dear Girls Above Me,

"I pretended to take out my wallet but he never stopped me! Who makes a hot girl split the bill?!" The guy you still slept with.

Dear Girls Above Me,

"I'm responding 'with my BF tonight.' He won't know if I mean boyfriend or best friend!" You're like The Da Vinci Code of texting.

Dear Girls Above Me,

"I can't keep saying I have my period to this guy; it's been 3 months, and he's becoming suspicious." I knew girls did this.

Dear Girls Above Me,

"I can't believe I'm 24 and I haven't even had my test-marriage yet!" Calm down, your rehearsal soul mate is out there somewhere.

Dear Girls Above Me,

"I knew Kevin was in love with me when he said it was okay to pop his back zits." Did I just hear the opening to your wedding vows?

CHAPTER SEVENTEEN

"**O**ne little push-up . . . Two little push-ups . . . Three little push-ups . . . Four little—ehhh, I'm done." Building up the lats sporadically throughout the day of the date may not be effective if you prefer to use things like logic. At the right angle, with the light dimmed just enough and your eyes squinted with the correct level of strain, I promise you there's kind of a difference, sort of. After an impressive seventeen-message e-mail thread with Katie Rosenfeld, my high school crush, I was ready. It was time. I was 100 percent confident in every aspect of tonight's date. Only, I wasn't sure if she knew it was a date or not. Also, in the event she knew it was a date, I was a little rusty on today's dating protocol, so I'd been taking (stealing) one-way advice from two girls who could confidently tell you what color shirt Robert Pattinson would wear on any given Wednesday because they'd memorized his laundry cycle. But other than those things, I was 100 percent confident in every aspect of that night's date.

Before heading to my car, I took one last look in the mirror to pep myself up. Typically this would have had the opposite effect and drained my confidence, but that day was a new day. My body was in tip-top shape, if you were Stevie Wonder, and my apprehension about the new ways of dating had been temporarily relieved due to some choice advice from the girls above me.

It was a cool, crisp Friday evening. Traffic was light, the windows were down, a breeze was in the air, and I was behind the wheel cruising, with Ace of Base crushing it as they usually did when blared through my speakers. Not "The Sign," as if I was some Johnny-come-lately. No. I'm talking about "All That She Wants." You know, the good stuff. Right now, if my penis could have spoken it would have said, "Put me in, Coach, I'm ready to play." Somewhere around the second verse of Ace of Base's supremely underrated song, I began to pay attention to the lyrics. "All that she wants is another baby, ooooh yeah yeah. . . ." The "ooooh yeah yeah" notwithstanding, I found the lyric to be troubling. I immediately thought of: "Ugh, he showed up with a condom. I so would've fucked him if he hadn't expected to fuck me."

I was torn. This was the longest red light of my life. In a panic, I immediately turned off Ace of Base, an act of betrayal I would have never conceived of as an option five minutes prior. I began to question everything I had ever learned from Mrs. Tamblyn, my seventh-grade sex-ed teacher. I was quite sure she was adamant about *always* practicing safe sex and never relying on your partner for a condom—"Bring your own!" But the mere fact that I jotted those sex-ed notes down on paper attached to my Trapper Keeper was enough to tell me that times had changed.

The girls above, specifically Cathy, were offended when a guy brought condoms, expecting to get some. Did I listen to Cathy and Claire or did I listen to my seventh-grade sex-ed teacher? Maybe in this day and age it's okay for the girl to supply the condoms. Did I risk it? If something sexual were to happen, would I potentially be blowing it if I wasn't prepared? Should I bust a quick U-turn and go home to get some condoms?

This would prove tricky on multiple levels. The most obvious and pressing issue being that I didn't even have a condom to bring. Remember, I'd just gotten out of a serious long-term relationship, and in this serious long-term relationship other birth-control measures were taken. My last purchased box of condoms had expired sometime in the Mesozoic Era.

At this point, I wasn't sure what the right call was. It's audacious enough presuming that you'll get laid on the first date, but I couldn't even say for certain that this *was* a first date. It's not easy being me. To a much lesser extent, it's not easy being men.

Let's be honest, right before having unprotected sex, most members of my tortured gender don't voluntarily say, "Wait, hold on. Before I venture into a place of incredible warmth and happiness, let me roll into a slimy suffocating balloon that smells like a hospital." Guys can't help but live in the moment. We use our heads, but not the smart ones. If I wasn't going to get condoms, I needed a plan B. Wait, Plan B! Could I convince her to take—no, on second thought, let's not go down that dark road.

It was judgment-call time. I was pulling up to her block and had to make a quick decision. Condom or no condom? A Shakespearean conundrum if ever there was one. I decided to go with condom. I mean, what was I doing here, right?

Luckily, there was a liquor store, as well as a CVS, right in her neighborhood. I knew both places were sure to sell condoms. For me, picking which store was a clear no-brainer. As dirty and presumptuous as buying condoms before a first date was, I thought the

least I could do was procure them from a drugstore. Purchasing condoms from a pharmacy, as opposed to a liquor store that sells *Barely
Legal MILF Magazine* (what does that even mean?), would somehow
classy the whole thing up. See, I was thinking of Katie.

I think I've mentioned before how reliable I am when it comes to
showing up to a place on time. For this reason I wasn't too stressed
about my CVS detour making me cut things close. I had plenty of
time to spare. Confident in my choice to go with condoms, I strolled
through the CVS trying to find the condom section. I can never find
the section I'm looking for in a grocery store. Typically I have no
problem asking an employee, but when it comes to condoms, not
gonna happen. Even at the expense of being late, I'd prefer to hopelessly roam the vast CVS wasteland like Moses before asking someone to point me in the direction of condoms.

Ten minutes later (I'm lying; it was fifteen) I found the section.
Needless to say, I had about seventeen different kinds of strokes trying to figure out the type of condom to buy. If I were a girl, I'd surely
notice what type of condom my sexual partner decided on, and then
I'd judge him accordingly.

With me, it's not so much you are what you eat. It's more you are
what brand of condom you decide to wear when having sex. Okay,
I'll admit the latter doesn't quite roll off the tongue like the former,
but I'm not trying to design a new bumper sticker here.

MY CONDOM OPTIONS

Twisted for Her Pleasure: I actually do care about her
pleasure. I'm a pleaser by nature. I'm the kid at his own
birthday party who can't have a good time unless he knows
that all the guests are also having fun. But as far as twisted

condoms go, if I was a girl, I'd think that a guy who was so
desperate to please me that he needed the extra help of a
bent, curled piece of latex to do what he couldn't was at best
a loser. Also, the lime-green wrapping ain't putting anybody
in the mood. That alone was enough for me to veto.

Lambskin: Do I even have to explain?

Magnum: Makes me think of Tom Selleck. Which, believe
it or not, isn't someone I like to think about during sex,
awesome mustache notwithstanding. (And that's the *only*
reason I'm not going with Magnum. *Only. Reason.* You think
I'm lying, don't you? Well, I'm not. There's no other reason
why I wouldn't go with Magnum. You believe me, right?)

Ultra-Thin for Extra Sensitivity: All I'll say is, it's been a little
while. . . . Good night, Charlie. Next.

Thick-Ribbed for Longer-Lasting Excitement: Why not just
call them "You Feel Nothing" condoms? If I didn't want to
enjoy it, I would've just stayed home and listened to Cathy
and Chad have sex. Also, who wants to last so long anyway?
It's like, sometimes enough is enough and Letterman has a
cool guest booked.

I didn't know which brand or type to get. I'll be the first to admit
how little I understand of marketing, but Trojan seems to me to be
the most poorly named condom brand one could possibly come up
with. Named after the Trojan Horse, a huge wooden horse given to
the Trojans as a surrender gift by the Greeks to end a war. Hidden

inside the wooden horse was a fighting force of Greek soldiers who broke through the wood and destroyed the entire city in a surprise massacre sneak attack. Yeah, I want to think of little soldiers breaking through wood, sneaking their way into enemy territory, claiming it as their own, while I'm trying to have protected sex with a girl I haven't seen since Justin Timberlake was a member of 'NSync.

Fuck it, I thought, and went with Durex.

On my way to the cashier I was pretty calm due to the fact that I still had ten minutes to pick Katie up and I was already on her block. Using the soothing technique of positive visualization I learned from my mom, I envisioned an evening that was smooth sailing from here on out. Only thing was, though, thinking about my mom reminded me that I'd forgotten to call her back that day. My mom views forgetting to call her back as my actively deciding to not call her back because I hate her and I'm waiting out her death. I could see her standing by the phone waiting for me to call her back just so she could yell at me for forgetting to call her back.

"You never called me back."

"Mom, this is me calling you back."

"No. This is you calling me back because you forgot to call me back."

"But, I'm calling you back *right now,* so what's the difference what my intention is?"

"Someone's beeping in on the other line. I have to call you back."

The mind games. I knew what she wanted to talk to me about anyway; she was planning our annual family reunion and she wanted to get everybody's availability to better plan the . . . to better plan the . . . Oh. Shit.

I was at the register, cursing the guilt I would inevitably face after returning my mom's phone call to apologize for not returning my mom's phone call, when Katie walked right in. What kind of moron architect would design a CVS checkout aisle that ends right at the main entrance?! There was no mistaking it. When she walked in, I was the first thing she saw. More specifically, I, buying condoms for our first date, was the first thing she saw. I grabbed as many bags of chips as possible, hoping to conceal my rubbers. *Mayday.* Brace for impact.

I saw that she saw. She saw that I saw that she saw. I was stunned. I couldn't speak. Unfortunately, she was able to.

"Charlie?"

She had the same voice. A more mature version, but almost exactly as I had remembered it. And, of course, she looked stunning. I was pretty much in heaven, but the little sealed items in my hands were trying to drag me down into the underworld. "Yes," I replied.

"Oh my God, this is so crazy!"

"Yes."

"I'm so embarrassed to be bumping into you right before our date."

"Yes." Wait, did she just say *date*? At least we cleared that up.

"I ran out of mascara and—well, ya know, typical girl stuff."

"Yes." That *yes* was genuine. I knew from Cathy and Claire that mascara to a woman is as necessary as maximum-hold hair spray is to Donald Trump.

Then the inevitable happened. She looked down at my arms full of cornstarch and latex. "Are you buying condoms . . . and chips." That's not a typo. Yes, she technically asked a question, but to hear her say it, it was a statement.

I guess it was time to come up with something other than *yes*.

"These . . . ? Oh. Yeah. They're not for—oh, you must think . . . No. That's so embarrassing. These aren't for, like, tonight." I left things open; maybe I was talking about the chips?

"They're not?"

"God no!"

"Well, what are they for, then?" She was onto me.

". . . I'm going out of town soon. . . . I'm taking a trip. . . . I have a family reunion to attend and—"

"You're buying condoms for a family reunion?"

"Umm . . . you like Cool Ranch Doritos?"

The good news was that I found out my meet-up with Katie was undoubtedly a date; the bad news was it only lasted a few seconds longer than my first hand job. No Doritos were had that night. It was a muggy, humid drive back home. Traffic was heavy; the windows were up, smog was in the air, and I was behind the wheel riding the brakes as the sounds of car horns and nighttime construction crews drilling into the cement of the 405 penetrated my car. No doubt the only kind of penetrating that would happen that evening. There was no Ace of Base to be played. No joy to be had. Right then, if my penis could have talked, it would have said, "Coach, I'm seriously considering switching teams, you're not ready for me to play."

As I delicately slid my key into the front door, I was praying to the Man above me that Pat wasn't home. He knew of my date and was excited for me to get back out there, as any close friend would be. This wasn't a story I was ready to laugh about, and the thought of having to relive it through explanation was something that made me physically ill. I didn't want to face Pat or anybody else who knew me.

As the door opened, I remembered that Pat and his crew were catching a fireworks show at Downtown Disney, so I was safe for a few hours. I never thought I'd ever be so grateful for the existence of Disney. I went into my room, barricaded the door, and hoped for an earthquake. Well, pretty soon, the walls were shaking, but it was no earthquake.

"If it's called pre-drinking before you go out, what's it called when you continue drinking after you get home?" Claire belted to Cathy over an upbeat Drake song.

"It's called Lindsay Lohan," I responded without even thinking, almost like a reflex.

The music continued to blare with no end in sight. The girls were hosting a pre-drinking party before going out. I knew I was in for trouble, because the last three pre-drinking gatherings they held had resulted in everybody getting so trashed that they decided not to go to the club they were pre-drinking for in the first place—sort of like tailgating before a football game and then not going to the football game.

I know I said I didn't want to face anybody who knew who I was, but that didn't mean I wanted to face two girls who *didn't* know who I was, especially these girls and their pre-drinking friends. (I'm looking at you specifically, Becca.) I mean, the disaster of tonight's non-date with Katie was a direct result of their voices bouncing around in my head, causing me to get flustered. In my normal daily life, I have enough trouble constantly second-guessing myself, but tonight I was triple- and quadruple-guessed by these girls above.

How on Earth did I allow them to infiltrate my neurotic brain so easily? I tried to shake their conversations from my mind, but the louder the walls thumped from Drake, the louder they managed to talk over it all. My apartment ceiling continued to pulsate.

Shake, shake, shake.

"I need to know right now if we're sunbathing on Sunday Funday

so I can get rid of any peek-a-boo pubes." Nice way to start the
workweek, I thought, cringing.

Shake, shake, shake.

"I hope that guy Kieran meets us out tonight. I'm talking about
'strong cheekbones but needs to lose the Harry Potter haircut'
Kieran." "Is there any other kind of Kieran?!" I wanted to sarcasti-
cally shout up to the heavens.

Shake. Shake. Shake.

"Anyway, I wasn't into Kieran at all until he called me outside of
booty-call hours just to tell me that he's into me. . . . Also, he texted
me a pic; he lost the Potter haircut, now it's more in the style of
Ryan Gosling circa *Drive*." Congratulations on using *circa* correctly.

Shake. Shake. Shake.

The night crawled on at a tortured pace. I couldn't sleep. And it
wasn't the girls above. I kept thinking about how that guy fumbling
for condoms at CVS wasn't me. I had gotten myself all worked up
for a date that I'd kept thinking I wasn't prepared for. It became a
self-fulfilling prophecy. I knew I could've done better. It may have
been too late to salvage things with Katie, but I at least could attempt to salvage some dignity. I wanted to apologize.

I stood in the center of my room and took in the many options I
had to connect with her. Did I continue to communicate with her
via Facebook message thread? How about straight-up e-mail? Would
a text be inappropriate after an impromptu CVS condom splurge? I
could apologize @her. Should I write her a handwritten letter and
send it off by way of the Pony Express? I was wasting time. In my
gut, I already knew the answer.

It was like Cathy said that one time: Drinks are text-approved, but
dinner deserves a phone call. (Using that logic, with the way events

unfolded at CVS, I should have sent her a singing telegram.) As her phone rang, I wondered what odds a Vegas sports book would give somebody gambling on whether or not Katie would take my call.

"Yes, Charlie?" Can't believe she answered.

"Can't believe you answered."

"Me either."

"I wanted to apologize."

"You apologized at CVS. Then we both went our separate ways, which I think was for the best."

"I know I apologized, but I didn't explain. I want to be honest with you. Please. Just give me two minutes and I'll never bother you again."

For the next two minutes I tried something I hadn't attempted since my breakup: total honesty. I was done pretending that I was something other than myself. I explained to Katie how devastated and insecure my breakup had left me. I told her how my absence from the dating game caused me to make poor choices. I even admitted to eavesdropping on the girls above me. Sharing a few specific tidbits didn't hurt either. Girls like to feel more superior and smarter than other girls, and Cathy and Claire gave that to Katie.

After it all poured out of me, there was a long silence on the phone. Not as long as the one that followed her catching me buying condoms before our date, but it was a silence nonetheless.

"The image of your face when I walked into CVS was pretty amazing. I don't think I'll ever forget it."

"Can we try this again sometime?"

"I'd like that. But next time I would prefer it if you wouldn't prematurely buy condoms five minutes before picking me up for our date."

"I promise you, I'll never do anything prematurely around you ever again—" I was already a few too many words into that sentence before I could save myself.

THE GIRLS ON SPORTS

Dear Girls Above Me,

"You hear that? I think the guy downstairs is having gay sex! He keeps screaming out DEREK." Nope, just watching the Lakers game.

Dear Girls Above Me,

"I bet this Arnold Palmer guy named a drink after himself just to be a celebrity." Now he can retire and take up a sport like golf.

Dear Girls Above Me,

"Rachel Zoe needs to find these teams better outfits. This yellow's seriously offensive." I bet the Steelers call her at halftime.

Dear Girls Above Me,

"Who do you think has the biggest dick on the Lakers?" Can't you just be quiet and let me enjoy this win—definitely Ron Artest.

Dear Girls Above Me,

"I know he really likes football, maybe I'll get him tickets to a Raiders game or something." The Raiders moved out of LA in 1995.

Dear Girls Above Me,

"He's on some fantasy team, but don't you think he's too small to play football?" I can't wait for you to go to one of his games.

THE GIRLS ON CARS

Dear Girls Above Me,

(Phone) "Mom, I'm not saying you did this on purpose, but are you aware that my car has no seat heaters?!" Classic bad parenting.

Dear Girls Above Me,

"Oh my God, one of my wheel-tire thingys is flat!
What the hell should I do, get a new car?" Seems like
your only option.

Dear Girls Above Me,

"I look fat in my photo light ticket! Why is the camera
at such an unflattering angle?" I think you're missing
the point here.

Dear Girls Above Me,

"Ellen DeGeneres is funny and all, but it's really weird
how much she loves her car." Her wife's name is
Portia.

CHAPTER EIGHTEEN

One lazy Sunday afternoon Pat and I headed to the laundry room with only a dollar twenty-five to our name. With our quarters combined, we had just enough money to share one load of laundry without having to go get more change. Pat's laundry basket was full of clothes that looked like a rainbow threw up inside of it. I tried warning Pat that his bright colors would never stand a chance in the wash with my darks, but he remained confident in his aquamarine briefs.

"Hey, once you're done watching the Laker game, do you mind if I put on last week's episode of *The Real Housewives of New Jersey*?" he asked me as we walked down the hallway. I told him sure, as if I didn't plan on watching that myself right after the game anyway.

Cathy and Claire had inadvertently gotten me hooked on *Real Housewives* a few months earlier. If I was going to be forced to listen to them discuss the trials and tribulations of Teresa and Melissa, I wanted to at least put a couple of faces (face-lifts) to those names. . . .

Sure, I may have gotten slightly invested in those trials and tribulations, but I'm nowhere near ready to admit that. All I'll say is that Teresa is one vapid excuse for a human soul.

Anyway, inside the laundry room, we found Cathy on her hands and knees with her head halfway inside one of the dryers. Pat and I shared an excited look, the same one we would have given if we had seen a real-life cast member from *Saved by the Bell*. (Except Dustin Diamond.) It was rare that I got to see either of the girls in the flesh. At this point they had become voices in my head more than real people. The girls above were sort of like Jiminy Crickets to my Pinocchio. If Jiminy Cricket carried a Balenciaga tote bag.

Cathy was busy searching for something, and I was fairly certain she hadn't heard us enter the fluorescent room. Both Pat and I stood there in silence, not wanting to startle her in her dryer hunt. She needed all the brain cells she could muster, and if I was the cause of her bumping her head in the laundry room, I would be forced to listen to her talk about it with Claire for the rest of the day. No, thanks.

I figured my regular voice saying, "Hello there," would be much too blaring, and if I said it in a whisper, it would be much too creepy. So instead I took one of our quarters for the laundry machine and dropped it to the ground. The chime of a coin coming into contact with a dirty linoleum floor seemed like just the right amount of noise to get her attention. Unfortunately, it backfired horribly. Cathy was surprised and slammed her head into the top of the dryer, yelling with an echo, "Bitch whores," as our quarter rolled its way underneath the machines.

"Oh Mylanta, you scared the crap out of me," Cathy said with her head now poking out.

"I'm sorry, I tried to be subtle about it."

"It's okay. I'm more upset that one of my thongs is missing. You didn't come in here and take it, did you?"

"No, we don't steal thongs after Labor Day," Pat responded. Nice one, Pat.

Cathy got up from the ground and approached us. "Sorry, how rude of me, I'm Cathy," she said with a hand extended.

I don't know why I was surprised *again* that she had no recollection of meeting me on several different occasions. How many lanky bearded guys did they know? And was I possibly in the middle of an *Eternal Sunshine of the Spotless Mind* situation? This could all have been a simple memory-erasing mix-up. I decided to give Cathy the benefit of the doubt.

"I'm Charlie," I said, as if for the first time.

Pat followed suit with "And I'm Pat."

"Nice to meet you boys." I was so glad I had been able to provide her that pleasure five times and counting. Incidentally, I never get Cathy and Claire mixed up. Even though they seemingly share a brain, there are many subtle differences between them. You get to discern them over time, like the tiny facial variations that allow you to gradually distinguish between identical twins.

DIFFERENCES BETWEEN CATHY AND CLAIRE

- Cathy is a five-foot-nine-inch brunette with hazel eyes; Claire is a five-foot-two-inch blonde with blue eyes.
- Cathy has a scar on the right side of her abdomen from when her appendix was removed at age five. Claire has a similar scar on the left side of her abdomen from when she fell off her dad's boat, which was parked in the driveway.
- Cathy never wears her cute strappy purple sandals unless

Claire also gets to wear her low-cut turquoise top with the
bedazzly jewels. This was part of the Wardrobe Accord
of 2011.

- Cathy has a tan line around her left wrist because the only
time she wears a watch is when she's timing her tanning-bed
sessions.

- During "that time of the month," Claire wears knee socks
because her ankles get swollen.

- Cathy is a low C-cup; Claire is a high B. And I'm just now
realizing the inappropriate nature of this list.

As Cathy moped her way back to the dryer in search of her thong,
Pat carefully put his clothes into the washing machine, one flamboy-
ant color at a time. I looked underneath the washer in hopes that the
quarter was in close reach, which of course it wasn't. It lay heads-up
at the very back. So I rolled up my sleeves and went right in. It's un-
believable what makes its way into the crevasses of a shared laundry
room. The deeper my hand traveled, the grosser the items I came
into contact with.

A toothbrush. What kind of person cleans their teeth and their
clothes at the same time? Probably David Spade.

A signed headshot of David Spade. I would have taken it if it hadn't
been personally signed to someone named "My Shrimp Guy."

A green gummy bear covered in hair. If it had been a red one,
I would have considered cleaning it off for an extension of the
Five-Second Rule.

A soggy light-pink slipper. Though I wondered which Cinderella from the building it belonged to, I didn't know how "charming" I'd look combing the building for her.

My fingertips finally grazed the quarter. I reached a little bit more in order to secure it between my two fingers, avoiding the rat droppings to the left. Finally, my meal ticket to a fresh pair of socks. As I stood up, Pat was loading my clothes into the washer, along with his own. Washing our clothes together to save a dollar twenty-five was something we had done many times. I had never thought it to be out of the norm, until I looked over at Cathy and saw her reaction. She looked as if she wanted to hug the both of us. It was at this moment that I realized Pat and I were both wearing matching T-shirts and jeans.

"Can I just say it's so sweet that you guys wash your clothes together? You two seem so in love," she said with such happiness.

I was surprised by this labeling of myself as gay. Not so much offended that someone would think I'm attracted to men as insulted that someone would think I couldn't do better than Pat. I'm not gay, but if I was, I wouldn't settle for the first guy who stuck an umbrella in my drink.

"Oh, no, no, no, sweetie. We're not homosexuals," Pat responded a little too fabulously.

Cathy's smug look made it very clear that she didn't believe him. She gathered her clothes, giving up on the lost thong, and on her way out she gently patted me on the back, as if she felt sorry for me. So not only did she think we were a couple, but she thought I was the abused partner in the relationship. Did that make me a "bottom"?

Pat chuckled like a giddy schoolgirl. "I can't believe she thought we were a couple!"

At that moment, I felt as if we were both living a lie. There was no doubt that Pat was fabulous. But we were both in the closet about his sexuality. He as a gay man hiding his homosexuality and I as that gay man's heterosexual roommate, facilitating his casual denial.

It's not that I didn't want him to be gay; in fact, it's the opposite. I really wanted him to be gay. I just wanted it to be official so he could be as gay as humanly possible, not just in the closet, but all over the house. I thought about what that would be like. We'd be able to openly discuss men without Pat's obligatory asides about how balls are not as sexy as breasts. Pat, the most fabulous guy I know, would then be able to bring equally fabulous guys home to spend the night. Pat, his lover, and I could stay up late watching horror movies and bake gluten-free cookies together during the super-scary parts. At night I would wear earplugs out of respect, allowing Pat the freedom to make a bit of noise, just as he did for me when I had a girlfriend. Then in the morning I would wake up the boys by way of a soothing bell, which would let them know that their fresh-fruit yogurt parfaits were ready to be eaten. Then, in the afternoon, we would all go shopping and stop off for a late brunch. There were so many places I never got to go. . . . Okay, this tangent is becoming a smidge too elaborate. But my point is that I wanted Pat to live happily ever after as a gay man.

So, now the question was, how could I myself emerge from the closet and then turn and yank my roommate out after me, so gently that he would feel as if he'd strutted out of there all by himself?

"I wonder if Cathy thought we were a couple because you were acting all gay on your hands and knees looking for that quarter," Pat said while casually applying some cherry lip gloss.

"That must be it," I responded. "I'll try to watch that in the future."

A week later, while in line to get my morning soy chai latte and blueberry scone, I overheard a very interesting conversation between the two elderly gentlemen in front of me.

"I even cut Brussels sprouts from my diet, but my gas is still incredibly pungent, or so my wife says."

This was followed by something even more interesting, not to mention relevant to this chapter:

"Did you hear that tonight kicks off the gay pride parade in West Hollywood? Are you going?" the guy with gas and a Ron Weasley–looking toupee asked.

"Oh, it's this weekend? What a glorious event. I remember the days when I used to sip pisco sours and march in nothing but sunglasses and a boa." This guy was literally Pat in fifty years.

"Well, I can't stand it! It practically gridlocks the whole city, and no matter where you look all you see are cheery men in assless chaps."

"What's wrong with cheery men in assless chaps? The parade gives gay men and women a place to go where they feel accepted. It's what got me to finally admit I was homosexual!"

"You're homosexual? I thought that was just a phase in the seventies."

". . . Do you mean seventies the decade or seventies the age?"

". . . I'm not sure."

The odd couple's banter, so much like a conversation Pat and I were primed to have forty years from now if I didn't get him to come out immediately, gave me an idea. What if I were to take Pat for a drive and "happen" to stumble upon the gay pride parade? If the traffic was as bad as future-clueless-me suggested, then Pat would be forced to sit in my car and gaze out into a world of oiled, glistening leather and perfectly waxed chests. There would be no better place for Pat to finally admit he was gay. My plan seemed foolproof. And I know it sounds stereotypical and that it wouldn't be ideal for every gay roommate in the world, but given Pat's fabulousness, it was perfect for him. This was finally the safe haven he needed, and as his dear friend, I was going to share it with him. I sent Pat a text that read, "Pisco sours and joyride around this fabulous city?"

PISCO SOUR RECIPE

4 ounces pisco brandy
1½ ounces lemon juice
1–2 tablespoons sugar

MY PISCO SOUR RECIPE

8 ounces cheap brandy
2 squeezed lemons from the neighbor's withering tree
5 tablespoons powdered sugar

I wasn't messing around. Needless to say, Pat was in.

"Oh my God, this beverage is to die for!" Pat shrieked as I poured him another. He must have been so thrilled I was mixing him a drink for the first time that he completely overlooked the fact that it tasted like hard children's lemonade-stand lemonade.

"All right, so, ah, should we go for a little drive?" I asked him as he stared back at me cockeyed.

"Wait, Charlie. Hold your pony just a second. First will you tell me the story of when you were a kid and realized you were chubby?"

Every single time Pat gets drunk, he begs me to tell the story of when I used to be fat and then pretends that he's never heard it before. I have no idea why he showed a particular fondness for this story. Maybe my emergence from the fat closet was an incidentally relatable social allegory. Maybe he just found humor in picturing me as a young portly boy with long wavy locks and a love of Looney Tunes shirts. Regardless, I really wasn't in the mood to relive my plus-size years, but I also knew we weren't going anywhere until I did. I figured a bit of self-humiliation was a small price to pay to get Pat to come out of the closet. So, I caved and gave him what he wanted.

There was no scientific explanation for my weight gain, but for some reason, between the ages of nine and twelve, I got quite plump. My mom believes it was an "emotional reaction" from witnessing her getting mugged on the streets of New York City, but I think it had more to do with the discovery of peanut butter M&M's. On Halloween I would trade away all other types of candy for peanut butter M&M's and then hoard them under my bed for the year. The bursting of my belt buckle was minor in comparison to the satisfaction I got when a peanut butter M&M burst in my mouth.

Looking back on it now, my main problem was that I didn't realize I was becoming overweight. It was as if my recently added fat was blocking a signal to my brain that was saying, "So . . . you're looking a little husky, my friend." But this self-denial was not the case for everyone else around me. My dad recently admitted that when he used to watch me play soccer, as I was galloping down the sidelines after the ball, he would whisper under his breath, "Look, there goes my son, Fatty McDowell. Oh, and he took a tumble to the ground. Big surprise."

"All right, so I guess the story begins—"

Pat stopped me. "Tell it like you normally do. With my favorite opening line." Ugh, all right . . .

"There was once a time in my life when I had bigger tits than my sister. . . ."

It was the summertime after fifth grade, and I was in the meatiest state of my life. I was with my family vacationing on Martha's Vineyard, a place we had been going ever since I was a toddler. But this summer was different from the others; something magical was in the air, and that was because Primo's Pizza had just opened up about a mile away from us. I was excited to try the place that some of my "islander" friends described as "the best thing to happen to the island since the nude beaches." As a twelve-year-old who had just discovered masturbation and loved to eat, this looked like it was going to be an incredible summer.

I'll never forget the first slice I ever ordered from Primo's Pizza. It was a simple cheese slice. I had no idea at the time that one slice would start a chain reaction of many slices in the days to come. But the pizza was that good. Thin but not frail, cheesy but not lame, oily but not enough to want to soak up with a napkin.

My first week I eased into ordering pizza slowly, only getting one slice. But the second week I watched the kid in front of me, a true visionary, as he demanded, "Two slices of cheese off the rack." I had never heard of such a thing. What was this "off the rack" that he spoke of? My question was answered when his pizza was handed to him in under ten seconds, instead of the usual fifteen minutes. So, "off the rack" meant to forgo the heating-up process and to take the lukewarm pizza as is. That wasn't illegal? Genius. As you can imagine, I followed suit.

By week four I was eating "three slices of cheese pizza off the rack" every single day and was even pouring on extra Parmesan. I went from being a cute pudgy kid who loved peanut butter M&M's to a fat-ass who was addicted to pizza. But the sad part was I was still in denial about my growing girth. That is, until week five . . .

"Three slices of cheese pizza off the rack, please," I said directly to Primo himself in my soft polite voice. I considered a fourth slice but noticed there were only three pieces left on the rack and there was no chance my hungry belly was going to wait around for another pizza to get made.

Unfortunately, the place was jam-packed and it was hard for me to tell whether Primo had heard my order or not, as he was busy rolling the dough for a brand-new pizza. I started to get a little frantic. The other register had just opened and the teenager next to me looked very hungry. What if he knew about the "off the rack" program?! Then he would be the one enjoying the last of the slices, while I waited around for Primo to get his act together.

"I'll take three slices of cheese pizza off the rack, please," I said once more, this time a little louder and with more bravado. But yet again, Primo did not acknowledge my existence. My blood pressure was running on yesterday's pizza slices, and I was beginning to get cranky.

I eavesdropped on the kid next to me as he ordered: "Can I please have two slices of pepperoni and a slice of cheese . . ."

Oh, thank God, he knew nothing of the rack.

". . . off the rack."

That son of a bitch! Now there were only two slices of cheese left on the rack, and I was sure that the rest of the kids in line were starting to understand the benefits of the no-heating process. I needed to act fast. It was now or never. I took a deep breath, cleared my throat, and prepared my voice for a level that Primo was sure to hear.

"Give me my damn pizza!" My prepubescent voice ricocheted off of every pot and pan in the joint. Not only had Primo become aware of my presence, but the entire pizza place had as well. I was slightly embarrassed, but relieved that this little mishap would now get straightened out and soon I would be enjoying my pizza.

Primo marched toward me. He did not seem happy. "You're going to need to calm down, miss." My body froze. Did he just call me *miss*? I wondered. Impossible, I must have heard him wrong. I bet he meant to say *mister* but got bored halfway through the word and called it a day at *miss*.

"Excuse me?" I asked, reverting back to my soft polite voice.

"We're very busy today. But I'll get it for you now, little girl," he responded.

Still in shock, I looked down at my body and realized for the first time . . .

". . . that you had tits bigger than your sister's," Pat chimed in, putting an end to my tragic story.

"Yep."

"Well, did you end up eating those two slices of cheese off the rack?" he asked.

"Of course. But after that I never had a slice of Primo's Pizza again," I responded.

"Aww, fat little Charlie. Rest in peace."

"You ready to go for a joyride in my car now?" I asked, jingling my keys.

"Hells. To. The. Yeah! Let's go drive like the mad men—oh, I love that TV show—that we are!" He always has to one-up me.

THE GIRLS ON SINGING AND LYRICISM

Dear Girls Above Me,

(singing) "Ovvvulation. Ovvvulation. Ovulation, ovulation, ovula-a-a-tion." You're not allowed to be around men today.

Dear Girls Above Me,

(singing) "The answer my friend, is blow jobs in the wind, the answer is blow jobs in the wind." So I see you figured it out.

Dear Girls Above Me,

(singing *Aladdin*) "I can show you my tits. Shining, shimmering, hard nipples." You didn't even have boobs when *Aladdin* came out!

Dear Girls Above Me,

(while throwing up) "I blame it on the
a-a-a-a-a-alcohol." I'm pretty impressed you had the
determination to say it like that.

Dear Girls Above Me,

(singing) "When the moon hits your eye, like a big
pizza pie, that's *vagina*. DaDaDaDaDaaa." Did you
guys bake pot brownies again?

Dear Girls Above Me,

(singing) "I love Zac Efron cause he's so delicious,
gone goldfishin'." Thanks for getting this stuck in my
head at the DMV.

Dear Girls Above Me,

"I want a guy who's gonna meet me half way, like
the Black Eyed Peas song." I want a girl who doesn't
quote the Black Eyed Peas.

Dear Girls Above Me,

(upset) "And on top of that Fergie was wrong, big girls do cry." Please stop living your life to the words of the Black Eyed Peas.

CHAPTER NINETEEN

It was a brisk night, but I decided to put the top down on my fifteen-year-old convertible anyway. This way Pat and I would feel as if we were a part of the gay pride parade without having to get out of the car. Pat's skinny body was shivering, but he was too drunk to notice or care. I could tell by his exaggerated scoffs that he was not happy with my music selection. Pearl Jam had way too much electric guitar and too many metaphorical lyrics, not enough of an electronic beat, and certainly no Auto-Tuning. But this was Pat's night, and I wanted everything to go smoothly, so I changed the radio station until I found something I knew he would bob his head to.

"This is definitely the Pussycat Dolls' best song," he said, hinting to me that I had found the station he wanted to listen to. He then belted out every single lyric from the song without missing a beat. As if that weren't impressive enough, he knew all of the words to the next song as well. And the next. And the one after that. I tried to think of just one song to which I could sing every lyric. The only one that came to mind was Billy Ray Cyrus's "Achy Breaky Heart." A classic never dies.

I think a lyrical memory is something you're either born with or you're not. Since Pat is able to listen to a song just once or twice and remember it, he was clearly born with this talent. Cathy and Claire, on the other hand, not so much. I mean, they can remember lyrics all right, but they're never the correct lyrics. Everyone has had their fair share of misheard lyrics, but these girls take it to a whole new level. I know this because at least once a day, often while I'm just about to fall asleep, they start singing these malapropisms at the top of their lungs.

Here are my favorite "lost in translation" lyrics from the girls above me:

KATY PERRY
"FIREWORK"

THE REAL LINE:
" 'Cause baby, you're a firework."
THE GIRLS ABOVE ME SING:
" 'Cause baby, you love firewood."

MAROON 5
"MOVES LIKE JAGGER"

THE REAL LINE:
"I've got the moves like Jagger."
THE GIRLS ABOVE ME SING:
"I've gotta prove I'm a jaguar."

Edit: They eventually did figure out that last one, but they don't seem to know who Mick Jagger is. Claire thought he was the movie reviewer for *Rolling Stone,* to which I gave partial credit.

MICHAEL JACKSON
"SMOOTH CRIMINAL"

THE REAL LINE:
"Annie, are you okay?"
THE GIRLS ABOVE ME SING:
"Annie, eat your own cakes."

THE BLACK EYED PEAS
"BOOM BOOM POW"

THE REAL LINE:
"Boom boom boom, gotta get-get."
THE GIRLS ABOVE ME SING:
"Yum yum yum, get a Kit Kat."

DR. DRE AND SNOOP DOGGY DOG
"NUTHIN' BUT A 'G' THANG"

THE REAL LINE:
"Ain't nuthin' but a 'G' thang, baby."
THE GIRLS ABOVE ME SING:
"Wearing nuthin' but a G-string, baby."

ADELE
"ROLLING IN THE DEEP"

THE REAL LINE:
"We could have had it all. Rolling in the deep."
THE GIRLS ABOVE ME SING:
"We could've had to crawl. Oh, and the meat."

GUNS N' ROSES
"SWEET CHILD O' MINE"

THE REAL LINE:
"Whoa, oh, oh, sweet child o' mine."
THE GIRLS ABOVE ME SING:
"Ho, ho, ho, the child is blind."

EMINEM
"LOVE THE WAY YOU LIE"

THE REAL LINE:
"Just gonna stand there and watch me burn."
THE GIRLS ABOVE ME SING:
"Just gonna stand there and watch Bieber."

SUBLIME
"SANTERIA"

THE REAL LINE:
"What I really wanna know, my baby.
What I really wanna say, I can't define."

THE GIRLS ABOVE ME SING:
"Well, I really wanna know, Jan Brady.
What I really wanna say, I can't eat limes."

Pat sang along to the radio with enough vivacity to rival Little Richard. Sure, he was drunk and a little looser than normal, but the amount of passion he conveyed through each and every syllable was something to be seen.

"Come on, sing with me!" he said as he held his imaginary microphone to my lips. I felt as if I were trapped in the opening-credits sequence to *The Hills*.

"I don't sing," I responded.

"What are you talking about? I've heard you sing in the shower before!"

"Yeah, but I haven't done that in a long time."

"Since when?" Pat asked.

"Since . . . I don't know." I wanted to change the subject, but my drunk, irritating roommate wouldn't let me.

"Charlie . . . since when?"

Oh, wow, he pulled the first-name card. How had he turned his "coming-out night" around on me? To be fair, he didn't yet know he was going to come out. "Well, if you must know, the last time I sang was in Las Vegas," I said.

"Vegas? What happened there?"

"Something I would like to forget . . ."

I have always been someone who finds karaoke to be incredibly uncomfortable. To me it's a lose-lose experience. If you're really bad at karaoke, then everyone judges your painful squawking performance, and if you're really good at karaoke, then there's something sad and depressing about you. I'm also convinced that when you're singing, you think you sound a lot better than you actually do. I've participated only one time in this obnoxious activity. As I said, I was in Las Vegas, which was bad enough to begin with, and I was somehow coerced into getting up onto a stage in the middle of a trashy casino to sing Seal's "Kiss from a Rose." I'm not going to lie, I quite love that song and felt as if it were the hymn that best represented me, and the Batman franchise. So I decided to go ahead and give it my all: "There used to be a graying tower alone on the sea. . . ."

I'll be the first to admit that I started off a little rocky, but by the time the chorus kicked in, I was definitely *American Idol* top-five-contestant-worthy. "Baby, I compare you to a kiss from a rose on the gray," I belted out passionately, of course, from a kneeling position. By gauging the people's reaction in the casino, I figured that I was singing at about an eight out of ten (I even got an elderly lady to glance up from her slot machine). But more important than that, my choreography added heft to the emotional performance, which scored me at least a 9.5.

I don't remember much from while I was up there, which had nothing to do with alcohol and everything to do with my transformation into the body of Seal, the original artist, minus the facial scarring. When I saw my friend Justin filming the concert from the front row, I was reminded for a minute that I was not Seal. His gigantic grin was an infuriating distraction, especially during the second verse, when I tripped up a bit. But I was happy for the documentation and was definitely going to ask him to post it on Facebook so all my ex-girlfriends could see how far I'd come. There's nothing more gratifying than having a girl who once loved you wish she was still your main squeeze. To me, this video was well worth all of the countless hours of heartache and pounds I'd gained from eating away my feelings.

"Now that your rose is in bloom . . ." Dramatic pause. "A light hits the gloom . . ." Turn my back to the crowd and have a personal moment. "On the . . ." Turn back around and look up at the ceiling while slowing raising my fist above my head. "Graaaaaaaaaaaaaay." Wait for the applause . . . wait for it . . . and . . . there's Justin's clap and a few other unknown adoring groupies.

I hopped off the stage and immediately grabbed Justin's video camera.

"Dude, that was hilarious," he said as I pressed PLAY.

What did he mean by hilarious? Since when was a sincere pitch-perfect performance humorous? I looked down at the screen. The beginning was a little shaky, but I knew that the chorus would make up for it. Then, when the chorus came in, I was paralyzed by how bad I sounded. Not only that, but the dance moves that I had believed to rival Michael Jackson's looked more as if I were channeling Psy in the "Gangnam Style" music video. Was it possible that Justin had quickly doctored the video and this was an elaborate prank?

"You were so funny up there," Justin said with a chuckle that made me want to punch him in the face.

"Thanks. I felt like the room needed some comedy," I responded, completely disheartened.

"Well, you sure gave it to us. Oh, man, I can't wait to post this on Facebook!"

"Oh my God, I totally saw that video on Facebook! You were pretty awful," Pat chimed in.

"Thanks." Geez, talk about kicking a dog while he's down.

"Sorry, I'm drunky. So where are we going, anyway?" Pat asked.

"Wherever the wind takes us, my friend." Pat brings out the cheesiness in me. There was no one else on the planet I would have said that to.

I steered our vehicle on a southwest course, and it was only a matter of minutes before we arrived in "Boys Town." I had done my
research and knew the exact street to drive down in order to get
stuck in the most traffic (something someone who lives in L.A. has
never done). A couple of blocks away I could hear the rumblings of
a catchy beat, which was basically the same sound that was coming
out of my car's stereo. Pat was in his own little drunken world with
no idea what we were about to "stumble" upon, until, all of a sudden, one specific musical note caught his attention. He perked up,
seeming completely sober, and looked around for the origin of this
sound.

"Was that the opening note to Gaga's 'Alejandro'?" he asked.

"Umm, I'm not sure," I responded, wondering if it had been a
rhetorical question.

As I made the final turn, almost at Santa Monica Boulevard, Pat's
question was answered. In front of us was the most vibrant spectacle
I had ever seen. Thousands of people, all different racial types, men
and women of every age, stood in front of us in the celebration of
being gay. The energy that filled my convertible was electric. It sort
of felt all of a sudden like stepping in front of a high-powered fan,
except this fan blew ultra-gay air. And, yes, the DJ, who was wearing
only a sock (and not on his foot), was blasting Gaga's "Alejandro."

I glanced over at Pat, whose surprised reaction made him look as
if he were a kid seeing the castle at Disneyland for the first time (or
so I'm told). I would not have been shocked if he had stood up in my
car and screamed out into the glittery parade, "Honey, I'm home!"

"You idiot! Now we're going to be stuck in this traffic!" he shouted
at me, pretending to be actually pissed off. I guess this wasn't going
to be as easy as I thought.

We sat in my car, totally gridlocked, watching as the floats crept by one by one. Pat pretended to be miserable, but he was not able to cover up his initial excitement when a theme he liked marched in front of us.

"Oh my God, they're totally dressed as McKinley High School faculty members from *Glee!*" Catching himself, he added, "The female babes on that show are super sexy."

As Pat remained conflicted, I sat there totally enjoying myself. The parade offered the thrill of a circus, except these participants had all of their teeth and were incredibly good-looking. However, I was most impressed, although not surprised, by the creativity and artistry of each passing float. Every one of these mobile structures showed such individuality, apart from one theme that seemed to connect them all: rainbows. The winner, if I had been a judge, was a re-creation of Rainbow Road from *Super Mario Kart*. The float was made up of two massive figure-eight rainbow tracks. On the tracks were people dressed up as each Mario character. They sat in homemade go-karts, racing each other in circles. They replicated it almost exactly like the video game; the only difference was that in their version, Luigi was a transvestite.

All right, it was time to begin the process of broaching the subject of the day with Pat. My hope was that I wouldn't need to outright interrogate him and that he would come out with it, literally, in the flow of a conversation. He had been given more than enough time to process the extravaganza in front of us. How could he deny his true sexuality any longer after seeing the joy on those sailors' faces aboard the "Butt-Pirate Ship"? Even I considered embarking on their vessel and helping them hoist up the rainbow mainsail. Plus, I secretly wanted one of their colorful papier-mâché parrots for my shoulder.

"Hey, Pat?" I looked over at my roommate.

"Yeah?" He continued eyeing the parade as the grand finale made its way down the boulevard.

I probably should have just simply asked him the proposed question. He was one of my best friends, and apart from one major roadblock, we told each other everything. He was one of the few people in my life who had seen me at my happiest and my lowest moments. And although his "I've so been there" relationship advice was terrible because he had so never been there, I still appreciated every word. I now wanted to be there in the same way for him. Just as real friends don't let friends drive drunk, well, real friends also don't let friends act straight when they are gay. It was time.

"Don't you think it's beautiful that there's a place where gay men and women can go to feel accepted?" Thanks to that guy in the coffee shop, I had my introduction.

"Umm, yeah, I guess so," he responded suspiciously.

But that didn't back me down even for a second. "I mean, look out there. What do you see?"

"Well, I see a guy dressed in lederhosen swinging around his nipple tassels."

"Yeah, but beyond that, what do you see?"

"Okay. I see a group of men in flip-flops and Speedos, and on their asses it says 'U.S.gAy,'" he answered.

"Look through them, Pat!" Had he never heard a metaphor before?

"Well, I'm trying to, but there's a huge advertisement for Nair in the way!" he yelled right back. I guess not.

"You're not understanding me, Pat."

"Understanding what? That's what I see!"

"You don't see a bunch of people being honest with themselves? Feeling truly accepted for who they are? You don't see real human connection out there? People who are so in love with one another and know that no matter what society thinks of them, they would rather die than not be together? You don't see any of that?"

Pat squinted his eyes, trying to find the float I was talking about. But, sadly, I could tell that I hadn't even made a dent in his protective armor. He shook his head.

"Can we go home now?" Pat asked in a somber voice. He put his hoodie up and cranked the music, letting me know he wasn't interested in communicating any longer. I guess I had tried to pull him out of the closet with a little too much force.

My plan had failed miserably. And worse than that, I had upset my dear friend. I looked out into the sea of sparkling men, taking in their good spirits one last time. I made a mental note to return to next year's festivities, but to remember to bring a blanket and a girlfriend. Who knows, maybe Pat would even be a part of the parade by then. Possibly on the "Skittles: Taste the Gay-bow" float? They seemed to be having the most fun.

When we got home, Pat disappeared into his room to take a phone call, a real one (I could hear the person on the other line), not a fake one like I usually do to remove myself from an awkward situation. I was left alone with my thoughts. Thankfully, the girls above me were home so I could distract myself with some background chatter. Unthankfully, they were discussing "how swollen a vagina gets for the week after childbirth." But then, something useful actually traveled from their apartment, through the vent, and into my room.

Somewhere between post-childbirth vaginas and *Real Housewives of New Jersey* analysis (I was pleased that both of them shared my opinion that Teresa's an opportunistic bitch), Cathy and Claire discussed their friend Jasmine, or as they refer to her, Jazz Hands. Apparently, Jazz Hands's makeup addiction is getting out of hand—er, out of jazz hand. Cathy and Claire were worried that her excessive purchasing of makeup products was masking, quite literally, an inse-curity she had due to slight facial scarring from years of acne. They brought it up to her a few times in a "nonjudgmental way" (I'd love to hear those conversations), but Jazz Hands would clam up and get defensive.

"Sometimes, it's like, we just assume people don't already know themselves. Like how Teresa on *Housewives* has no clue what a wretched whore she is. But sometimes they really do know. And all we can do is let them figure things out at their own pace while letting them know that we're there to support them," Cathy philosophized.

Holy shit. Did that just happen? This profound insight that pre-sumably formed in Cathy's brain and traveled out of her mouth with articulate execution had just made me recognize that I was going about this entire Pat thing all wrong. In an instant I was guided to the realization that my job was to be there for Pat when he was ready to come out on his own terms. It was never about Pat coming out, it was about Pat letting me in.

After the excitement of my newfound awareness subsided, I sat there stunned that I was actually guided to this realization by the girls above me. I couldn't help but wonder if there was more to them than I initially thought. Were they philosophically in tune with certain cosmic insights that we "normal people" couldn't possibly fathom? Was I living beneath the modern-day, female versions of Proust and Nietzsche, if Proust and Nietzsche had inside access to the new Manolo Blahnik line that you "can't even get until next sea-son"? I silently sat there, petrified that I had horribly misjudged the girls above me—

"Sorry, I completely missed what you just said about Jazz Hands, I was Google Imaging swollen vaginas after childbirth. And FYI, I now understand why Angelina adopts those African babies."

Okay, maybe I didn't entirely underestimate them. Thanks for bringing me back down to earth, Claire.

Later that night, I was in the bathroom, making sure my receding hairline hadn't subsided any further since last night's inspection. One strand seemed to be missing. Probably from the stress of my day. When I began brushing my teeth (the second time), I heard a knock at the door. Pat poked his head in.

"Hey, thanks for getting me drunk tonight."

"Yeah, no problem," I said with a mouth full of toothpaste.

"Also, the parade was really . . . colorful."

"Yeah. It was, wasn't it?"

He nodded. "Okay, well, good night."

"Good night, Pat."

I was climbing into bed, getting ready to call it a night, when I heard a familiar song echoing through the walls of our apartment. An unspoken acknowledgment that can only come from someone who has a flair for the fabulous. Playing softly from Pat's room, I heard . . . "There used to be a graying tower alone on the sea. . . ."

THE GIRLS ON HOLIDAYS

Dear Girls Above Me,

"Supposedly if you get wasted the night before New Year's, your hangover isn't as bad on New Year's."
Words from a true alcoholic.

Dear Girls Above Me,

"I don't understand weather talk, but it says there's a 10% chance it's going to rain on New Year's. Is that high?" Are you high?

Dear Girls Above Me,

(phone) "Mom, if I come home for Thanksgiving, I want calorie signs beside each dish." That was all the Native Americans wanted too.

Dear Girls Above Me,

"She's dressing up as a pumpkin? *Just* a pumpkin!? So shady, I don't trust this bitch." Agreed, never trust something not slutty.

Dear Girls Above Me,

"We should celebrate by going to the hospital and looking at newborn babies!" Or you could celebrate *Labor Day* by getting a job.

Dear Girls Above Me,

"She was a major buzz kill talking about death and war. I wanted to be like, relax, it's a holiday weekend!" Happy Memorial Day.

Dear Girls Above Me,

"What the hell does Easter have to do with Jesus anyway?" You don't know? He's the one who hires the Bunny.

Dear Girls Above Me,

"So far my biggest disappointment of 2011 was realizing that real bowling is way harder than Wii bowling." You've had a rough year.

Dear Girls Above Me,

Throwing a Cinco de Mayo "partaay" over the weekend means you're just getting drunk on a Saturday. Regardless, Happy Ocho de Mayo!

Dear Girls Above Me,

"I hate St. Paddy's Day cause I look fat in green
although getting pinched secretly turns me on." I live
under you, it's no secret.

CHAPTER TWENTY

Whenever the girls above me say the words *I have the best idea everrrrr*, I know that something terribly bad is going to happen. I can't recall there ever being an occasion that their "best idea everrrrr" was even a moderately good one. And not only that, it changes on a daily basis. So that means that yesterday's "best idea everrrrr" really only lasted for twenty-four hours, instead of its promised "everrrrr," because now all of a sudden there is a new "best idea everrrrr." When I start to calculate what today's "best idea everrrrr" is going to be in a few days, I get dizzy and need to lie down. I think it might have to do with an overload of R's.

What's even harder is overhearing ideas that Cathy and Claire believe to be exceptional but that I know from their past experiences will only bring them sorrow, disappointment, and a trip to the gynecologist. But it's my duty to respect their integrity and protect the stable ecosystem of their apartment by not interfering with them. I'm not going to pretend it's been easy, because it hasn't. There have been many times that I've wanted to lend a neighborly hand, but I have had to learn to let Mother Nature follow her own course and allow the girls to make their own mistakes.

I witnessed the girls so distressed that they had to wait "a whole 'nother day" for the *Bachelor* finale, even though I knew it was on live TV at that very moment. It was driving me crazy knowing that they were missing it. I came very close to yelling out "Employee!" while I listened to Claire practice for her entry-level-job interview: "So, that's why I want to be your employer." And for a month I had to listen to Cathy learning a Spanish "phrase a day" in preparation for her "trip to Italy!"

Knock on wood, these little mistakes and mishaps haven't caused the girls any permanent damage. I would feel such guilt knowing that I could've saved them from acquiring a nasty STD (some people have good "gay-dar"; well, I have good "STD-dar") but instead was forced to keep quiet so as not to blow my cover, although there was one specific incident where I came very close, so close that I was inches away from their door, getting into position for a Kramer entrance. But this was a life-and-death situation, and I couldn't just sit there eavesdropping and do nothing about it. I didn't care that I was breaking nature's code and proving to have no future career as a National Geographic cameraman. This finally proved that my top-notch stalking skills were beneficial to their survival.

Cathy speaks extra loud whenever she's on the phone with her mother: "Mom, can you text me your green bean casserole recipe? Claire and I wanna make it for dinner. Best idea everrrrr!" I immediately called my friend and canceled our biweekly bingo plans. I happened to be remarkably familiar with a green bean casserole. In fact, it's really the only thing I know how to cook. I don't want to come across as a total arrogant asshole, but I am pretty much the red

Power Ranger when it comes to green bean casseroles. Ever since my grandma Nell taught me her secret recipe, I've practically been able to prepare it in my sleep (although I'm not encouraging sleep-cooking; it can be quite hazardous, to say nothing of fattening). I've memorized all of the ingredients, measurements, and ideal cooking and cooling times. I figured the girls could use a professional spotter just in case things got out of casserole control.

Up until this point, the only dish that the girls had made success-fully was peanut butter and jelly on white bread (not toasted). Of course, I'm not able to visibly see the outcome of their sandwiches, so I can't fairly judge how presentable they might be, but from the sounds of their orgasm-like moaning. Unfortunately for my little sous-chefs, most of their other kitchen experiences have been fail-ures. Even the simplest of meals seemed to be too much for them, as indicated by some of their unsuccessful attempts: Toaster Strudels (burned), canned soup (tried microwaving in the can), chicken pail-lard (they got lost on step two), and hard-boiled eggs (they thought that by just dipping the eggs into boiling water they would be ready).

My plan was to synchronize my cooking of my grandmother's green bean casserole with theirs in order to psychically guide them to at least one cooking success. Since my well-practiced dish was guaranteed to turn out, if I were to prompt them along the way so they would unwittingly correct their typical errors, their dish would be a success too. If I heard them veering off track, like mixing the ingredients in the wrong order or forgetting the secret component that should be a part of all green bean casseroles (Cheez-Its), then I would make a squawking sound out my window that would, I hoped, snap them back on track. In hindsight this plan made little to no sense, but it was getting me out of my apartment and forcing me to cook something that Rachael Ray calls "therapeutic."

I contacted a couple friends to see whether I could get them to join me in this night of synchronized cooking, but none of them was fully grasping my proposition.

"So, you're cooking the same meal as the girls above, but not actually making it *with* them? And on top of that they don't even know you're doing this?" my brother-in-law Jesse asked. It sounded so abnormal coming out of his mouth.

"You're not understanding. Okay, think of me as that sweet little rat in *Ratatouille*. I'm just making sure that they don't screw up their dish," I said, pleading my case.

"Yeah, but in *Ratatouille* the guy is fully aware that he has a rat tugging on his hair. How is that even close to the same thing?"

"Okay, well, this is a slightly different, less realistic version."

"I don't know, brother. I think your version would make a really fucked-up animated movie."

I will admit that if I hadn't known my own wholesome intentions, this could very well have been a scene from a bad slasher film, but I honestly had zero plans to chop up Cathy and Claire into bite-sized pieces and bake them into my casserole. First of all, throwing in additional ingredients that weren't a part of my grandma's original recipe would really have pissed her off if she were alive (don't worry, Grandma Nell, you can rest in peace), and also dicing someone into pieces for consumption is against the law and evil and stuff.

I had struck out with my friends, so it looked like grocery shopping was going to be a solo mission. There are two grocery stores within walking distance of my apartment building. One of them is Ralph's; the other is Whole Foods. Even though I lie to my mother about "only eating organic foods," because she is a true believer in *everything* organic, I much prefer Ralph's for my basic shopping needs. Not only does Ralph's provide me with cheaper items and wider aisles, it also happens to be the place where on one incredible day I flirted in the checkout line with Julia Roberts. I know, I know, she's a tad older than me and happily married or whatever, but you should have seen the way she smiled at me when I placed the plastic divider between our food items. It was almost as if she didn't want it to be there. Like a happy way of showing me that she wanted my bleach to be closer to her papaya without any impediment. Regrettably, due to the shock of her acknowledgment of me, I stood there frozen. Julia checked out, both figuratively and literally. I watched as she drove off, out of my life forever, probably to go pick up her kids from school or something. If I could go back and do it all over again, I would have lifted that germ-ridden divider, just to see what could have happened. Who knows, maybe my life would have turned out completely different. Or at the very least I think I would have made a wonderful male nanny to her children.

As it turns out, Cathy and Claire were putting on their TOMS shoes to go to the grocery store at the same time I was lacing up my Vans.

"I think we should go to Whole Foods to get the ingredients. It won't save us money but will save us on calories, fo sho," Claire yelled out to Cathy.

I have never been, nor do I see myself becoming, a calorie counter. In fact, for this particular dish I believed the more the calories the better. But I didn't like the idea of watching the girls walk one direction toward Whole Foods while I walked the other way to Ralph's. We planned to cook the same thing; we should have been using the same-brand contents. So I made an agreement with myself that I would go the healthier route this time around (Sorry, Grandma).

Once I heard the girls head out the door, I counted to twenty before leaving my apartment. There's nothing worse than having to walk a few blocks directly next to people you aren't hanging out with. They look at you out of the corner of their eye, as if you're listening in on their conversations, which in my case I would be. But if you speed up your pace, then you increase your chances of walking funny and/or pulling a hamstring, and if you slow down, then you get agitated with the little progress you're making. I've found that the best thing to do in these moments is to pretend as if you are answering your phone and say, "I haven't heard from you in almost ten years." This will give you the opportunity to naturally stop dead in your tracks, forcing the people to continue on without you.

Once I got to Whole Foods and spotted the girls I instantly transformed into Jason Bourne. . . . Okay, maybe Mr. Bean is a more accurate depiction, but in any case it was exhilarating to camouflage myself behind the organic eggplants (I was wearing a dark purple shirt) and watch them as they shopped. I was not used to seeing them in the flesh. I had become a specialist when it came to understanding their voices, but I knew very little about their mannerisms. Just from listening to Cathy and Claire, I learned how to decipher the meaning of each and every inflection of their speech, probably understanding them better than anyone else in my life or in theirs. I know that after sitting in rush-hour traffic, Cathy gets really quiet, only wanting to be left alone, but Claire is completely oblivious to this: "Will you drive me to Starbucks so I don't have to look for parking?" I know that when they are starving, they pretend not to be: "I'm not hungry! Stop saying I'm hungry! Why do you think I'm hungry? You're the one who's hungry!" And I can always figure out when it's time for Claire to start sobering up for the night: "If I'm drunk would I be able to do this—ouch! You just let me poke myself in the eye!"

As I stared at my upstairs neighbors examining a can of green beans, I couldn't help but feel sadness about our one-sided friendship. I had never before heard such completely uncensored and honest conversation. Not even my ex-girlfriend spoke to me as candidly when we were together. But the truth is that Cathy and Claire know very little about me. Not only that, but most of the time they don't even remember who I am or they still think I'm Stephanie's boyfriend. And for some bizarre reason, watching them in the canned-food aisle at Whole Foods made me want to change that. I wanted these girls to know me—the real me, not the eavesdropping me.

Still crouched behind the eggplants, I got ready to make my move. I had no idea what I was going to say to them. Maybe I would help them shop for the green bean casserole ingredients while voluntarily giving them the CliffsNotes to my life? I was sure if they knew I got my first hand job with SPF 50 sunscreen as lotion they would feel a lot closer to me. At least I would hope so. Or if that didn't do it for them, then the story about the time I went to see *Love Actually* in the theater and ended up getting into a hair-pulling fight with the enraged little man who was kicking the seat behind me was sure to bond us.

As I stepped away from the ugly purple vegetables, allowing myself to be detected once again, I got a whiff of a familiar pungent smell. A body-spray fragrance that only a d-bag would dare wear. And judging by the amount that was forcing its way into my nostrils, this d-bag was close. Real close. I turned around.

"I like staring at their asses too. Downloading some visuals for your spank bank? File saved," said the Con-Man, who was inches away from my face.

"Huh?" Couldn't he just get sucked into the black hole that was where his personality should have been?

"How about this . . . I'll take the blonde, you take the brunette, and then we'll do a switcheroo."

"What? No," I replied, backing up to regain my space once more.

"Fine. You take the blonde, I'll take the brunette, and then we'll do the switcheroo? Bro, that's the last scenario I can think of, so if you say no, then I'll have no other choice but to assume you like dudes."

"I'm okay with that," I responded.

While he thought about this for a while, he made a face that looked as if he were constipated. I wondered if this was actually his "thinking face" or if he felt the need to show me his clogging problem in the supermarket. Both were equally likely. "You're okay with liking dudes or you're okay with the plan of me macking on the brunette?" he replied.

I figured the best thing to do at this point was pretend as if I had lost my hearing. At the very least that would confuse him enough to give me time to make a run for it. When I looked up to see what the girls were doing, they weren't there. I glanced over at the dairy aisle, knowing that milk was a key ingredient to the casserole, but they weren't there either. I examined every inch of the store in plain sight, but the girls were nowhere to be found. On top of that, Conor (I refused to refer to him as the Con-Man in my inner voice anymore) was still blabbering on about "tag-teaming the bitches" who lived above me. Due to a particular aversion to Axe body spray, a general distaste for Conor's overall being, and a bizarre protectiveness I had for the girls above me, I lost my shit.

"Conor?"

"I think you mean the Con—"

"Conor?"

"Yes?" he replied.

"If you ever refer to my neighbors as 'bitches' again, I'll hit you so hard that not even mama will be able to say I knocked you out," I growled out loud while simultaneously realizing it made no sense; my apologies to LL Cool J. Today was a good day. He stood there traumatized, or maybe confused, having no idea how to react. I glanced at his pulsating biceps, which were about the same size as my waist, and at full flex they could grow to dimensions similar to my chest size. At any particular moment he could have literally destroyed the face where my beard grew. Instead he looked at me with what I believed to be respect, something he had never given me before. He and I both knew I had no chance against him. But that didn't matter. I had earned admiration from the biggest douchebag in my building.

Just then a familiar voice caught my attention at the checkout counter. Cathy and Claire were in the middle of purchasing their items, well on their way to preparing their green bean casserole. I needed to get a move on.

"Are we good?" I asked him.

"We're good, bro," he replied.

"Enjoy your protein shake."

"I always do," he said as he took a sip, leaving a chocolate mustache above his lip.

I grabbed a shopping cart and made a speedy dash for the canned green beans, stopping only a few times to sample the weird cheeses. Whole Foods has a lot of weird cheese samples.

THE GIRLS ON READING

Dear Girls Above Me,

"Wait, when it's a hardcover, it's a novel, and when it's floppy, it's just a book?" All you need to know is it's available on tape.

Dear Girls Above Me,

"So this is fiction or nonfiction? I'm confused, why can't we just say real life or fake life?" Okay, Harry Potter is fake life.

Dear Girls Above Me,

"The Bible is an actual book you can read? I thought people just did chants and stuff from it." Oh dear God above me.

Dear Girls Above Me,

"He wanted to know the last book I've read and all I could think of was *Goodnight Moon*." And didn't your mom read that to you?

THEY COULD BE MOMS SOMEDAY

Dear Girls Above Me,

"Women always complain about getting older, but I'm totally excited for my MILF years." So are your future son's friends.

Dear Girls Above Me,

"I just saw a parent with her child on a leash! I'm so gonna do that with my kids." You should also look into designer body armor.

Dear Girls Above Me,

"I watched a special on conjoined twins and all I could think about was karate chopping them to freedom." You should be a doctor.

Dear Girls Above Me,

"I think I'm pregnant—Wait, does the Barneys sale last all of December?!" Umm, can I react to the first part instead of the sale?

CHAPTER TWENTY-ONE

"Okay, so now we have to set the cooking timer thingy to twenty-five minutes," Cathy screamed out to Claire, who sounded as if she were rummaging through the cupboard.

I sat in my sink, acutely focused, with a ready-to-cook casserole beside me. My glow-in-the-dark novelty cooking timer (thanks, Mom) was in hand and all prepared for synchronization.

"Found it. Oh, and it's pink! So cute!" Claire giggled.

Yeah, but can it glow in the dark? I remember thinking. The one-sided cooking competition had clearly begun.

"Did you say set it for fifteen minutes?" Claire asked.

I waited patiently. How does the word *fifteen* sound even close to *twenty-five*?

"No, you idiot. I said twenty minutes."

No, you didn't, *you* idiot. You said twenty-five minutes. I looked up at the ceiling and prayed that she would correct herself.

"Setting the timer to twenty minutes . . . right . . . now!"

I had no plans to sacrifice my own casserole just to stay

synchronized with the girls, so I set my timer for twenty-five minutes. Anyway, it was safer for Cathy and Claire to come up a bit short
than to discover their oven was up in flames. Plus there was a good
chance it would take them some time to discover that Kleenex do
not make effective cooking mitts, which would give the casserole
the additional time it needed. Clearly, I took my casserole making
incredibly seriously.

Now all I had to do was wait, and I happened to have the perfect
amount of time to watch one of my half-hour TV shows saved on
my DVR. My problem is that I always end up spending more time
deciding which show to put on than I do actually watching it. You
can't blame me, given that I only record the stuff worth watching,
like *Cash Cab* and *Sister Wives*. After scrolling back and forth between
the two for several minutes, I realized I no longer had time to watch
either and turned my TV off. I've tried watching *Cash Cab* in install-
ments before, but you really lose the flow of the story. Like, where
was this guy going again?

As my casserole baked, I sat comfortably in my kitchen sink, with
my computer across my lap, watching YouTube videos and writing
down the wisdom coming from above me. After listening to these
girls for almost a year now, I've developed a strategy for when and
when not to be attentive. This is not necessarily a rigorous plan to
live by, but it at least gives my brain and ear canals a chance to know
when I should be alert (because they are most likely going to say
something interesting) and when I should relax (because I am about
to be seriously bored).

ALERT

Around the time they've taken too many Patrón shots.

Anything to do with boys and dating.

Whenever they started off a sentence with "I've made a huge mistake."

While they are on the phone with their moms talking shit about each other.

During any natural disaster.

RELAX

Around the time of year when *American Idol* auditions are nearing.

Anything to do with shopping and high heels.

Whenever they start off a sentence with "I need to tell you about this ingrown hair."

While they watch *Sex and the City* reruns.

During any "fashion disaster."

"Oh my God, did you hear that Jen got her boobs done?" Claire blurted out.

"No. Way. No. Way. No. Way!" Cathy responded.

Hmm, what category did this fall under? I guess I could have relaxed on this one, considering the conversation concerned one of their friends and not them, but at the same time boob jobs are almost always fascinating. So I decided to be on the alert.

"Supposedly she went all Anna Nicole Smith on us."

"She died?!" Cathy screamed.

"No! She got boobs like Anna, but they are totally alive," Claire reassured her.

"Oh thank God. I mean, I don't really like Jen, but I don't want her to be dead or anything."

I was really happy I'd stayed and listened.

"Facebook! I bet she posted pictures of her new tatas on Facebook!" And with that the girls stampeded into their living room. In order for me to have gotten a full listening signal, I would have had to follow them into my living room. The only problem was I had really wedged myself and now I was stuck in my sink. I tried maneuvering my caboose from side to side, but due to an awkward angle and the maple donut I had wolfed down that morning, I wasn't going anywhere.

Out of nowhere, I heard a timid knock on my door. There was a split second where I wondered if the girls could have made it down to my apartment within those seven seconds. As much as I might wish, tweets don't self-destruct (Inspector Gadget style) after reading them, so these girls could conceivably discover my snippy 140-character jokes at their expense. Too bad Twitter doesn't have some sort of fail-safe device that instantly wipes all the evidence, like in *Conspiracy Theory* when Mel Gibson flips a switch and it burns everything in his apartment. Knowing me, if I ever installed such a switch, I would accidentally flip it later that night when I got up to pee.

Anyway, it wasn't them at my door, because I could hear the rumblings above me of a debate about breast size: "Those are D's, Claire!"

Again, a knock at my door, this time a tad bit louder. I sat hopelessly among dirty dishes, unable to reach the door's peephole to see who was on the other side. I felt just like the guy who got stuck between rocks and had to cut off his own arm in order to free himself, but instead of considering a dull knife to get the job done, I eyed the dishwashing liquid beside me.

I figured the worst-case scenario was that Tania and her frightening poodle, Penny, were at my door, wanting to pay Marvin an afternoon visit. The best-case scenario was that it was the delivery guy needing my direct signature for the *Shark Week: 20th Anniversary Collection* I had ordered on Amazon. I rarely, if ever, had let someone into my apartment just based on the sound of his knuckles on wood, but I really wanted to see the "Air Jaws" people had been praising in their reviews.

"Come in," I hesitantly called out.

There was a long overly dramatic pause before my door slowly creaked opened. This could only belong to one person. The actual worst-case scenario . . . My ex-girlfriend.

She stood serenely in my doorway. I had no choice but to match her calm due to my restricted position. But on the inside I felt just like George Clooney's fishing boat in *The Perfect Storm,* right as it was entering that huge wave of destruction. . . . Spoiler alert: Based on her expression she seemed to be just as confused to see me as I was to see her. Although her confusion most likely had to do with the fact that I was hanging out of my kitchen sink.

"Are you okay, Charlie?" she asked.

I had imagined a million different scenarios in my head for what it would be like to bump into my ex for the first time since our breakup. Somehow I forgot to visualize this one.

"I'm great. How are you?" I said, responding the only way I knew how to from a sink.

"Are you stuck in there or something? I mean, do you need my help—"

"No, no. I'm good. Just lounging. Doing some Internet browsing," I said back to her.

We sat there in silence—well, I sat there; she was standing, unencumbered. I had no idea why after all this time she'd shown up to my apartment unannounced. Did she need some cash? She had about twenty times more money than I did, but maybe after our breakup, she had turned to gambling as a coping mechanism. Or was it a possibility that she had come to collect her electric toothbrush? I sure hoped not, because during my anger stage in the phases of grief, I had used her Sonicare to clean the Thai food streaks I had left in my toilet.

"Can I come in?" she sweetly asked.

I pretended to consider her question for a short time. I didn't want her thinking she could just march back into my life so easily, regardless of the fact that she could. "Sure."

She wore the vintage 1987 Lakers T-shirt I had let her borrow the first time she spent the night at my apartment. I couldn't help but believe this was a conscious decision on her part. She looked the same, possibly a few pounds skinnier, but this was only noticeable because it had been so long since I had last seen her. As she walked toward me, I was surprised by how dispirited she seemed. I was used to seeing her as the life of the party, bubbly, zestful, and always prepared to sing a number from the musical *Rent*. Now she looked disheartened and lifeless.

"You have a beard."

"I do."

She came in to hug me. I tried my best to reciprocate, but I had trouble lifting my upper torso. I could tell she felt as if I were being standoffish, which seemed to make her more interested in me. If I had only had the restrictions of a kitchen sink to sit in during our relationship, we very well might still be together.

"Why are you sitting in a sink, Charlie?" she asked. Fair question.

I could have told her all about the girls above me, but I wasn't sure how not to come across as super creepy. So I whipped up an alternative. "This is where I've been eating my meals."

"Not at your dining table anymore?"

"No. Why? Because it's a table surrounded by chairs? What if everyone always colored inside the lines?"

"That's a point. . . . So, how's the writing been going? Still working on that 'great screenplay' you used to talk about?" she asked.

"Oh, you mean 'Channeling Erica'? Yeah. I'm almost done, actually. Just polishing up the ending." Truthfully, I was on page eighteen and I had completely made up that title. The actual name was "Untitled Charlie McDowell Shitty Ball Hair."

"I can't wait to read it," she said in the most genuine way she knew how.

"So . . . What are you doing here?"

She looked up at me with her beautiful eyes, not knowing how to respond.

"I just feel so lost."

"How come? Everything seems to be going well in your life. A wonderful career, family, and I would bet you have a special someone as well. . . ." Thanks to Facebook I already knew the answer, but I wanted her to think I didn't check her page daily and hadn't discovered she was indeed "in a relationship."

"We broke up."

"I know. You don't have to rub it in."

"No, not you and me. Me and Tone."

"Tone? Please tell me that's his DJ name," I begged.

"I'm pretty sure that's the name his mother gave him."

"So you went from dating me, Charlie, to a guy named Tone?"

"Well, there were a few in between, but yes," she said, hitting me with another dagger.

"'A few' meaning 'three,' though, right?"

"I don't know, Charlie!"

I was beginning to come to the realization that relationships are mostly about the balance of power. If you have all of it (her), then there is very little hope for the other person (me) to gain any sort of respect. This Tone guy sounded like a real asshole, but who knows, maybe he was just a normal guy with a ridiculous name who got his heart broken like me. And maybe that was her superhero strength: to lure men into her charmingly decorated lair, where she gradually sucks the "relationship power" out of them.

"You know, some people might think Charlie's a weird name," she said.

"Yeah. So did you just come over to give me a pep talk or . . . ?"

"Charlie, I came here to tell you that I think I made a big mistake."

Damn it, she really was my kryptonite. Deep down I knew that she wasn't the amazing person I had made her out to be, but up until this point I had been so infatuated by the idea of her that I wasn't able to think clearly. And even still, somehow she found a way to point her tractor beam directly into my heart. I needed to break free from her Jedi mind trick, but I couldn't do it alone. I wasn't strong enough. I needed something, a sign, an immunity, or at least a foreseeable way out of my sink.

And just like that, a miracle happened. Through the stucco and plaster ceiling I heard the ringing of a cooking timer going off. For me, it was a spiritual awakening; for the guardian angels who live above me, it was the alarm notifying them that their green bean casserole was ready. Without liquid soap or any other lathering lubricant, I shot out of the sink like a cannonball. It's funny how a little motivation can give you the power to accomplish impossible feats. This was my version of the mother who lifted a car to save her child (mine was easier on the back). I realized that while catching up with my ex-girlfriend, I had completely forgotten about the girls above me, who were nowhere to be heard.

"Don't you have a response?" My ex-girlfriend examined me, realizing that I wasn't the same guy she used to walk all over. But all I could do was picture Cathy and Claire's casserole smoldering in their oven. Due to the timer miscommunication, I now had less than five minutes to track them down and try to find a way to shepherd them back into the kitchen.

"Hold that thought," I said as I ran out of the kitchen, searching for an audible signal from the girls.

I stopped and listened for them in the living room. They weren't there. Next I checked Pat's room (he was away at work). Still nothing to be heard. I did, however, spot an opened condom wrapper in his trash can. For a moment, I was offended that he hadn't gossiped with me about it the next morning.

I continued my search in the bathroom. I imagined how annoyed my ex-girlfriend was getting in the other room, but I kept my focus on my priorities. Suddenly, I remembered that I had my own casserole to tend to. The cooking timer was still ticking, but I didn't want to follow in the steps of the girls above me and forget about my dish.

"Hey, do you mind taking my green bean casserole out of the

oven?" I called out to her while I listened for the girls through my bathroom window.

There was a lengthy pause. "Are you serious? I don't know how to do that. Charlie, what's going on with you?" she yelled back at me.

"Just take out the casserole with an oven mitten and place it on the counter!" I couldn't believe she was messing around with my casserole.

Sadly, this was probably the most I had ever asked of her. She made that rather apparent in my kitchen with her overly theatrical scoffing noises. "You never cooked anything for me before," she muttered under her breath. She was right. I only did *everything else*.

I proceeded into my bedroom (directly below Claire's room), where I found the girls still analyzing Jen's breast implants.

"I think the right one is a little lopsided."

"Hmm. I don't know. It probably just has to do with those hideous bras she always wears," Claire said.

"Okay, I'll bet you a soy chai latte that her boobs, or at least the left one, is at least a double D," Cathy proposed.

"You're on, bitch. There's no way she's two cups bigger than Gisele."

It became fairly clear the girls had completely forgotten about their casserole and hadn't heard the cooking timer from the other room. Speaking of cooking timers, mine finally expired. The twenty-five minutes were up. From now on, with each second that ticked away, so did the chances of my somehow saving their casserole. I looked around my room for an object that I could use to bang on the ceiling, hoping the noise would jolt them back to reality.

Between a skateboard, a *Dora the Explorer* beach towel, a floor fan, and a large wooden salad bowl (please don't ask what that was doing in my room), I decided that the skateboard was going to make the most racket. I could only imagine the horror on Mr. Molever's face if he knew I was planning on attacking his precious ceiling with a transportation device. But that wasn't enough to stop me. Something needed to be done. So, I stood on my bed, gently bounced up and down to give myself some extra momentum, cocked the skateboard back, and flung it up toward the ceiling.

With my eyes closed, I expected to hear a thunderous echoing sound bouncing off every wall in my apartment. Instead it sounded more like what I imagined I would hear if someone punched a fist into a bucket of Jell-O. I glanced up at my ceiling, which my skateboard was now a part of. The wheels had punctured the cheap plaster job, and it dangled there on its own, looking like some bad hipster art installation.

"Did you just fart?" Cathy asked her roommate.

"No. Did you?"

I needed to find another way to get to them. Not only to have a chance at salvaging their casserole, but to save them from burning down their apartment as well.

I left my skateboard suspended and headed back into the kitchen, where my ex-girlfriend was sure to be pissed off. For the first time ever I had no interest in seeing her. I imagined that partly had to do with the casserole mayhem, but I also believed that I was starting to realize she was not "the one."

She stood there with an oven mitt on her hand and a bitchy look on her face. My perfectly baked casserole sizzled on the counter beside her.

"What was that noise?"

"Oh. I think my neighbors farted." I shrugged. Admittedly, I'm not the world's fastest thinker.

"Don't you have anything to say to me?" she desperately asked.

The hundreds of things I had rehearsed over and over in my head to say to her were nowhere to be found. I couldn't even muster up one of them. I think she realized this and decided to get closer to me so I would get a whiff of her blissful scent. This was something that had always worked in the past. As she approached me, she transformed from irritated bitch to seductive wench: slightly pouting her lips, running her finger along the collar of my favorite T-shirt, tilting her head down and gazing up at me with her giant blue eyes. Being the typical male that I am, this was very hard for me to resist.

She leaned in and pressed her lips against mine. It was exactly as I had remembered. Peerless. Passionate. And powerful . . . But not as powerful as the burned-casserole smell that came wafting in from the window. My eyes opened wide, while she remained in the moment.

"Wait, stop," I said as I pulled away from her.

I could tell she didn't believe I was strong enough to resist her powers. "Why? What's wrong?"

"Nothing. I just can't do this." The scent of smoldering casserole grew stronger.

She paid no attention to me (reminiscent of our relationship) as she leaned in to kiss me once again. But I pulled back.

"I'm sorry, but I just don't want to be with you anymore." I finally said it out loud. It was a good thing my family wasn't there to witness this, because they would have cheered at the top of their lungs and done a jig.

"But I thought you loved me. You texted me 'Everything I have ever done has been for you' just recently." I could see how that would be confusing to her.

"I did love you. Even recently. But I don't anymore." I had no idea what had come over me. But I felt content for the first time in a while.

She eyed me, searching for a way to look deep into my soul to see if I was speaking the truth. I let her in, just so she knew that we were over. When she finally got it, she appeared to be upset, but not any-where close to breaking into a scream cry. We stood there in silence.

"So now what?" she asked.

"Well . . . First I'm going to give you a hug. Then you're going to leave. And then I'm going to go save the lives of my upstairs neigh-bors. Okay?" How's that for taking initiative, biotch? Oh, I forgot to mention that she used to tell me that I never took initiative.

I could sense that she was in shock and didn't want to be touched, but I hugged her anyway. We said our good-byes: "I wish you the best of luck," "Send love to your parents," "This doesn't mean we have to block each other from looking at our Facebook profiles"— you know, typical stuff like that. In the hallway I gave her one last "sexy face" look (but it was more something for her to remember me by) and then bolted up the stairs.

When I arrived at Cathy and Claire's apartment, the smell of charred canned green beans was at an all-time high. Did they think these were normal cooking smells? Oh . . . I guess probably. I was so disappointed that they had ruined yet another meal, especially one that I had given so much of myself over to. But I put my feelings aside and tried to come up with the best plan of action.

I didn't want the girls to see me. All I really had to do was get their attention to the kitchen and let them discover their catastrophe on their own. So I rang the doorbell, probably seventeen times. I was pleased with my approach until I saw Sally (my agoraphobic old neighbor) staring at me in terror through her cracked-open door.

"Sorry, Sally. Everything's all right. No need to worry—" She immediately closed the door, but not before reminding me that I had to pick up Marvin's poop from the grass out front.

I darted back downstairs to my own apartment just in time to see—I mean hear—my plan work flawlessly before my very own eyes—ears!

"Holy Kardashians! Our casserole is burning alive!"

I sat back, this time in a chair, with a piece of casserole cooked to perfection and listened as Cathy and Claire stomped all over the place, attempting to clear the smoke from their kitchen. Even though I knew it was their own fault, I felt remorseful that they had gone to all this trouble and just happened to get sidetracked by a pair of fake boobies. Who knows, maybe if I had seen a picture of those breasts, I might have also forgotten all about the casserole.

Although I knew I wasn't supposed to feed "the animals" in their natural habitat, I made the decision to go ahead and do it anyway. I had more than enough green bean casserole to go around, and I thought it would be amusing to listen to them try to figure out how it got outside their door.

"Claire! Claire! Look what's outside our door!"

"What is that?!"

"It's green bean casserole!"

"What?! Did we do that?"

There was a long pause. I had an enormous smile on my face.

"You know what? I think we did!"

LOST IN TRANSLATION

Dear Girls Above Me,

"She's waiting on the results of her biopic. It better not be life threatening." Although her life story might make a nice biopsy.

Dear Girls Above Me,

"I'm so sore! It's like 10,000 spoons when all you need is a knife." And once again you haven't referenced that lyric correctly.

Dear Girls Above Me,

"She was totally bragging about changing a flat tire. Who cares, that's why they invented AA." Pretty sure you're missing an A.

Dear Girls Above Me,

"She said I'm way too PC! Umm, excuse me, but I've *always* been a Mac girl." I'm sure your iPhone has a politically correct app.

Dear Girls Above Me,

"The rain is like two swords; it makes my nipples
look great, but it also makes my hair look like death."
Double-edged sword?

Dear Girls Above Me,

(walking out the door) "Wait, getting a CAT scan
doesn't involve like a real cat, right?" Only if it's
raining cats and dogs.

Dear Girls Above Me,

"So the 'right to bear arms' has nothing to do with
acting like you're a bear?" No, but it totally should.

CHAPTER TWENTY-TWO

Nothing's worse than waking up to the piercing sound of a mal-functioning fire alarm. I'd even prefer waking up to an actual fire. Sure, the alarm would still be going off, but at least, in the event I escape, I'd have an opportunity to tell people I'm a survivor. I've always wanted to survive something. Not necessarily something as depressing as, like, a Holocaust type of thing, and I think even sur-viving a plane crash would prove too intense for me. I'm just not a plane crash/Holocaust kind of survivor. Something like a nice little contained fire in the laundry room is more my speed. I don't think that's too much to ask.

The fire alarm jolted me to life one cold early-winter morning. The sound was so earsplitting, I couldn't help but feel pity for poor Marvin's super dog hearing ability, a power I normally would have envied and killed to have. Unfortunately, there was no fire in sight, so it didn't look as if I'd have any surviving to do, unless surviving hearing loss counts.

I stood there in the hallway, in only my boxer briefs (I know what you're thinking—that sounds emasculating—but my boxer briefs had baby deer on them, so clearly I was exuding pure unadulterated testosterone), and tried to figure out how to destroy the alarm to end this horrible sound. I knew for a fact that Mr. Molever would use any excuse to keep my entire security deposit anyway, so surrendering myself over to the logic that I'd be financially obligated no matter what, I figured, why not go to town and have some fun? Cooler heads *didn't* prevail, so naturally I grabbed my decorative samurai sword from off the wall. This obnoxious chalky-colored disk with a blinking red light was going to suffer a painful death by way of ancient Japanese euthanasia; I would give it an honorable death.

I took a swing at the fire alarm as if it were a candy-filled piñata. And just like every childhood birthday I attended, I completely missed and instead knocked off the only thing I had put on the wall, my framed autographed Marg Helgenberger headshot. I threw myself at the falling Marg, snatched her from the air, but not without slamming my right shoulder into the wall. The pain was instantly blinding, but I would have done it all over again for Marg. Despite the pain I raised the sword above my head once more, focusing any chi that I possessed on the evil little smoke detector. Just as I was about to conquer, Pat opened his door and by way of hand motion ordered me to cease the attack.

Pat was in a pair of bright red American Apparel underwear. We both stood there shirtless, the only difference being that my skin was as pale as a baby's bottom and his was the color of Snooki on Mars eating an orange at sunset. The uproar was too loud for us to hear each other, so we communicated through a made-up sign language:

ME: Hands opened and out to the sides. ("Why not?")

PAT: A pointed shaking finger and a look of disappointment. ("Because it's too violent.")

ME: Same position as I was in but more exaggerated. ("Well, then what should we do?!")

PAT: A deep knee bend, pointing to his shoulder, a look at the alarm, and a swift tugging motion. ("I'll hoist you up to the alarm and then you jerk it off"—oh, wait, "and then you pull out the battery.")

ME: An unflattering grab of my flabby belly. ("I'm too heavy for you.")

PAT: Opening the door a little wider to reveal an equally spray-tanned guy in matching underwear. ("But not for the both of us.")

ME: A wide-open mouth, tilted head, and not-so-subtle look at this surprising turn of events. ("Is this your boyfriend?!")

PAT: A finger across his lips with a chill-out look. ("It's a little too early for titles.")

ME: A scrunched forehead and proud nod. ("Play on, playa!")

PAT: An impassioned acknowledgment of the fire alarm. ("Can we turn off this sound already, please!?")

Pat's officially gay! Yay! Now I had even more anger toward this fire alarm, because it was ruining the "Pat's Coming-Out Fest" I had fantasized about planning. I was going to rent a bouncy castle and everything! I even knew a girl who knew a girl who did group in-home spray tans, which I was willing to try for such an occasion. Okay, I needed to focus.

The three of us stood directly underneath the ill-tempered alarm. Even with our hands covering our ears, the sound was still excruciating. I bit down on a Phillips-head screwdriver, in that "handy pirate" sort of way, and prepared myself to take down the beast. The two brave souls beside me each dropped down to one knee and hoisted me up. My right butt cheek rested on Pat's shirtless shoulder, while the left cheek took a seat on his boyfriend's. In order to gain my balance, I had to remove one of my hands from my ears, which damn near killed me. Not only that, but I got very little sympathy from the foundation of our human triangle, even though they had no idea how much louder the ringing was at my elevation.

At this point I was just inches away from the eye of the beast, the blinking red dot in the center. Even with my ears covered up, the sound waves found a way to irritate an already existing headache. I swiftly tried to grab the screwdriver from my mouth but was forced to recoil in pain. This thing had a genius defense mechanism: It was too small to destroy from a distance and too deafening to do anything about close up. But I needed to find a way to get to that battery. I tried once more, this time even faster, except once again the sound was just too powerful. Maybe if I screamed at the same time the noise wouldn't seem as loud? "AAHHHHH!" Oops, that just made me drop the slobbery screwdriver on Pat's big toe, which he did not seem to be thrilled about.

The screwdriver settled beside Pat's boyfriend, whom I hadn't been properly introduced to due to the raucous alarm, so in my head I named him Ferdinand. And out of nowhere, Ferdinand pulled out some crazy Cirque du Soleil move by picking up the screwdriver between his toes and, with me still perched on his shoulder, grace-fully lifted his leg all the way up and placed it gently back into my mouth. The move was too awe-inspiring to even consider the un-sanitary nature of it. Did Ferdinand have a sister? I wondered.

I had been awarded a second chance from an acrobat, and I was not going to let him down. Even with my ears plugged, the siren was beginning to drive me insane. Pat and Ferdinand were locked into position and ready. So I attempted the assassination of the fire alarm once more. I let go of my soon-to-be-damaged ear and began unscrewing the machine parts as quickly as possible. With its face hanging by a wire, the intensity of the alarm became almost unbear-able. I felt as if there was a good chance I was going to pass out and topple over, ruining this great cheerleader triangle we had going on. But I was able to stay strong, especially when Ferdinand assisted me once again, this time by reaching up and covering my exposed ear with his own hand. He was truly a contortionist. If Pat didn't lock this guy down, I would.

I finally dismantled the shrieking alarm from the ceiling and force-fully yanked the battery out. But . . . nothing happened. The wail continued, powered by God knows what. This little alarm had gone more rogue than I expected. I looked down at Ferdinand for advice, but he was just as confused as I was. I didn't even bother consulting Pat, because quite honestly I wasn't really sure what he brought to the table anymore.

The only other option was doing something about the wires that connected to the fire alarm from somewhere in the ceiling. In look-ing back on it now, I should have gone directly to Stanley and had him take care of the problem. He was getting older and probably at that age where he would have been losing his hearing, which would have made him perfect for this job. But once again, I needed to be the hero.

I called out to the boys, "Brace yourselves," which didn't do much good because they couldn't hear me anyway. I pulled those pesky wires with everything that I had. One of my many problems in life is that I close my eyes whenever I do something even remotely physical; this proved to be a gift and a curse during the Great Hide 'n' Seek Game of 1997. However, in this particular circumstance I was happy not to have seen everything:

The Good News: The insufferable noise came to a stop!!!!!!!!!!!!!!!! (Notice how many exclamation marks I used to make the news sound even better? Yeah, there's a reason for that.)

The Bad News: In pulling out the wires from the ceiling, a chunk of the ceiling decided to come with it. We three toppled to the ground, plaster and all. And as if that weren't enough, a plumbing pipe that had been somehow attached to the inner workings with which I had just tampered burst, and horrible-smelling brown water came raining down on us. . . . Ferdinand wasn't God after all.

The three of us were slammed into the middle of a poo sandwich. As the spilling began to subside, we all tried standing up on the slippery surface. This took us a minute or so, as we skidded and flopped around like ice-skating fishes. Just when we thought we were stationary, Pat attempted a move toward the bathroom and pulled us all back onto the floor with him. And as if this moment couldn't have gotten any worse, we heard our front door unlock. The only other person with a key to our apartment was Mr. Molever. He frantically swung the door open with Stanley by his side. They both stood there, traumatized, as the three of us lay on top of one another in only our underwear, covered head to toe in chocolate rain.

"Sweet mother of pearl!" Stanley yelled.

For the first time in his life, Mr. Molever was speechless.

"This is not what it looks like," I said back to them.

"Unless it looks like three strapping young men in their underwear mud-wrestling in a vat of shit," was added by a voice in our crap-covered man pile.

"Not now, Ferdinand," I muttered to a room full of people, none of whom was named Ferdinand.

THE GIRLS ON SCATOLOGY

Dear Girls Above Me,

"If a car is out of gas, can you fart into it to make it drive?" Meet you in the parking lot in 10.

Dear Girls Above Me,

"Eww, Cathy. Was that a regular fart or did you just Queefer Sutherland?" You have 24 hours to never say that again.

Dear Girls Above Me,

"Well if you still have diarrhea tomorrow we need to get you some of that ex-lax stuff." Putting out the fire with gasoline, huh?

Dear Girls Above Me,

(regarding her loud fart) "Exactly why I'll never move in with a guy. Who wants to give *that* up?" I guess I'm the lucky one then.

Dear Girls Above Me,

"In getting colonics, we basically paid 75 dollars to take the biggest shits of our lives." Ha, mine was only 7.99 at Chili's.

CHAPTER TWENTY-THREE

After a forty-five-minute Purell shower, I found myself sitting unresponsive on Mr. Molever's faux-leather couch as he calculated the damage I had caused. I was wondering if there was a way to somehow pin this whole thing on Ferdinand. Although I knew that would be a tough sell; he has very trusting eyes.

Mr. Molever wore his thick prescription glasses as he number-crunched on his annoyingly loud calculator: "Two hundred for the plumbing . . . Seventy-five—make that a hundred and seventy-five for the cleanup. Twenty-two dollars for the replacement fire alarm . . . Six dollars and ninety-nine cents for a new battery . . . Okeydokey, I'll need you to sign your John Hancock here . . . and here . . . and here . . . and here. . . ."

"But this entire ordeal was the result of a malfunctioning fire alarm that I had absolutely nothing to do with. Shouldn't that be considered in your calculations?" I pleaded.

"Here are the words I just heard come out of your mouth, Charles: 'The traffic light wasn't working properly, so I took a chain saw and sawed it in half, causing it to crash down on multiple cars and one unfortunately located small business.' Then, as a result of the mass confusion and hysteria due to the missing traffic light, it turned into a free-for-all of cars going in all directions and slamming into one another, culminating in a fifty-four-car pileup. And after a massive search-and-rescue mission comes to a grueling, time-consuming end, the police, and most likely National Guard, finally approach you to ask why on earth you caused all of this. And you say, 'The traffic light wasn't blinking correctly.' I imagine that as you're placed in handcuffs, on your way to prison to serve your life sentence, the judge will probably have a good chuckle at your 'malfunctioning traffic light' defense."

By the time Mr. Molever finished his rant I was willing to pay whatever he asked in exchange for him to simply stop talking. Finally, he carefully folded the savings-draining documentation in half, then into thirds, and placed it neatly into a manila envelope. He then removed the documentation, smoothed it flat, then folded it in half, and again into thirds, and again put it back into the envelope.

Next, he searched around his immaculate desk for something but was unable to locate the item. When he asked whether he could have a minute to find whatever it was he was looking for, for some reason I nodded. The way he asked for a minute made me kind of, sort of, feel bad for the guy. Was it possible I actually felt the tiniest bit of compassion for this lunatic? Thirty seconds ago I had wanted to kill him, but now I strangely thought about embracing him and letting him know that it was all going to be okay. Then I started wondering what "it" could be.

His apartment felt as if no one but he, and maybe an occasional unsatisfactory tenant like me, had set foot in there in years. He had no pictures of family or friends on the walls, only a couple of perfectly centered pieces of art that you would find in the discount section at Target. The main bit of decoration, besides the "Welcome Home" mats in every entryway, were the neatly organized folders that lay stacked on top of one another. There must have been twenty piles, each arranged in different colors. Tacked above each mound was an apartment number and a picture of each tenant. Putting aside the general creepiness of the layout, something suddenly dawned on me. In some messed-up—really messed-up—way, his tenants were the only family he had. He viewed himself as our parent. As I came to this realization, I glanced over at the section for 2C and found a photograph lifted from my Facebook page of me surrounded by beekeepers. Yes, I had been on a scavenger hunt in an apiary, but that's another story. Seeing my picture only further confirmed my theory. Just like most parents, Mr. Molever somehow got past the privacy settings on his "children's" Facebook pages and sifted through personal pictures, most likely jumping to silent yet judgmental conclusions. Or maybe I'm reading way too much into this and I just have severe untreated mother-privacy issues that I need to deal with on my own time.

Eventually, Mr. Molever found what he was looking for. He was holding a red ink pad and a stamp attached to a gavel-like handle. He politely took back the envelope, dipped the stamp into the ink, and hammered it onto the cover of my folder. After a few awkward seconds of his grunting and pressing down with all of his might, he lifted the imprint, which read, CONFIDENTIAL. Are you kidding me? That's what I had been waiting for?

"You can never be too sure who's going to want to take a look at your documents. Don't worry, this stamp will scare them off," he said.

If only such a stamp existed for my Facebook scavenger-hunt

photo album. "Thanks, Mr. Molever." I was almost out the door when, just as he does so well, Mr. Molever had more parting words.

"You're gonna want to go ahead and inform the girls who live above you that they shouldn't flush their toilet for the next twenty-four hours, unless you would like more of their waste pouring into your apartment," he said with a wildly entertained laugh.

In the barbarity of the moment, it had not occurred to me that the sewage, which had so profusely showered down on us, had been that of the girls above me. I wouldn't go so far as to say that this made the unpleasant experience all right, because that would be psychotic bordering on fetishistic, but I would be lying if I said I didn't feel slightly better about the whole thing.

No doubt knowing where the shit came from caused momentary relief, sort of like how eating a hot dog at a baseball game is somehow more mentally acceptable than eating one at a movie theater. Regardless, though, I never again wanted to put myself in a position where I'm finding comfort in the fact that the people who defecated on my face were sanitary enough.

SOMETIMES THEY FIGHT

Dear Girls Above Me,

"We need to talk." Uh oh, are you guys okay? "Did you switch over to iced coffee without telling me?" That bitch!

Dear Girls Above Me,

"Cathy, talk to me! I can't eat, I can't sleep, I can't pee, knowing you're mad at me." Don't let Cathy mess with urinary system.

Dear Girls Above Me,

"You can't go on birth control, your tits will get bigger than mine! We had a plan!" Does this plan involve small boobs and a baby?

Dear Girls Above Me,

I don't normally weigh in on your fights, but "whose hypothetical older brother would be hotter" is serious stuff. Sorry Claire.

Dear Girls Above Me,

"I can fully admit you're better at yoga, but it's totally offensive you're claiming to be a faster texter." Umm, should I leave?

THEY LOVE THEIR PSYCHIC

Dear Girls Above Me,

"The psychic said I have a serious stalker in my life!"
I much prefer "a friend who always listens," thank you
very much.

Dear Girls Above Me,

"The psychic said that in a past life I hung out with
Jesus! Does that mean I've, like, walked on water?"
No, he made you swim.

Dear Girls Above Me,

"My tarot card lady told me that babies bring people
money. Maybe I should have one?" I see no harm in
testing it out.

Dear Girls Above Me,

"The psychic said I'll marry a redhead! I can't have
fire crotch kids!" I think their pubes will be the least of
their problems.

CHAPTER TWENTY-FOUR

I knocked on Cathy and Claire's door without hesitation. My intense motivation didn't come from a place of confidence, but from the fear that I wouldn't make it to them before they used their toilet again. Thankfully I could faintly hear them analyzing a text message from somewhere in their apartment. As usual, their voices were too overbearing for them to hear me, so I tried knocking again, this time much louder. Their conversation ceased, followed by the monotonous sound of high heels walking on fake wood floors.

"Who is it?" Cathy called out.

Completely forgetting that they did not know my voice the same way that I knew theirs, I stupidly responded with "It's me." For the record, I'm not an "It's me" type of guy. I didn't even "It's me" my ex-girlfriend and I was with her for years. I don't "It's me" my parents, and I don't "It's me" my friends. I'm against all "It's me"–ing not because I think I'm above it, but because quite often when you hear "It's me" you immediately know who it is and wish that "me" was "anybody else."

I was able to hear consulting whispers between the two girls: "Should we open it?" "What if it's a kidnapper who's going to force us to become sex slaves like in that movie *Taken*?" The girls have a bizarre habit of watching a movie and becoming so immersed in it that they think the lives of the characters are comparable to their own. This was especially worrisome after Claire watched *Dangerous Minds* and thought it would be fun to become a substitute teacher in South Central.

The door creaked open. Two sets of eyes under mascara-coated eyelashes gaped at me. They did not have a favorable track record of remembering who I was; plus my beard always seemed to freak them out, so I knew I had only a few seconds before the door closed in my face.

"Do you know who I am?" I asked.

Cathy and Claire inspected me further. Once, I thought, just once, could I not be so forgettable to them? I know I'm not exactly Michelle Pfeiffer when it comes to first impressions, but I would like to think I have enough "geeky charisma" to make an impact by the third or fourth viewing.

"We totes know who you are, silly," Cathy said to me. Finally. The sixteenth time was totes the charm. They swung their door open hospitably.

"Yeah, you're Stephanie's lawyer boyfriend. How's all the law stuff going?" Claire asked.

I'd gained confidence too soon. I really needed to track down Stephanie's boyfriend and kill him. I didn't like knowing that there was a better and smarter version of me out there somewhere.

"Cathy and Claire, I'm Charlie, your downstairs neighbor."

Their faces lit up, just as they do every time I remind them who I am. "Charlie!" And with that they whisked me inside their apartment.

Before I could form my next thought, let alone construct it into a coherent sentence, I had a glass of mimosa placed in my hand by Cathy. The three of us cheers-ed one another and just like that I was a part of their Sunday Funday tradition I'd heard so much about.

Not sure if it was the "bubbly bit of heaven in a glass," as Claire called it, or the fact that a mimosa is quite refreshing after you get shat on, but I actually let my guard down. For the first time since these girls had come into my life, I finally stopped analyzing every little detail and got out of their heads (and my own) for a little bit. We were actually conversing, which led to smiling, which evolved into actual relatable human laughter. This was something new; I was laughing with them. This made me laugh even harder.

Since laughter is indeed contagious, it was only a matter of time before they let their guards down and joined my madness whole-heartedly. The three of us belly-laughed for quite some time, all with unique styles. I went with the "silent laugh," which every so often included sudden unattractive gasps for air. Cathy chose the "horse laugh," which was one long impressive guffaw, accompanied by the head movements a horse makes when it neighs. Claire joined us with the "model laugh," which meant she was more concerned with her appearance during this group chortle than the actual chortle itself.

I had heard Cathy and Claire suddenly erupt into hysterics before, but this was my first time being "one of the girls." Dare I say, I was actually happy to be there. Until out of nowhere Cathy shifted from hysterically laughing to hysterically crying. It took me a moment to figure out this new direction, since laughing and crying share quite a similar face, but once I did, my chuckling mellowed.

"Are you okay?" I asked.

She was sobbing so hard she couldn't even get a word out. Claire consoled her by wiping away the streams of mascara running down her cheeks. I prayed that her crying would not last as long as our laughter had. What were the rest of us supposed to do, cry with her?

After a few hiccups, Cathy spoke. "We know why you're here."

She did? "You do?"

"Yes," Cathy responded.

How was she aware of the burst pipe in my ceiling that was giving me a chance to experience their bodily waste? And more important, why was she crying about it? If anything, I should've been the one emotionally affected by this. As well as Pat and Ferdinand.

"Look, girls, I'm only here to tell you—"

"How much you hate us. We know!" Cathy belted out as her weeping resumed.

"Hate you? What are you talking about?" Oh, no, was this the code red? Could this have been the moment I had been so fearfully awaiting? The day Cathy and Claire discovered my letters to them blasted all over the Internet for others to enjoy? Was it time to finally face the music?

"Didn't you come here to complain about us like the other neighbors did?" Claire asked.

Hold the music. "Umm, no," I responded.

"So you're not here to file a noise complaint?" Cathy said.

"Wait, there are neighbors who filed noise complaints?" I asked.

"Three of them."

"One more and we'll get depicted from the building," Cathy said, on the verge of tears once again.

I couldn't believe there were others who could overhear Cathy and Claire's conversations. This whole time I'd thought I was the only one. And three of them actually used the energy required to fill out that binder full of Mr. Molever's excruciatingly long and tedious complaint papers? What losers. All because of a couple of sweetly naïve party girls, who were maybe just a tad bit loud sometimes? A strange emotion took over my body. The feeling was reminiscent of a time when I was younger and the owner of a toy store accused my sister of stealing a set of the Calico Critters elephant family. I was enraged that this man would even consider my sister to be a toy poacher, regardless of the fact that I could see multiple trunks bulging from her pocket. Even though my sister did have a childhood thievery problem, I did not like someone other than me commenting on it. Was I experiencing a similar sense of protective possessiveness over Cathy and Claire? Only I was allowed to complain about them; anyone else was an interloper. Had over a year of their conversations become my stolen elephant family? I believed so.

"Does that mean you aren't going to get us kicked out?" Claire asked.

Cathy and Claire looked at me with the weight of their destiny in my hands. Of course, a part of me thought about how I could put an end to my upstairs neighbors once and for all. But then I thought that if they weren't living above me, it would just be someone else. With my luck a couple of gaming nerds would move in and spend hours discussing all the locations of Zelda's secret flutes. And that wouldn't help me at all, because I'd discovered those locations years ago. I would much rather have benefited from knowing the "exact location of a girl's G-spot," even if that meant suffering through all of Cathy and Claire's constant chitchat and spontaneous parties. Plus, let's be honest, I would miss them way too much.

"Of course not. Why would I want to get rid of the two best neighbors in the building?" I said with ever-so-slight exaggeration.

The girls leapt up and tackled me, wrapping their arms tightly around my body. "Oh, neighby!" they said simultaneously. The time elapsed between making a decision and then regretting that decision could never be shorter than it was for me after the two of them used the term "neighby."

Regardless of the state of my own apartment—a piss-and-shit-stained hallway, a skateboard hanging from the ceiling, and indentations in the wall from when I had really great pretend sex with Bridget—I couldn't help but sit there with a smile on my face.

"Well, I'm sorry you wasted this fancy champagne on trying to win me over for no reason," I said.

"That's all right. We were going to get totally wasted from it tonight anyways," Claire replied. I already knew this information from a conversation I had previously overheard, but I feigned ignorance.

"Wait, why did you stop by here in the first place?" Cathy asked, reminding me I had something seriously important to tell them.

I then explained to the girls what had happened just a couple of hours earlier . . . well, sort of. I don't feel as if anyone should know that you've bathed in their bodily waste. That should not be the foundation of a new friendship, one I hoped to have with the girls, so I tweaked the story just a tad.

"So there's this exceptionally cute little family of mice living in the walls between us, and I've figured out that if you flush your toilet just one more time, a pipe is going to burst and flood their little home, leaving them confused and gasping for air, which won't be there because the water will be rising too quickly, and they'll have no choice but to hold each other's little tiny claws and with their little beady eyes wide open, accept their fate. . . . Death by doody," I said in a completely unrehearsed rambling sentence.

"Oh my God, we love mice!" See, I already knew they loved mice, so I used psychology. "We don't want to kill them!" Claire continued.

"So you can't flush your toilet until I've gotten the problem fixed, okay?" I asked.

"Okay! We won't!"

When I got back to my putrid-smelling apartment, Pat and Ferdinand were cuddled up on the couch wearing germ masks and viewing the latest episode of *The Real Housewives of Beverly Hills,* each clutching a Swiffer. I wasn't upset that they'd paused midclean to watch TV; I was upset because they started watching *Housewives* without me and now I'd be forced to come in as it was ending. Why not just tell me Bruce Willis is really a ghost and get the whole thing over with, Pat?

The two of them really missed out. Because now they wouldn't be able to hear my analysis on the state of the season. For example, Pat wouldn't ever get to hear me say that I'm really proud of the way Camille matured between seasons one and two. She was faced with such adversity, with the divorce and all, but instead of going to Dr. Paul Nassif (Adrienne's husband) and getting more Botox and collagen injections, Camille retreated to her multimillion-dollar Malibu home and really worked on herself. Unlike Kim; don't even get me started on her! The way she embarrassed Brandi at that manicure party—

"Do you wanna watch with us?" Pat asked through his mask, interrupting my mental recap of season two.

"Thanks, but I'm gonna finish cleaning the hallway," I replied. The subtext to that being "There's no way I'm watching this unless it's from the beginning, I don't even like missing the opening-credits sequence."

I got the third industrial-strength Swiffer they had purchased and began to work through the sludge methodically, almost hypnotically, and saw the grain from the fake wood start to emerge. I was really getting somewhere. As I mopped, swept, and bagged the mess, stopping periodically only for Purell breaks, I began to think about my empty walls (minus Marg Helgenberger, of course). It was time to fill them. I was already picturing my massive Muhammad Ali painting overwhelming the hallway, my vintage James Bond posters filling the living room, glamour shots of Marvin dressed in a tuxedo lined up on the mantel (and he really got into it after the ninth costume change), and my prized Lakers bobbleheads lining the kitchen window. I was going to make my place mine.

The floor was sparkling; now all I had to do was buy about fifty candles and be sure to keep them far from any throw pillows. As I thought about the kinds of hardware I would need in order to make all the changes I wanted to make, I heard the unmistakable footsteps of the girls above me. I smiled, thinking that if not for them, I wouldn't have had some of the many profound insights I'd had that year.

But were they technically insights, since I'd overheard them without permission, or would they be considered more eavesdroppings . . . or . . . What? . . . Wait. . . . Oh, shit.

"Oh nooooooo!!! The mice!!!!!! Oh nooo!! I'm so sorry, little mice!!!!" Claire screamed desperately.

With that, a flood of water poured through the open ceiling, and once again, there I stood, drenched in their wisdom, their insightful eavesdroppings.

ACKNOWLEDGMENTS

I'd first like to thank the people who are mentioned in this book. Whether you're my family, my friend, or my barista at Starbucks, you've been an influential part of my life and I wouldn't have stories to exaggerate without you. Some other people I would like to acknowledge: Linda Gillespie (my real-life Mary Poppins), Ali Mann Fenton, Jody Chapman, Eric Kranzler, Enrico Mills, the Mara family, the Webster family, Dave Hackel, Eric Haury, Alyson Hannigan and Alexis Denisof, Joanne Wiles, Zachary Levi, and Kobe Bryant.

Pam Felcher, I'm grateful for your laughter and for helping me make sense of what I was trying to say. You truly are the Rose Marie to my Dick Van Dyke. . . . Whatever the hell that means.

This book wouldn't be the same without the enormous amount of work done by Justin Lader. Luckily he owed me after I saved him from almost sticking a metal knife in a toaster. Who doesn't know not to do that!?

I'm very appreciative to Simon Green, C. C. Hirsch, Kenny Goodman, Anna Thompson, and especially Suzanne O'Neill (my editor extraordinaire) for making this idea something more than a collection of tweets. Suzanne, you set the "editor bar" very high with my first experience of writing a book. I hope to always work with people as encouraging and talented as you. And you'll be glad to know that I can finally spell Christian Louboutin without having to Google it.

I'd like to express immense gratitude for the hardworking people at Three Rivers Press: Catherine Cullen, Lisa Erickson, Meredith McGinnis, Campbell Wharton, Mauro DiPreta, and Tina Constable.

If you actually read the book and didn't just skip to the acknowledgments, then you know I can often be an insecure neurotic mess. Roon, thank you for always being there and lifting me up.

I have the most caring family. They are Mary, Malcolm, Ted, Kelley, Lilly, Charlie, Kate, Jesse, Katrina, Beckett, Finn, Seamus, and Clementine. Mom, thank you for infinite amounts of love and support and for choosing me as your favorite child. I'm honored and I won't let you down. Dad, as a kid I listened to you tell extraordinary stories, later to find out that you invented about 80 percent of the details to make them more entertaining—which is pretty much the synopsis of *Big Fish*. But more important, you're the reason I wanted to become a storyteller. Thank you.

Lastly, I would like to acknowledge the girls above me, Cathy and Claire. Without your wonderful insights on life and your deep affection for alcoholic beverages, none of this would exist. We have quite a complex relationship, which you sadly know nothing about. If you read this book one day, I give each of you permission to slap me across the face, but then let's three-way hug, okay? More likely, if you read this book and don't realize it's about you, I hope you find Cathy and Claire as lovable as I do.